DRUID'S DUE

A NEW ADULT URBAN FANTASY NOVEL

M.D. MASSEY

MODERN DIGITAL PUBLISHING

1

I sensed the creature's presence—or rather, the Druid Grove detected it and then conveyed that information to me. This wasn't my first rodeo since becoming stranded in the Void, and it was a given that the creature I hunted also hunted me. Hidden as I was behind foliage and obfuscating magic, there was little chance the beast would see me after it materialized in our tiny, city-block-sized pocket dimension.

With a thought, I instructed the Grove to keep me hidden while I changed locations. My experience with the various monsters and entities that had previously emerged from the Vast Nothingness told me they were sneaky bastards, one and all. Some were capable of slipping between realities, many were highly intelligent, and all of them were inherently malevolent as a matter of course. I had no reason to suspect anything different of this particular interloper.

Slinking soundlessly to a position ten yards distant, I turned around to observe the place where I'd been concealed just moments before. As expected, a creature materialized there, its bulk obscured by the dense canopy of leaves, vines, and branches such that I only glimpsed a flash of flaccid, corpse-like gray skin. The thing appeared to be quite large, and the thoughts and images the Grove conveyed via our bond confirmed that assessment.

As I'd learned while we were both still in stasis, the Druid Grove used a nonverbal, telepathic form of communication, one that I mostly understood despite its limitations. I simultaneously received images of a fifteen-foot-tall thorn tree, a Kodiak bear rearing up on its hind legs to attack, and an ominous, threatening darkness. The Oak also sent me sensations of caution and trepidation, and while I knew they were not my own emotions, I felt their effects nonetheless. I sent a message back that, yes, I understood—and to tone it down so I could focus on destroying the thing.

The Oak's presence in my mind receded, allowing me to stalk the intruder undistracted. As far as I could tell, the Grove didn't have "feelings" per se, but I sent it my gratitude just the same. I received an image of a lion savaging a jackal, then a peaceful forest glen. Obviously, all was well between us, because the Grove wanted this thing gone as badly as I did.

Time to make the chimichangas.

Not wanting to take any chances, I stealth-shifted to increase my odds of surviving the coming encounter. When I "stealth-shifted," I retained my human form and appearance while increasing my muscle and bone density to become stronger, faster, and more injury-resistant. Once I'd partially shifted into my Fomorian form, I slipped through the undergrowth as I moved to a flanking position on the beast, relying on the Grove's magic and the dense plant life to keep me hidden. Although I could've used Gunnarson's cloak of invisibility to obscure my movements, I deemed it too risky for use with a creature that could phase in and out of planar existence. The cloak employed some unknown magic to phase shift the wearer so they were just on the other side of reality. Thus, using it actually drew the attention of creatures with the ability to move between realms. After nearly being killed by a human mage while wearing the cloak, I'd learned my lesson.

Unbeknownst to me, this particular trespasser had gained planar shifting and inter-dimensional traveling abilities by merging with a symbiote that had attached itself to his head. While the symbiotic link had apparently destroyed the magician's eyes, it had also granted him extensive psionic capabilities, including three-hundred-sixty-degree "vision" in multiple planar spectrums.

Thus, the cloak remained in my Craneskin Bag, and I relied on the Grove, my wits, and nature to keep me safely hidden as I stalked this latest interloper.

It didn't take long to achieve the angle I wanted, roughly behind and to the left of our unwanted visitor. I crept forward, moving my right hand across my body so I could quickly slip it inside the Bag to draw my weapon. Again, my reasons for waiting to open the Bag were similar to the reasons why I didn't use the cloak, and why I wasn't currently wearing Dyrnwyn on my hip. Powerful magical artifacts shone like beacons to creatures of the Void, and opening any extra-dimensional containers would also alert such creatures to my presence.

The thing stayed hidden in the foliage, alternating between sniffing the ground and turning its head this way and that to look for me—but thankfully, never in my direction. As I closed the distance between us, its shape and form were revealed. Standing roughly twelve feet tall, it was vaguely humanoid and covered in thick folds of dead-looking, hairless gray skin. Its bald head was large and round, with an almost simian face that bore an elongated, dog-like snout. The monster's arms reached almost to the ground, each ending in clawed hands with three multi-jointed fingers and two opposable thumbs.

I was about to draw my blade and spring on its back when it took a step forward, moving awkwardly, almost ponderously, following the trail I'd left just seconds prior. As it moved, those thick folds of skin and flesh rolled and shifted with it—not so much like sacks of jelly, but more like leaves and detritus disturbed by some unseen thing beneath.

A shambler, that's what it is. A dimensional shambler.

The way it moved, it reminded me a bit of the eponymous creature from that old Sid and Marty Croft show, *Sigmund and the Sea Monsters*—except this monster didn't appear to be friendly, at all.

That single step didn't take it far, so I adjusted my stance to compensate for the slight change in distance. Then, in one smooth motion, I leapt forward while drawing Dyrnwyn from the Bag. I moved very, very fast in my stealth-shifted form— equal perhaps to a young vampire or mature 'thrope.

For that reason alone I'd expected an easy kill, especially since Dyrnwyn's blade was blazing like the sun. It did that in the presence of evil creatures, and this thing was definitely rotten to the core. When it was lit up like this, the sword would slice through flesh and bone like a hot knife through butter.

While still airborne, I swung the flaming sword at the creature's back, intending to cut it in two from shoulder to hip. But instead of meeting with the satisfying resistance felt when sharp steel parted flesh and bone, there was no impedance at all. My blade met empty air as the monster vanished, like a wisp of smoke disappearing on the wind.

Shit.

My head whipped around as I looked over my shoulder, checking to make sure the shambler didn't materialize behind me and rip my head off. Finnegas had never spent much time teaching Jesse and me about inter-dimensional threats, choosing instead to focus on the Earthbound creatures we were most likely to encounter. However, during a recent case I'd had a run-in with an exceptionally polite demon who'd made every attempt to make me his next meal. I'd since initiated an independent study of extra-planar entities, and had come across a brief passage on dimensional shamblers in one of Finn's texts.

As I recalled, they were slow, lumbering creatures, and therefore preferred to move via dimensional teleportation versus physical ambulation. Despite their clumsiness, they were quite strong, and typically made sport of preying on humans by popping into our reality and snatching them into another dimension. Once there, the shambler could snack on their prey at will, without the constraints of gravity and physics to slow them down.

Obviously, the inherent danger in fighting this thing was that it could appear anywhere and at any time, attacking and retreating back to whatever parallel dimension in which it preferred to reside. That meant I'd only have a split-second to react when it showed up again, leaving a very narrow window for any counterattack.

I sighed inwardly. Finnegas always said, "Once you're clued into the World Beneath, there are no easy days."

How right you were, old man.

I needed open space to maneuver, so I asked the Oak to provide me with a clearing where I could make my stand. Instantly, the surrounding plant life receded into the soil beneath my feet, making way for lush, green grass that grew to ankle height underfoot. Simultaneously, the forest retreated all around me until I stood in a clearing roughly thirty feet across.

That'll do. Now to—

A brain-rattling blow interrupted by thoughts. All I saw was a large gray blur that popped into existence a few inches from my face just before it slapped me silly. The force of the blow snapped my head back as I somersaulted across the clearing. Dyrnwyn went flying as I landed in an awkward heap, my thoughts swimming and my limbs turning to jelly as I tried to stand.

Well, this isn't turning out as I planned.

The Grove flashed a warning at me, more an impression of danger than a coherent message. On instinct I rolled to my left, just as the creature appeared above me to slam a clawed fist into the ground where I'd landed. I received another cautionary communication and rolled again in the opposite direction, once more narrowly avoiding being smashed by the shambler's massive hands.

Desperate to avoid being turned into Colin-goo, I waited for the next proximity alert from the Grove, then extended my hand to release one of my go-to emergency spells right in the thing's face. It was a flash-bang cantrip, designed to emit an intense burst of sound and light that would temporarily confuse, blind, and deafen an enemy.

The shambler took the spell full in the face, and it roared with an unearthly keening wail before disappearing again. Even with my eyes shielded by my other arm, the luminous flash seared a bright white spot in my vision that would last for several seconds. I only hoped that the beast was worse off, so I could get my bearings and devise a better plan for defeating it.

Unfortunately, I was still disoriented from that initial, devastating surprise attack, and I couldn't think clearly enough to come up with anything other than running away. And in a pocket dimension the size of a football field, that wasn't a very good plan.

Think, Colin—think!

The effects of my spell would wear off momentarily, and I couldn't dodge the creature's surprise attacks forever. I growled in frustration as I stood and stumbled toward the gleam of Dyrnwyn's hilt in the grass several feet away. I was still a few wobbly steps from my weapon when the Grove set off alarms in my head.

Do something, dumbass! I admonished myself, attempting to stir my still addled brain into action.

Apparently, the Druid Oak thought I was addressing it directly, rather than chiding myself for my lack of mental alacrity and decisiveness. In mid-stride, I felt the ground beneath me surging up to encase my feet. In the blink of an eye it spread over my ankle, calf, and knee, then it reached my legs and waist. I observed in horror and fascination as a thick, chitinous, bark-like skin grew up from the earth below, encapsulating my body head to toe in the span of perhaps half a second.

Something struck me—or rather, it struck the bark-skin surface that currently protected me from the dimensional shambler's onslaught. The blow lifted me off the ground and sent me flying across the clearing. I landed a few seconds later with a resounding crash, able to move normally and otherwise no worse for the wear. Somehow, the "armor" that the Grove had provided me was able to articulate at my joints so it didn't restrict my movement. That was all well and good, until I began to panic due to the fact that I couldn't see or open my mouth.

I can't breathe, I can't breathe, I can't breathe!

A series of images of fish breathing underwater flashed through my mind. Experimentally, I expanded my lungs and found that, yes, I actually could breathe. The air was warm and it had a loamy taste to it, but respiration was not an issue. Eyesight, however, was.

I still can't see.

The Grove replied by sending me an image of an owl turning its head all the way around. Then, it sent an image of a forest with owls on every branch of every tree.

Ah—I think I understand.

While I was in the Grove, my connection to the Druid Oak made it incredibly easy to use my druid senses to "feel" what was going on around me. Thus far, I'd only used that connection when I needed to check on the Grove's recovery. And since there was currently no animal life in the Grove, it made little sense to me that I should use my druid talents to monitor my surroundings.

Yet, if I was interpreting the Oak's message correctly, it was telling me I didn't need to borrow a mammal's or insect's eyes to see what was happening inside the Grove's boundaries. Apparently, I could use the Grove itself to surveil my demesne.

And this is my domain. No creature from the Void is going to come in my house and run the place.

The Oak sent me feelings of warmth, which I took as a note of approval, or perhaps that it shared my sentiments. I relaxed my connections to my normal faculties—sight and sound, primarily—and reached out with my druid senses to the Grove.

The sensory input nearly overwhelmed me.

Normally when I used my druidic powers to surveil the area around me, I borrowed the senses of an animal, like a squirrel, or a fox, or a sparrow. However, this reminded me of the time I'd used a bat's sonar to locate Commander Gunnarson when he was invisible—multiplied by a factor of ten. It was like having 360-degree vision, and simultaneously being aware of every blade of grass, every leaf, and every inch of ground for a hundred yards all around.

I "saw" the entire Grove all at once, and felt each living thing as well, down to the smallest moss, mushroom, and fern. It was mind-blowing, to say the least, and it took an enormous effort of will not to lose myself in the sensations I experienced.

It's too much—turn it down a bit!

The Oak responded by filtering a good deal of the data the Grove was sending me. Now, instead of receiving information from every single plant around me, instead I only shared a link with the trees, and nothing else. It was still a lot to take in, but much more manageable than the initial onslaught I'd suffered moments earlier.

Thanks. Now, show me where the shambler is hiding.

My awareness zoomed in on a spot about twenty yards

away that shimmered like a desert mirage. It appeared the trees could sense the shambler's presence while it remained out of phase, just on the other side of this reality. Since I couldn't "see" the shambler's location in that parallel dimension, the Oak showed its location in a way I could understand. It sort of reminded me of how the Predator looked to Arnold when he fought it in the jungle.

Ain't got time to bleed—nor to fuck around. I need to end this.

From what I could tell, the shambler was scoping me out, reassessing the threat I posed before it went in for the kill. The flash-bang cantrip and sudden growth of my bark-skin had made it skittish, so I'd have to draw it in with subterfuge. I stood up slowly, pretending I was still shaky from the creature's last attack, stumbling a bit to sell it hard. The shambler slowly began to stalk toward me, still shifted out of phase where it thought it was safe.

I need a plan, and fast.

If I wanted to kill it—and I did—I'd have to anchor the thing to this reality. The only way I knew how to do that was to keep it from phase shifting.

Oak, show me how it transports itself between dimensions.

An image flashed through my mind of the creature as it had appeared when I'd first seen it—a tall, gray, hulking thing with alternating tight and loose folds of skin that were reminiscent of an undead Chinese Shar-Pei. The image in my mind zoomed in on the thing's hands, or more specifically its fingers, which twisted and contorted in a peculiar pattern just before the creature disappeared.

Ah ha, so that's how it does it—by using good old magic. My own fingers weren't capable of copying those patterns, which was probably why human mages found it so difficult to learn dimensional travel. However, knowing that the beast required the use of its hands to phase shift gave me an idea. I sent the Grove a few very specific commands, then stumbled to a knee while I waited for the shambler to appear.

The otherworldly predator approached me inch by cautious inch, still concealed from human sight, but not from the sensory powers of the Grove. I continued to feign injuries, despite the fact that I was still encased in several inches of pliable bark-like armor. I only hoped it'd be enough to protect me when the thing struck again, because I doubted the Grove could carry out my commands in time to prevent the shambler's next attack.

Soon the creature was nearly on top of me, and I tensed for it to strike. In an instant, perhaps less than the blink of an eye, it phased into existence and swung one of those massive clawed limbs at me, striking me full in the chest so hard I flew a good twenty yards. Despite the armor the Grove had provided, the force of the attack knocked the wind right out of me. I landed hard and rolled awkwardly, spinning limp as a rag doll until I came to a violent stop against the trunk of a tree.

From somewhere nearby, I heard a loud roar that trailed off into a despondent wail. Yet my body was currently in panic mode, and my lizard brain rated the noise an insignificant distraction compared to my current desperate need for oxygen. My diaphragm spasmed and my chest heaved in an attempt to draw air into my lungs, but in spite of my survival instincts, I forced myself to look across the clearing.

There, the shambler struggled against dozens of vines, roots, and creepers that had sprung up from the ground to trap its limbs. More importantly, the Druid Oak had obeyed my commands and wrapped several smaller tendrils of root and vine around and between the thing's multi-jointed digits. This temporarily prevented the shambler from phase shifting, but I knew it would soon use its size and prodigious strength to break free.

Seconds later, I was finally able to breathe. As my lungs filled with air, I tried to call Dyrnwyn to me. Normally, this was a piece of cake; it was simply a matter of using my link with the wood scales that covered its hilt to telekinetically bring it to my hand. However, my mental commands went unanswered, and the shambler was starting to break free.

Must be the bark-skin armor interfering. Shit!

I looked up at the creature as I struggled to my feet. It had snapped all the ropy vines and roots that held its left hand, and was shaking the remnants from its fingers like a dog shaking a thorn from its paw. Once it was completely unfettered, it'd phase out and I doubted I'd trick it the same way twice. The damned thing could stalk around here at will then, waiting for me to sleep so it could strangle me and take me back to its own dimension for a snack.

I simply could not let that happen. Too much was at stake.

"Get me out of this armor—now!" I shouted, my voice ringing out across the clearing. The shambler's head snapped toward me, and by the look in its eyes I suspected it understood me. The Oak sent me a series of images detailing various ways the shambler might dismember me. "I don't care, just do it!"

I felt a note of discord through my link to the Grove, but it complied. Instantly, the bark shriveled away from my skin and crumbled into dust. With a thought I called Dyrnwyn to my hand, and as the warm hilt slapped into my palm, the blade ignited like a white-hot road flare up and down its length.

I bounded toward the creature, using a bit of my Fomorian strength to propel me at speed across the clearing. Time seemed to slow as the shambler used its free hand to tear at the remaining bonds that held it. It ripped out of the vines and roots that constrained its remaining hand, opening those simian, baboon-like jaws and arching its neck as it roared to the sky in triumph.

Don't count your inter-dimensional chickens just yet, Wrinkles.

What the creature failed to realize was that two of its fingers were still wrapped tightly by small threadlike vines. It tried to shift out of existence, but noticed its mistake too late. The shambler looked at me, its glowing yellow eyes reflecting the brighter light of Dyrnwyn's blade—along with the realization that the predator had now become the prey.

Those yellow eyes tracked the blade as it swooped down. Not at its neck, because that was out of reach. No, my target was the creature's means of escape. The flaming blade flared briefly as it sliced cleanly through the shambler's arms, one at the elbow and the other just above the wrist. As I landed I dropped and spun, pivoting to chop one of its legs off at the knee.

I rolled out of the way, extinguishing Dyrnwyn's blade with a thought. The shambler was still alive, but not for long. As it fell, black blood spilling onto the soft grass beneath it, more vines and roots sprung out of the ground to wrap it up like a spider encasing its prey. The Grove pulled the now helpless beast down, down, down into the loamy clutches of its bosom, and as the shambler's cries faded away, I had no pity for it at all.

"Better you than me, motherfucker," I muttered.

Clucking my tongue, I spared it one final glance before it sank completely into the rich dark soil, where it would feed the Oak's recovery and bring us one step closer to returning home.

2

There are things more dangerous than shamblers lurking in the Void, dark things best left alone to pursue whatever vile and horrific designs a being of pure evil might devise. Pro tip: If you find yourself in the Void, the last thing you want to do is draw their attention. I discovered this the hard way, which, upon much reflection, is how I often learn such things.

Unfortunately, drawing attention to myself out in the very literal middle of *nowhere* had been unavoidable. Much to my dismay, my efforts to repair, replenish, and regrow the Druid Grove acted as a beacon in the cold, absent reaches where we drifted. Magic and energy—especially the vital life energies of the Grove—were anomalies in the Void. Whatever dwelt in or traversed the desolate spaces was eventually bound to notice their presence.

I'd ended up here after Jesse had fooled me into having sex with her, impersonating my other ex-girlfriend so convincingly I'd had no idea who it was until it was too late. By that time, we'd both been locked in the throes of the

Grove's claiming ritual, a sort of tantric, primitive mating rite that required me to—ahem—*contribute* my DNA directly to the Grove, sealing the bond between us.

The betrayal and violation I felt over that single deceptive act could not be understated, although I understood why she'd done it. First, she was bug-fuck nuts—a side effect of too much magic being pent up inside a partially-human body that had never been meant to contain it. And second, the human side of her still loved me.

Jesse, having been resurrected in the dryad body of the Druid Oak's avatar, had inadvertently initiated the bonding ceremony, unaware of the consequences of such a union. Prior to that fateful evening, Finnegas had begged me to do it of my own accord. I'd refused, simply because I hadn't wanted to cheat on Belladonna. Plus, I'd thought the whole idea was barbaric and more than a little misogynistic to boot.

Despite my misgivings about the manner in which it had occurred, I was thankful I'd bonded with the Oak, and through it, the Grove as well. Because of our connection, I'd instinctively determined what I had to do to restore the Oak to its former and intended glory and heal the Grove. It was now my sole mission, because if I didn't nurse the Oak and Grove back to health, all three of us were doomed.

Although I was the one who'd damaged the Druid Oak and Grove in the first place, Jesse had goaded me into it. Then, she'd tricked me into sleeping with her, and that had saved the Druid Oak—but it was still pretty fucked up, all things considered. The good that resulted from that deception might very well have balanced out the bad, but I still didn't know if I'd be able to forgive her for it.

That personal dilemma weighed heavily on my mind, and I often found myself wishing I could go back to the way things were when Jesse and I were young. They say you can never go back, but I wondered—if Jesse were human again, could we rewind the clock? Would it be possible to reset our relationship, and put all that craziness behind us?

I honestly had no idea, but that particular philosophical quandary would have to wait. Presently, I had bigger issues to contend with.

As I'd discovered, the Oak was never meant to be weakened, mortally wounded, and cut off from the Earth, which was ultimately its primary source of magic. Certainly, the Oak generated its own magic, as did all living creatures, but in its injured and infirm state it lacked the ability to self-rejuvenate. It was unable to return to Earth, never mind traveling to any other plane or location. That's why I'd been slowly nursing it back to health with my own magic, all while rebuilding the Grove as well.

And it *was* coming back to health—but slowly, ever so slowly. Forming matter in the vast empty reaches of the Void meant it had to be transported from somewhere else. While magic could bend the laws of physics, it could not cheat them completely. I was no more capable of creating matter than any other magic-user, and thus was bound by the laws of conservation.

Thankfully, my Craneskin Bag had provided a sufficient amount of mass to get us started. The damned thing had accumulated tons of junk over the centuries, and I got the impression it would be glad to be rid of it. So, I'd cleaned out the Bag and fed the useless contents within it to the Grove.

No matter what I fed it, the Grove happily sucked all manner of matter underground. There, it rapidly decomposed, after which it was used as the raw building blocks for creating earth, water, and plant life. But once I'd relieved the

Craneskin Bag of any and all superfluous items, I'd then had to use the Oak's enfeebled magic to transport matter from elsewhere. The process had started slowly, but as the Grove healed, it began to acquire matter on its own at a steady pace. Unfortunately, our efforts were still insufficient to bring the Grove's magical protections back online, so we were still vulnerable to intrusions by unwanted visitors.

When completely healthy and whole, the Grove and Oak were protected by wards and magical barriers of immense power. Those spells kept the Grove hidden in the vast reaches of the Void, while also preventing anything that did happen upon it from entering its boundaries. In fact, its primary method of self-preservation was both simple and ingenious —it promptly zapped itself somewhere else whenever it felt threatened.

To my shame, I'd screwed that all to hell when I'd damaged the Oak during my fight with Jesse. My Hyde-side definitely had one gear and one gear only—seek and destroy. The *riastrad* was a powerful weapon, but it was also a liability, because when I let it take over I couldn't think clearly.

After finding myself in this fix due to losing control after I'd shifted, I'd sworn to avoid fully shifting in the future if I could avoid it. As this little jaunt to the Vast Emptiness had proven, it was too damned dangerous to go directly to the nuclear option every time I found myself in a fix. It'd taken having to freeze myself in stasis and being lost in the Void to see the error of my ways. From here on out, I would think before acting, instead of relying on my Fomorian muscles to solve my every problem.

Once I get out of here, that is. Kind of hard to hold off on the nuclear option when you're fighting a nuclear war.

Speaking of which, it was a damned good thing my brain

hadn't stopped working when I'd cast that stasis field, or else I'd have been Thing food by now. And "Thing" was the only term I'd come up with to describe the entities that had attacked us thus far. Why they were here in the Void was a mystery, but I suspected it was because this was a place between places, a "non-dimension" between dimensions of sorts. If I was right, then it made sense that inter-dimensional beings would use the Void to hop between realities and planar spaces.

It was just my shitty luck that I was stuck here with them.

Soon after I'd started healing the Grove—"soon" being a relative term, since I had no way of measuring time at the moment—they'd started coming, probing at the outer edges of our little island in the Darkness. Some were relatively easy to deter, like the black, eyeless, winged creatures that were the first to appear in the Grove. The Oak's natural defenses had made quick work of that first wave, capturing the alien beings with ropy vines and then pulling them into the soil to help feed our rejuvenation efforts.

It was a good thing too, because at that time I hadn't managed to create a livable atmosphere—thus, I was still confined to my stasis field. Later, after I was able to move around again, I'd learned that those early trespassers were among the least dangerous inhabitants of the Empty Reaches. Granted, any creature able to traverse the Void was no joke, since it took a certain toughness to survive the complete absence of everything. Considering that anything capable of extra-dimensional travel must inherently possess magic or technology of an advanced variety, it came as no surprise that I found myself fighting for my life and that of the Grove on a routine basis.

I'd barely rested when the Grove alerted me to the presence of a being far more dangerous than the shambler. Based on the information the Grove was sending me, it was easily the most formidable of any Void creature I'd encountered thus far. I'd likely have come to that conclusion based on its size alone. However, it was the creature's appearance that informed me I was not dealing with your standard Void-traveling creep.

Apparently, I was about to face down the spawn of an Outer god.

Probing the ragged edges of the Grove was a huge, blackish-green, ill-shaped blob of tentacles, eyes, mouths, and legs. My connection to the Druid Oak had alerted me to its presence just moments before, jarring me from a meditative state in which I'd been trying to balance the water, soil, and gas ratios in the Grove. You'd think such a thing would be easy—it wasn't. When Void entropy had eaten away the original iteration of the Druid Grove, the little pocket universe lost a bit of the magical code that regulated such things. Eventually it would rewrite itself, but it hadn't happened yet. So, parts of the Grove were flooded, while others were nearly parched, and I'd been attempting to remedy that situation when the Thing appeared.

I didn't need to run to the edge of the Grove to see what was out there, because I noticed its presence as soon as I opened my eyes. Although perspectives and distances were weird in the Void, I estimated it to be at least fifty feet tall and just as wide. At first, I had no framework by which to classify the Thing, and frankly just looking at it was making me nauseous. Many of the creatures I'd run into out here had that effect—in fact, their "wrongness" was sometimes so overwhelming I had to shut my eyes and fight them while relying solely on my connection to the Oak.

The creature floated out there in the Nothingness, poking and prodding at the horribly inadequate wards and protections I'd constructed to protect my little pocket dimension while it healed. I'd considered myself a pretty fair hand at creating and casting protective wards back on Earth, but these creatures ate such barriers for lunch. I speculated that my wards would be stronger back home, where the solid firmament of reality would shore up the separation between spaces and things.

But here? Here the delineations and boundaries that seemed so natural and permanent back on Earth were much more malleable, and that made it easier for Void travelers to break through my defensive spells. Yet, that didn't mean the Grove and I were completely vulnerable—far from it.

"No rest for the weary," I said as I rose, stiffly, from my comfy spot by the Oak.

My ancient druid mentor Finnegas had taught me many things that had helped me survive to the ripe old age of twenty, and one of them was a simple battle axiom. *When in doubt, attack.* Heeding that advice had saved me out here countless times. I hoped it would do so again today.

I accessed my mental link to the Grove, checking to see which spells, defenses, and traps we had ready. The Oak and Grove might be healing, but they still possessed formidable power I could bring to bear in our defense. I'd also made a habit of setting aside resources in preparation for each new attack, and assured myself that we were prepared to deal with this intruder.

Yep, we are totally ready to fight the offspring of an Outer god. Right.

The thing I'd learned about these *Things* was that out there in the Void, they lacked substance and solidity. Like the shambler, most of them remained ethereal while traversing the Nothingness, so attacking them while they were out there was pissing in the wind. To fight them, I had to bring them inside the Grove.

Smaller creatures would enter the Grove willingly out of necessity in their attempts to hunt, kill, and devour the sole inhabitant—me. That tended to work in my favor, since the moment they entered or materialized here, I could hunt and kill them with impunity. Relatively speaking, of course, because killing some of them was easier said than done.

But a being such as this one? It would be more than happy to float out there in the insubstantial Darkness, ripping away chunks of life, matter, and magic to fuel its own continued maleficent existence. It would be a real challenge drawing in a creature of this size, but I'd been waiting for just such an opportunity. If I brought the creature's considerable carbon-based bulk into my little pocket of reality, and if I managed to kill it, well—I could then use its remains to complete my work on the Grove's restoration and recovery.

A corpse was just a corpse, after all—no matter how inherently, primordially evil it had been when alive.

Yet the cost to do so could be high. There was a reason why people went mad staring into the Void, and it often had to do with the Things they saw there. I was having a difficult time just looking at this abomination in its current insubstantial state. Once I brought it into this reality, its immense malevolent presence would likely exert a maddening effect on my mind.

I'd experienced it before, during my encounters with lesser beings. Presumably, most had been servants and supplicants of dark gods—alien races long-forgotten by man or perhaps worshipped as gods themselves in some dark corner of my world. Pale reflections of their masters, their presence still turned my stomach and weakened my resolve. Everything about them reeked of *wrongness*, and at times it was all I could do to resist curling up in a ball to be eaten.

The experience was reminiscent of the fear I'd felt when I battled the Maori god of evil. Whiro's avatar had emanated an almost palpable, abject terror that had paralyzed me and shaken me to my core. Thankfully, no Void traveler thus far had caused me to experience a level of dread like I had in Whiro's presence. But this Thing, this amorphous colossus of writhing appendages, eyes, and orifices—I suspected it might just come close.

I had a pretty good idea what it was and what had spawned it, based on recent research I'd done on inter-dimensional entities. If I was right, this Thing was a child of Yog-Sothoth, one of the most powerful of the Outer gods.

Yeah, this is going to suck, I reflected as I sent the mental command to the Grove to begin our assault. *Let's just hope it pays off.*

The great thing about my bond with the Grove was that I didn't have to contain its magic as Jesse had. She'd been bound to the Grove when her resurrected human body merged with that of the Oak's avatar, turning her into a direct conduit for the Grove's enormous power. Possessing and wielding all that magic had driven her insane, but as the intended caretaker of the Grove, I was in no such danger.

Now that I'd bonded with the Grove, I was master and commander of its magic, a conductor directing and orchestrating its flows where I willed, sending them where they were needed. It was much more of a symbiotic relationship than a forced one, since I served the Grove just as much as it served me. In dire emergencies, I suspected I could also act as a conduit for that magic—but after seeing its effects on Jesse, I had no intentions of testing the validity of my theory.

That thought, detected by the Grove's presence through our mental connection, caused the Oak to send me a series of images that assured me I'd come to no harm in channeling its energies. It sent me feelings of light and warmth, a mental impression of health and completeness. To top it off, it transmitted an image of me, wreathed and wrapped in leaves and vines, wielding its immense mystical energies like some dreadful green forest god who'd just discovered the existence of glyphosate.

The images, thoughts, and feelings had been meant to comfort me, but they had the opposite effect. All I could think of was mad-as-a-Hatter Jesse, a nascent nature goddess driven to the brink of insanity by channeling powers that were never meant for a human body to contain.

Grove, let's just hope it never comes to that. I felt a small, subtle emotional backlash through our connection. The Grove didn't like being called as such. It had a name, apparently, but I'd yet to suss it out. *Sorry.*

It sent me an image of a happy little forest grove on a bright sunny day, a gentle breeze blowing through the grass and leaves. The Grove was funny that way. It was mercurial, but never malicious as dryad-Jesse had been; it was quick to take offense, and just as quick to forgive. Its temperament reminded me of a small child, or a puppy—and in many ways, that's exactly what it was.

The creature snapped through one of my wards, releasing magical shockwaves that reminded me we had a primordial demigod to kill. I telepathically instructed the Grove to shoot thick, thorny vines at the creature, hoping we might encircle it so we could reel it in. As I watched the vines lash out at the horror, I flinched in anticipation of what came next.

Brace for impact.

The moment we made contact with the creature, panic washed over me in waves. My mouth grew dry, my limbs numb, and my heart began beating out of my chest. It was such a visceral, gut-churning fear, if I'd had anything in my stomach I'd have retched it all over the place. Terror and revulsion gripped me, my body felt leaden, and no matter how much I screamed at my muscles to obey, I couldn't get them to move.

Damn it!

Mentally, I strained and struggled, yet remained paralyzed with fear and disgust at the innate peccancy of the creature. Thankfully the Grove didn't experience fear as I did, so it had obeyed my initial commands. Vines whipped around the Thing, snagging and capturing it and then reeling it toward us. Soon, it would cross the barrier into our reality and manifest itself physically—an angry, fifty-foot-tall godling seeking something or someone to devour.

And crippled as I was by bone-deep terror and gut-level abhorrence, I was powerless to defend myself against it.

3

As the creature materialized in the Grove, the feelings of dread and horror intensified. My stomach muscles clenched up and then I was leaning over with my hands on my knees, dry-retching. Just when I thought it couldn't get any worse, the Thing opened every mouth it had, and each one screeched the same, ear-piercing syllables.

"Tekeli-li! Tekeli-li! Tekeli-li!"

The cacophony was like a thousand ice picks piercing my skull all at once. I sank to my knees, sobbing incoherently as something warm and wet began to run from my eyes, ears, and nose.

Make it stop make it stop make it stop!

The monster's hundreds of eyes locked in on me and the Oak. Without hesitation, the god-spawn began to ambulate toward us, slipping around, under, and through its constraints like a massive blob of self-healing gelatin. Rather than walking like an insect or mammal, the creature's strange, tentacle-like legs rolled it forward as if it were on a conveyor belt. As it moved toward us, new legs sprouted from its "chest," each traveling down until the suckered feet made contact with the ground. Those legs traveled in a continuous pattern from front to back, only to be replaced by new appendages that popped out of the Thing's body in a never-ending sequence, similar to the treads on a tank's tracks.

The sight both mesmerized me and filled me with even greater revulsion, causing me to shut my eyes for fear of having a complete mental break. Somewhere inside my mind, I knew the creature was getting closer, and I knew I had to act soon or die. Yet my conscious mind had retreated to a deep, dark place within me, where it sought some escape from the mental, emotional, and physical onslaught of the creature's psionic and sonic attacks.

Linked as we were, the Druid Oak sensed my predicament, and it began sending me a combination of urgent warnings and comforting thoughts. Unfortunately, my conscious mind wasn't accepting correspondence at the moment. Although on some level I knew the Grove was communicating with me, the messages weren't being received.

But the will to survive was a difficult thing to extinguish. While my conscious mind attempted to retreat, my more primitive self decided we were not going to be eaten and slowly digested over the course of several centuries by the spawn of some inter-dimensional god. Like it or not, my other half was coming out to play, and he was not amused by this creature's presence.

When my shift happened, it took about twenty to thirty seconds to complete the entire extensive, excruciating process. I would gain about four feet in height and several hundred pounds in mass. My bones would elongate and thicken, my muscles increased in size and density, my skin toughened, and my teeth and nails lengthened and hard-ened. The end result was that I transformed into something that looked like a cross between the Hulk and Quasimodo. When I was in control, it could happen faster if I'd already partially shifted, and slower if I started from my fully-human state.

But under life-threatening circumstances, my Hyde-side often decided to make an appearance in spite of my own plans to the contrary. When that occurred, the change was nearly instantaneous. In such cases, the Fomorian side of my personality became dominant, and I turned into a much more ruthless, war-like, and dangerous version of my normal self. It used to be that I had zero control when my other side took over, but eventually I'd found a way to integrate my two halves. These days, I remained cognizant and in the driver's seat when I went through a spontaneous change.

Yes, I was in control when the change happened—but my thoughts and emotions were heavily Fomorian-influenced. They were the race that once subjugated the Tuatha Dé Danann, a group of god-like entities that comprised the Celtic pantheon. And while the Tuath Dé eventually managed to throw off the yoke of subjugation placed on them by the Fomorians, the Fomoire never stopped being the badass supernatural race of warriors they were.

In short, Fomorians were god-killers, plain and simple. Meaning, my Hyde-side wasn't about to be intimidated by the offspring of a had-been god. In the instant my transformation from human to Fomorian was complete, the terror I'd felt vanished. In its place, I felt righteous indignation at the crea-ture's gall for initiating the assault in the first place, and determination to make it regret that decision.

As I rose, the god-spawn's screeching ceased—as did its

steady forward progress toward the center of the Grove. I stared at it with my two beady eyes, set as they were beneath a jutting, Cro-Magnon brow, and it stared back with hundreds of eyes that were possessed of every shape, color, and type.

I strode forward on tree-trunk legs until I stood within twenty yards of the great quivering mass of flesh and pestilence. Fomorian-me was confident that, despite our difference in size, this thing was going to be meat for my pot. Or, rather, for the Grove's pot.

Arms crossed, I spread my feet wide. Raising my chin as if speaking to a child, my challenge echoed across the Grove. "You fucked with the wrong pocket dimension, god-spawn. Now, you're going to pay the price."

Most of its eyes blinked—some once, others several times. The creature's multitude of mouths spasmed until every one of them had been drawn into a tight rictus, some curling up while others twisted down. The orifices then emitted a noise that was at first strange to my ears, until I puzzled out what it was.

Laughter.

The god-spawn replied in a chorus of voices, some high, some low, many otherworldly. It spoke in a garbled string of syllables, grunts, and clicks, yet I understood the creature perfectly.

"There are things older than your kind in the cosmos, Fomori, and I am one of them. Your threats are empty, but your bulk will fill my ninety-nine stomachs, each in turn, as I digest you slowly over the course of many millennia.

"Whoa, slow your roll there, Sarlacc. This is my turf, and I call the shots here."

"Be that as it may, your powers are insignificant compared to

my own. Your only choice is in how you will die—willingly, as a voluntary, sacrificial act of worship to my magnificence, or struck down in battle, as is inevitable if you resist."

I smiled a crooked grin that was all jagged teeth and hate. "Neither sounds very appealing. I'll take what's behind door number three."

"There are no doors here. Of what alternative do you speak?"

"The one where I rip your guts out and use them as garland for my Christmas tree," I replied, sending a message to the Druid Oak to grow me some weapons as I began to run at an oblique angle to my prey.

The Grove responded, and several saplings sprung up in my path. As I reached for the first one, the branches and leaves took the shape of fletching, and the trunk at the base narrowed into a sharp, leaf-shaped point. I snapped it off from the roots and threw it in mid-stride, aiming for a rather large cephalopodic eye in front. The shaft pierced the platter-sized orb cleanly, and the god-spawn roared in anger and pain.

I circled the creature, making certain I was out of reach of its tentacles but well within throwing range. With one spear throw after another I pierced its eyes and hide, repeating the tactic as I made three complete circuits of its monstrous body. Soon the thing's skin sported more than a dozen spear shafts, like a huge quivering pincushion made of flesh and evil that spilled black blood in rivulets.

But despite the many wounds I'd inflicted, the godling seemed none the worse for the wear other than being angered. Indeed, it soon began to suck the spear shafts into its body, spontaneously healing each wound as it grew new eyes to replace the ones I'd ruined. Clearly, attacking the monster by conventional means had been a futile attempt at best.

We need another approach.

Fire was out of the question, as the Druid Oak barely tolerated the presence of Dyrnwyn; if I started tossing fireballs around, the Grove would go nuts. Besides, I couldn't risk damaging the Grove while it was in such a precarious state. Acid was another option, and while I suspected it would work well on the creature, I didn't want to risk it for the very same reasons. Cold would likely have little effect, as creatures of the Void were used to the absence of warmth. That left a single alternative, and thankfully it was one at which the Grove was particularly adept.

With a thought, the Druid Oak received my message and obeyed my command. Six thick, tree-like vines shot up from the ground around the god-spawn, each bristling with thorns the size of my forearm that dripped with venom. Those vines grew rapidly, and when they reached a length greater than the height of the creature, they whipped up and around it, slamming into the interloper's body so the thorns pierced its hide.

I'd instructed the Grove to produce toxins that were necrotoxic, neurotoxic, and paralytic. The first would destroy soft tissue, hopefully faster than the thing could heal, and the others would interrupt the god-spawn's nervous system. Or so I hoped.

As the vines attacked the creature a second time, it roared defiantly as it used its many tentacles and appendages to tear the vines away from its body. However, the Druid Oak knew its business, and the thorns on the vines were barbed and detachable. Thus, when the beast ripped the vines away, their poisonous barbs remained behind, continually dripping their deadly payload into the god-spawn.

Soon the toxins began to take effect, paralyzing entire sections of the creature's body. In those affected areas, eyelids drooped shut, pupils became unfocused, mouths grew slack, and limbs went limp and flaccid. Yet this only served to enrage the thing even more, and unfortunately the Grove's ability to create new vines was limited by its current infirm state. I instructed the Grove to attack again and again with the same six vines, but the beast began to fight back.

Numerous tentacles and multi-jointed, insectile limbs sprouted from the god-spawn's hide in areas not affected by the toxins. Those appendages latched onto the vines, holding them out and away from the creature's body where they could do little harm. Then, the creature grew several crab-like limbs with large, wicked pincers on the end. It used these to sever the vines at the root, tossing them to the ground where they withered and died without their connection to the Grove's life-force.

Freed from its constraints once more, the creature renewed its efforts to reach the Druid Oak. Despite the partial paralysis caused by the Grove's toxic thorns, the god-spawn's speed was only slightly reduced. It simply shifted those areas that were paralyzed up to its back while bringing the unaffected areas to its underside. There, those areas were repurposed to provide the creature with a means of locomotion. New legs sprouted from the thing's chest and belly, and then it was off to the races once more.

Well, shit.

I had to act and fast, otherwise the beast would reach the

Oak and begin devouring it—and that would really put a damper on my plans for a Welcome Back to Austin party.

Oak, tell me something—that thing said it had ninety-nine stomachs. How many hearts does it have?

The Oak sent me back an image of a small copse of trees that numbered in the dozens.

Crap. Okay, how many brains does it have?

The image that came next was of a single, small sapling.

Jackpot. I chuckled when I realized the significance of the Oak's message.

I guess that tells me what you think of the god-spawn's intelligence.

I immediately received an image of a panda, one of the world's dumbest mammals.

Damn, that's cold. Now, show me where it is.

A minute later, I was standing in front of the god-spawn, my hands extended outward in supplication as I prepared to put my plan into action. If my calculations were right, this Thing would provide sufficient mass to restore the Grove's teleportation and dimensional travel abilities. In other words, if I took it down we'd be back at the junkyard in no time flat. My intended course of action to accomplish that feat was both risky and dangerous, but I was desperate to get home.

"Oh great and mighty, er, Thing—"

"You may call me Throdog Uh'enyth ot Soth," it said, interrupting me.

"Er, can I shorten that to just Throdog?"

"I will allow it, considering that you only possess the most rudimentary organs of vocalization. Continue."

"Oh great and mighty Throdog, it has come to our attention that you are more powerful than us by many degrees—"

The Grove sent me an image of a dog pissing on a tree.

"—and that we are not capable or worthy of opposing your all-powerful and ever-resolute will."

Now it was an image of a dung beetle pushing a turd ball up a hill. The beetle lost control of its payload, and the ball of crap and the beetle both tumbled back to the bottom of the mound.

"Obviously. Go on."

"For these reasons, if it pleases the great and mighty Throdog, we have decided to sacrifice ourselves willingly. In this way, by providing ourselves as sustenance to your supreme wickedness, we hope to establish some small bit of meaning for our utterly ephemeral and ultimately futile lives."

"As I said, inevitable. I shall devour you forthwith."

An image appeared in my head of a dodo bird walking off a cliff.

I knelt and bowed my head, hiding the smirk I fought to keep off my face. "If it pleases your puissant intransigence."

Although I kept my head bowed to maintain the ruse, I "saw" the god-spawn rolling toward me through my link to the Grove. As it neared me, a huge gaping maw appeared that split the creature from the ground and up its side to a height of ten feet or more. The newly-formed cavity was lined with numerous long, razor-sharp teeth, and within its depths a slimy black tongue lapped at the air as if it were tasting its next meal.

The creature continued to advance, and it took every last ounce of my self-control to avoid attacking it outright. The mouth loomed over me as the god-spawn raised itself up so it could gulp me down in one bite.

Now!

As that cavernous mouth enveloped me, the Grove covered me with a thick protective layer of bark-like skin, just as it had done to protect me from the shambler. I figured if Throdog took several millennia to digest something my size, between the bark and my Fomorian hide, it'd be a while before the acids in its digestive tract did me any harm.

I hope.

Once the jaws closed, the creature's massive tongue pushed me to the back of its mouth. Then, it swallowed me. Peristalsis did all the work after that, pushing me farther and farther into what served as the creature's alimentary canal.

Ugh, I can't even smell or see and I can tell how disgusting it is in here.

I had no idea which of its ninety-nine stomachs I would end up in, but that was not my concern. What did concern me was where I ended up in relation to the god-spawn's central processing unit. Hopefully I'd be within striking range, because I seriously doubted there was any sort of ambient atmosphere in here. While I could hold my breath for extended periods when fully-shifted, I could only hold this form for so long. That meant I might only get one chance to kill Throdog.

Better make this count.

Just as it had previously, the Grove provided me with a sort of three-dimensional view of the world around me. However, the primary information it provided me this time was the location of Throdog's brain—a dark, football-sized mass that was surprisingly small for a creature so large. As the smooth muscle that lined the thing's esophagus pushed me further toward Throdog's center, the black, crenellated object neared.

As I slid closer to the god-spawn's brain, I readied myself for my attack. The Oak had formed the bark-skin so the ends of my fingers and toes were sharp and claw-like. It wasn't the ideal weaponry, and certainly not my first choice for such a task, but it'd have to do. I waited patiently, allowing myself to be pushed through Throdog's esophagus until I was parallel with the vulnerable organ.

Then, I attacked.

Turning sideways inside Throdog's throat, I jammed my feet against one side of the slimy shaft and thrust my arms in the opposite direction. As I did, I extended my fingers like spears, so the sharp projections on the ends pierced the soft, smooth membrane like knives. Upon penetrating the surface layer of the god-spawn's throat, I met some resistance from the muscle on the other side. I pushed harder, making my entire body a single rigid structure.

As expected, the irritation I caused made Throdog's throat muscles spasm. But rather than crushing me, instead it forced me further through the side of the beast's throat. Immediately, I began clawing and tearing at the muscle and cartilage holding me back from my intended target: a quivering mass of fat and neurons not more than ten feet away.

By this time, I was free of Throdog's throat, but making progress now was like swimming through greasy latex rubber. I had to tear through muscle and connective tissue to fight my way ahead, pulling myself along inch by tedious inch. It didn't help that the god-spawn was going nuts all around me, and I hated to see what was happening to the Grove at the moment.

Still I pressed on, for what seemed like an eternity.

Throdog's bulk pressed in on me, and if I didn't know any better I'd have sworn he was trying to squeeze me to death. My lungs and muscles were on fire as my body cried for oxygen. I began to fade in and out, and it was all I could do to keep myself from taking a breath.

But finally, I reached my destination. Throdog's brain was dead ahead, encased in a thick, cartilaginous membrane. The tiny brain was obviously the god-spawn's only weakness, and I was pleased to see that it was woefully under-protected. The obvious play was to rip through the cartilage to get at the fatty tissue and nerve clusters beneath, but I knew that I'd likely pass out before I could cause enough damage to kill the huge, amorphous god.

Thankfully, I had a better plan.

I simply sliced a hole through the protective membrane, one large enough to allow me access. Then, I thrust my hand inside Throdog's "skull," and released the lightning spell I'd prepared before I'd allowed the god-spawn to swallow me. Electricity crackled and arced from my fingertips, spreading in all directions and striking the delicate nervous tissue in multiple places. Throdog's brain reacted to that insult just as a human brain would, by burning and short-circuiting as the many synapses inside the organ overloaded.

What I hadn't accounted for was the effect it might have on the rest of Throdog's anatomy. Electricity tends to release heat energy very rapidly when it meets with resistance, and in this case it was enough to instantly boil approximately one thousand gallons of god-spawn blood. Considering that water expands at a factor of 1600:1 when it turns from liquid to gas, it was easy to see where I screwed up. Add to that the volatility of Throdog's blood—because who knew what unknown elements were present in the blood of a god—and the effects were rather explosive.

And that's how you give a god an aneurysm—shit! was the last thing that went through my mind, right before approximately 15,000 cubic meters of fledgling Outer god exploded all over my Druid Grove.

4

S ometime later I awoke, curled up beneath the Druid Oak and nestled within a cozy bed of leaves and grass.

Nice to know the Grove was looking after me while I was out.

My muscles were stiff, but that could've been the result of lying in one position for an extended period of time. I sluggishly gave myself a once-over to determine if I'd suffered any serious injuries from the unexpected explosion of the god-spawn.

Once I verified that yes, all my parts were present and in the proper place, I checked to see how the Druid Grove was getting along. A quick visual scan of the surrounding area indicated that the Grove and Oak had wasted no time putting Throdog's remains to good use. I saw no trace of the disgusting creature's blue-black flesh, rubbery tentacles, cilia-like legs, or multitude of eyeballs.

Connecting with the Druid Grove through our mental link, I asked it for a situation report. It replied with a string of mental and emotional impressions, as well as a number of mental images, all of which together indicated that the Druid Grove had almost completely recovered. We were headed home.

Since I'd been stranded in the Void with the Druid Grove, I'd asked it many times what had happened to Jesse after I'd unintentionally claimed the Grove. Based on its replies, which usually amounted to images of caterpillar larvae in cocoons, birds in nests, and baby animals snuggled all cozy inside their dens, I had to assume that the Oak had transported her someplace safe. Physically, I knew she'd be safe—but mentally? I could only hope that she'd be able to recover from the trauma of being forcefully separated from the spirit of the Druid Oak.

Despite my misgivings, and whatever grudges I might have held against my ex for tricking me, I still considered it priority number one to check on Jesse and make sure she was okay. So, I instructed the Oak to take us directly to wherever she was just as soon as the Grove was capable of inter-dimensional travel. The tree replied in the affirmative, so I sat beneath it engaged in meditation while patiently awaiting the time at which we would finally be headed home.

When the hour finally arrived, there was no fanfare, no advance warning, nor even a message from the Grove to tell me we were about to traverse the normal boundaries of space and time. Instead, I felt a mental nudge from the Grove that roused me from my meditation, then the Druid Oak sent me an image of the junkyard and my bedroom inside the warehouse.

How the damn thing knew what the inside of my bedroom looked like was beyond me. Perhaps when we'd become mentally linked it was able to see and experience my memories secondhand. Or maybe it possessed sensory abilities that allowed its awareness to venture far and away from its physical location. If I had to guess, I would say it was a combination of the two possibilities. The Druid Oak and Grove were certainly not entities limited by any of the dimensional boundaries or physical laws that tied the typical human to a single temporal location.

Notably, the Druid Grove and Druid Oak *were* two interconnected, but separate entities—of that I had no doubt. It had taken me a while to suss that out, but after being connected to the Grove while in the Void, I came to realize that the Oak was the progenitor of the Grove. Much like a child is born from its mother's womb, the Druid Grove was for all purposes the offspring of the Oak. The two were connected but separate entities, each with their own "mind" and personality.

In fact, they were so thoroughly connected that I often found it difficult to determine where one ended and the other began. Certainly, I could communicate with each separately and simultaneously and task them with different purposes and functions. Yet, the delineation between the two was both fluid and elusive.

If I had to put their relationship in practical terms, the Druid Oak was the power, and the Druid Grove, its expression. It was a simple explanation—obviously the relationship and interconnection between the two was likely much more complex and nuanced than I currently understood. Yet for now, my limited understanding would at least allow me to interact with them in meaningful ways to pursue our mutual goals and needs.

Time to go find out what happened to Jesse—and see if she's still crazier than an outhouse rat.

I stood, unraveling my legs from the lotus position and

shaking them out to encourage circulation and deal with my residual muscle soreness. Then I laid a hand on the bark of the Druid Oak, apologizing for the hundredth time for damaging it and placing us in such a dangerous situation. The Druid Oak sent back feelings of warmth and encouragement. It was incapable of holding a grudge against its master —who could hold a grudge like nobody's business.

When a sentient magical construct is a better person than you are, you know you have issues.

After thanking the Oak for its gracious attitude and helping to keep us safe, I requested to be sent Earthside, back to the junkyard. I no longer had the need to walk widdershins around the Oak's trunk in order to travel to and from the Grove. Now that our connection was complete and whole, it took but a thought for me to travel from that little pocket dimension back to my home on Earth.

As I appeared in the junkyard, standing beneath the expansive reach of the Druid Oak's foliage, I was greeted by a rather peculiar sight. There in front of me, emerging like a sprouting seed from the rich dark earth, was Jesse. She lay on her side, curled up and naked as the day she was born. It occurred to me that she was effectively being birthed from the earth beneath the oak tree, just as if she were a nascent dryad rising up from the soil that gave her life.

For a moment I paused. Although she looked human, I wondered if she really had been made fully human again. Or perhaps she still remained partially or even fully dryad—and therefore, partially or perhaps fully insane.

I'd barely finished that thought when her eyes fluttered open and she took a sharp intake of breath. Then, a single word escaped from those cherry blossom lips I once knew so well.

"Colin?"

It's funny how a heart can break in an instant. Mine broke for her in that moment, seeing her so vulnerable and alone. It had been easy to maintain a level of distrust and animus toward Jesse when she was a dryad. Now, however, she looked very, very human—and very much like the young woman I once loved.

And still love? I guess the jury's out on that.

"I'm here, Jess," I replied.

Despite my misgivings, I immediately began to attend her needs. I pulled a jacket out of my Craneskin Bag, one of the few mundane items I'd chosen not to feed to the Grove, and draped it across her shoulders as she sat up. It was still night-time in the city, but based on the position of the stars, it'd be morning soon. If I had to guess, I'd say that we'd returned to the junkyard within a few hours of the time we'd departed.

Jesse pulled the jacket around herself and shivered, then tucked her hair behind her head self-consciously, her eyes avoiding mine. "Colin, I—am I alive?"

"Let's just get you inside, alright?"

She nodded, and I lent her a hand as she stood on shaky legs, like a newborn foal taking its first steps across the meadow. Jesse leaned against me, hesitantly at first and then with greater confidence as I walked her to the warehouse and my room in the back. The door had been left open, the light was on, and Belladonna's perfume still lingered in the air.

Thankfully, my bed remained intact. Although it was probably time for an upgrade. I'd pulled the rusted old bed frame from a pile of scrap in the yard. Ed had called the rust "patina," which still made me chuckle. I'd never move out of here, not if I could help it, because doing so would be abandoning my uncle's memory. *Still, my lifestyle could definitely use an upgrade.*

Jesse cleared her throat, and I realized I'd allowed my mind to drift. I shook off those stray thoughts and guided her to the only chair in the room.

"You should sit down," I suggested. She obliged, for lack of any other option. I grabbed a blanket off the bed and covered her with it, then pulled a bottle of water from my dorm fridge and handed her that as well.

She still wouldn't look at me, choosing instead to sip at the bottle of water as her eyes darted around the room. "You're sure I'm alive?"

"Yes, Jesse. As far as I can tell, you're alive and human again."

Jess shook her head. "Something's wrong. I'm—seeing things."

"It's probably just a residual effect of being made human again," I offered.

"I had no idea that things would turn out this way," she whispered. "The Dagda offered me a chance to be with you again, and I took it despite the consequences. I'm sorry for all the trouble I've caused."

I really didn't know what to do with myself in the moment, so I plopped down on my bed and followed her lead by avoiding eye contact. "Jesse, there's a lot that needs to be said, but right now I have to know—"

"Do I feel human?" She shrugged with her shoulders slumped and knees together, like a small child awaiting punishment. "I am, at least as far as I can tell. But there's still a little magic there—something that was left behind when I was separated from the Druid Grove's spirit. The question is, am I fully alive?"

"I don't get what you're saying."

Jesse waved my comment off. "It's nothing. Forget I mentioned it."

Since I wasn't getting answers from Jess, I sent a message to the Druid Oak.

What's wrong with her?

The Oak sent me an image of a seed, green and glowing, nestled inside Jesse's chest, alongside something dark and hazy. I took the seed image as a figurative message, an indication that some of the Grove's magic remained inside of her. As for the darkness, I had no clue.

"The Oak agrees that a bit of the nature magic remained inside of you."

She glanced up at me, and for the first time I noticed that her hair had changed. Jesse had taken to dyeing her straight, auburn locks a combination of plum purple and black in the months before she died. Now it really was black as midnight, save for a bright silver mallen streak at her widow's peak, where her hair naturally parted down the middle.

But that wasn't the only thing that had changed. Jesse's moss-green eyes—thankfully now very human-looking—shone like two emeralds, bright and filled with light and life. Yet she'd paled considerably, leaving her formerly-freckled skin an ivory expanse free of any mark or blemish. And standing in stark contrast to her milky white complexion, her lips were the color of dark cherries—or blood, take your pick.

If I didn't know any better, I'd have pegged her for a vampire, but her skin was warm and she had a heartbeat. Clearly, death and the Grove's magic had left its mark on her, in more ways than one.

"It talks to you now?"

I nodded. "It does, the Oak and the Grove both."

She sniffed and rubbed her nose. "Feels weird, not having it inside my head. Like something is missing, you know?"

"I can only imagine. We were stuck in the Void for a while —although it's only been a few hours here—and I've already grown accustomed to it myself."

Jesse pulled the blanket more tightly around her shoulders. "The Grove was falling apart, and had been for some time. What I did, it was desperation—you realize that, right?"

"Did you know what would happen?"

Her eyes darted away as she replied. "No. Back in Underhill, the Dagda had told me that if the Grove was ever in danger, and if you hadn't yet mastered its magic, then I was to seduce you. All I knew at the time was that he wanted you to claim the Grove. Obviously, he's a god and Tuath Dé, so I initially suspected he wasn't telling me the whole truth. But after I became part of the Grove, I acted entirely on instinct. Logic never factored into my decisions."

She's hiding something—but what?

Despite her transformation, I still didn't fully trust her. I chose to respond with a nod, because I was emotionally conflicted and didn't want to say anything I might regret. I'd done more than enough of that over the last few months, that was for certain. A quick glance at her bare feet reminded me that she was still a mess. Jesse had dirt between her toes and in her hair, and smudges here and there on her arms and face.

I clapped my hands on my thighs and stood. "Well, what's done is done. We can unpack all our baggage later, but for now we need to get you cleaned up and dressed. Then, we'll figure out how we're going to explain or hide the fact that you've come back from the dead—this time for real, it seems."

"For a time," she whispered, choking up and burying her face in her hands. Before I could ask her what she meant by that, she continued. "Do you know what? That whole time after I came back, I never once thought about seeing my family. Not once! You can't let them know, Colin—promise me that, please."

"Hey, don't cry now, we'll figure this all out." I reached out for her, hesitating for an instant before I laid a hand on her shoulder. "I promise, alright? Nobody has to know you're back."

Before I knew it, she'd wrapped her arms around my waist and laid her head against my stomach, at which point she began to cry in huge wracking sobs. For lack of any other option I held her close, rubbing her back and whispering that everything would be alright. But that's not how I felt.

Jesse's human again, the Druid Grove is repaired, and we're all back on Earth. This should be a time for celebration. So why does everything feel so wrong?

A few hours later, Jesse had cleaned up and gotten dressed in some clothes Maureen brought for her. While Jess had been showering, I'd called Maureen and then Finnegas, catching them up on all that had happened while simultaneously asking for their assistance. It didn't take long for the two of them to appear, Maureen fussing over the girl while Finnegas cried like a baby. Jesse had been like a daughter to him, so I gave them their privacy while they enjoyed their reunion.

I was sitting on the front steps of the warehouse nursing a beer when Finnegas finally came out to join me.

"So, what do you think?" I asked.

The old man shook his head. "Incredible, never seen anything like it. She's definitely been touched by the Oak's magic. Yet it seems that dying and being brought back to life —twice—has changed in her ways that I don't think we'll understand for some time yet. At least, not until those changes manifest completely."

"It doesn't seem like she retained much of the Grove's magic. Is she still a threat?"

Finnegas patted his pockets absentmindedly. "To us? No, not at all. As far as I can tell, her former personality has reemerged fully. But to herself?" He sighed. "She's been traumatized, my boy. We'll need to keep a close eye on her over the coming weeks, to ensure that she safely readjusts to life as a human."

"I won't let anything happen to her," I said, softly.

"I know you won't."

He sat next to me, patting my knee before carefully packing his pipe. I arched an eyebrow and suppressed a grin as I watched him complete the ritual.

"Back to the pipe? I thought cigarettes were your chosen poison these days."

He lit up and puffed on it a while. "Seemed appropriate."

It occurred to me that the last time I'd seen him smoke that pipe had been when Jesse was still alive. "Are you going to go back to dressing like a college professor, too?"

He frowned. "Pfah, I only dressed like that because it was good for business. No point anymore, now that Éire Imports is shut down." He had a twinkle in his eye I'd rarely seen in recent days. "I'm glad to know that everything turned out well. Jesse is more or less back to her old self, and you've claimed the Grove. Healed it up good as new from what I can tell."

"It wasn't easy, let me tell you." I took a deep breath, letting it out slowly. "You think Jesse will be alright?"

Finnegas tsked. "She's a tough one, always has been. The girl will pull through, with our support. The more pressing concern is how we're going to hide her, now that she's back."

"Hmm… yeah, I thought about that. Don't you think it should be her decision, who she tells and who she doesn't?"

The old man scratched his forehead. "Maureen seems to think—"

The loud screech of tires cut him off mid-sentence. We both stood, watching with interest as three large black SUVs with dark limo tint and government plates squealed to a halt in the junkyard parking lot. No sooner had they stopped than over a dozen men and women in black tactical gear poured out, guns drawn as they took cover behind the vehicles. Every barrel was trained on us.

"Fecking Cerberus. I was afraid this would happen," he hissed.

"Afraid what would happen?" I asked. "Finnegas, what's going on?"

He spat and dumped the cherry from his pipe bowl, tucking the pipe away as he leaned against a rusty metal support pillar. "We drew the attention of the wrong people, son." He turned his head and gave me a look that brooked no argument. "Whatever happens, leave the talking to me."

An athletic man with olive skin and dark, crew cut hair stepped out of the lead vehicle. He wore a Kevlar vest over a white dress shirt and black suit pants, a walking cliché if I ever saw one. His eyes were hidden behind a pair of mirrored aviators, and instead of a pistol he held a document in his hand. He swaggered up to the gates as if he owned the place, disdain written across his face.

I already hate this guy, and we haven't even been introduced.

The place was still locked up, which meant he was locked out. On seeing the lock and chain, the agent held his papers up like a cleric presenting a talisman against the forces of evil.

"Colin McCool! My name is Special Agent Mendoza. I'm from the Department of Homeland Security, and we have a warrant to search these premises. Open the gates and allow us to search the facility, or we'll cut the locks off and enter by force."

I looked over at Finnegas. "Should I warn Maureen?"

"Trust me, she knows. Probably on the phone with Borovitz and Feldstein as we speak."

"Finn, why is DHS here?"

He chuckled humorlessly. "They're not DHS, although that's what their badges and identification will say. You'd best let them in—and drop your wards, too. They're bound to have a few non-humans in the mix. No sense getting them riled up more than they already are."

Agent Mendoza called to us from the other side of the gate. "I'm running out of patience, Mr. McCool. Trust me, you do not want to do this the hard way."

I grabbed Finnegas by the shirt sleeve. "Who are these people?"

He rubbed his chin and scowled. "Lotta folks think the PATRIOT Act was written to fight terrorists. It wasn't. It was penned so people like Agent Mendoza and his crew could rendition good folks like Maureen and Jesse."

"Wait—you mean they're clued in?"

"Yes." He leaned in and whispered to me. "We're human, and so long as we don't show any sign of magical ability, we're safe. Do not work any magic, other than quietly releasing your wards—and definitely don't let them near Maureen or Jesse, you hear me? Whatever it takes, keep them out of sight, or we might never see either of them again!"

5

Mendoza and his agents split into teams of four, with two teams searching the warehouse and yard while he and the remainder of his people tore through our offices with a vengeance. They tossed papers everywhere, overturned desks, rifled through file cabinets, and ripped posters and pictures off the wall. Nothing was sacrosanct to them, and they took what they wanted, which was pretty much every written record and receipt. Finally, they shoved it all in boxes along with our computers, and packed them in their vehicles.

I sat to the side, fuming but saying nothing. Finn had warned me to keep my mouth shut until someone from Borovitz and Feldstein arrived. Mendoza stood in front of me, communicating on a walkie-talkie with his other teams. Apparently, they had yet to find Maureen and Jesse, so that was a plus. But something told me they weren't going to leave until they found whatever it was they'd come for—which I assumed was evidence of supernatural activity or involvement.

Mendoza marched up and hovered over me, hands on his hips. He was obviously trying to intimidate me, but it wasn't working. The agent whipped off his aviators, then he glared at me for what seemed like an eternity. Finally, he spoke in a low voice.

"Three major terrorist events in the span of two weeks, and you know what they all have in common?"

Finnegas smirked. "Don't say a word, boy."

Mendoza ignored the old man. "No? I'll tell you. A certain college student and junkyard owner was spotted by eyewitnesses at each scene. First, we have you on camera at a convenience store on the east side of Bastrop. You were in a late model Corvette with a tall, blonde female we have yet to identify. However, we have reason to believe she has ties to the Russian government." He showed me a picture on his phone of me, standing in line at the counter waiting to buy a slushy, a bag of caramel corn, and a pecan log. "This was just a few hours before that medical research facility got blown sky-high."

I did my best to appear disinterested. Mendoza swiped to another photo on his phone. It was of me again, this time barefoot in jeans and a t-shirt, running down West Avenue toward the collapse.

"This is a photo of you, taken by a bystander, at the scene of the building collapse in downtown Austin. You know, the one where eight hundred and fifty-seven lives were lost?"

"I thought the official number was eight hundred and forty-nine," Finnegas interjected, stone-faced.

The agent kept his eyes on me. "Yes, that was the official count." He swiped one more time. "And this is a photo of you, taken by a traffic camera in Glen Rose, the day of the meltdown at the nuclear reactor outside town."

The photo was blurry, but it was definitely me, running a red light in a rental car registered in my name. I silently cursed myself for needlessly being in a hurry that day.

Agent Mendoza leaned forward, hands on his knees, as he got in my face. "So tell me, McCool—how is it that you just happened to be at the scene of three major disasters that happened at three different locations, all over the state of Texas?"

About that time, a very well-dressed blonde with a very expensive haircut and highlights walked through our front gates. She wore a pencil skirt and matching suit jacket, a silk blouse, sensible pumps, and she carried a Burberry briefcase in her left hand. In her right she held a business card, which she extended to Agent Mendoza.

"Are you the special agent in charge?" she asked Mendoza.

"I am," he replied frostily.

"Kenzie Kupert of Borovitz and Feldstein, Attorneys at Law. Mr. McCool and Mr. Murphy have both retained the services of our firm. Are my clients being detained?"

"Not yet," Mendoza said with a curious gleam in his eye.

She turned her steel gray eyes on me. "Colin, you're not required to answer any of his questions. My Audi is parked in front. Go wait for me inside and speak to no one until I join you."

I shrugged and stood, but Mendoza motioned for me to halt. "Not so fast. We have reason to believe your client is a material witness in a case involving domestic terrorists operating on U.S. soil. As such, I have the right to detain him if I believe he presents a flight risk. And, I do."

Finnegas laughed while Kupert glowered at Mendoza. "Preposterous. My client is a law-abiding college student and a hard-working business owner. To claim that he has knowledge of any terrorist activities is simply ludicrous."

"Nevertheless, I do have the right to detain him—indefinitely, if need be." He motioned to a pair of agents who were standing by. "Grimes and Case, take Mr. McCool into custody."

"You have got to be fucking kidding me," I hissed. Despite my concern, Finnegas seemingly found the situation to be very amusing. I decided it was likely an act, meant to keep Mendoza and his team focused on us.

"You're definitely too pretty to go to jail, that's for sure," the old man chortled.

Kupert gave us each a hard look. "Please, not another word—from either of you."

Finn winked at the pretty young attorney. "Oh, I'll be fine, ma'am. Just minding my own business." He then nodded at me. "She's right, you need to keep your mouth shut."

I made the universal sign for zipping my lips and throwing away the key. Then, I held my hands up to show I didn't intend to fight being taken into custody. I figured it was better that I get arrested by these chumps instead of Maureen or Jesse, and I was pretty sure the old man would agree with me.

Mendoza smirked. "Wise choice, kid."

I flipped him off with both barrels and a smile. Mendoza's smirk turned into a snarl as he got up in my face, drill sergeant style.

"You want me to put you in cuffs? Keep trying me, kid, and I'll lock you in a hole so deep, every time you take a piss you'll be watering flowers in China. I'm begging you, keep it up and I'll show you how the Federal Government treats suspected terrorists."

Kupert was on her phone, and I overheard the words "U.S. Attorney" and "immediately." She covered the receiver as she addressed Agent Mendoza. "If that's the case, then we're going to need to see some formal charges. And, I want a copy of that search warrant."

Mendoza smiled at Kupert like a wolf eyeing a newborn lamb. "I'll get right on that, your highness." He turned to the same two agents he'd addressed earlier. "Didn't I tell you to take McCool into custody? Cuff him, damn it!"

I looked at my mentor. "Finnegas—"

"Just go with it, son. They have jack squat, and Mendoza knows it. This whole damned thing is nothing more than one big fishing expedition. Keep quiet, do as your told, and Borovitz's team will have you out in no time."

Meanwhile, the two agents had already jumped into action. Before Finnegas was through talking, they'd manhandled me out of my chair and slammed me facedown in the dirt and weeds. Soon I had my hands cuffed behind my back, and the bastards even zip-tied my ankles to the handcuffs. One of the agents continued to kneel on me, digging his knee into my spine. Kupert nearly had a fit.

"This is an outrage, Agent Mendoza, and your superiors will be hearing about this—"

"Agent Case, escort Ms. Kupert to her car. She can speak with her client when we're damned good and ready. Grimes, ease up on the kid. We need him to cooperate." Mendoza squatted next to me, leaning in close to whisper in my ear. "What your pretty little attorney doesn't know is that we don't answer to the Justice Department. Just wait,

McCool—once I get you someplace private, the real fun will start."

"Why, Agent Mendoza," I said aloud, "I'm flattered, but you're just not my type."

Finnegas guffawed.

"Shut it, old man," Mendoza snapped, "or I'll cuff you too."

The old druid gave an innocent smile and pulled out his tobacco pouch.

Mendoza looked like he was about to say something else to me when one of his agents came in over the radio. At the same time, screams and gunfire erupted in the distance.

"Sir, this is Agent Wurzel—we have a problem!"

Mendoza stood and grabbed his radio. "What is it, Wurzel?"

"Potential Level Five entity, headed your way. She took out Reagan and Cox without batting an eye. I've taken cover behind a stack of junked cars, but—"

Finnegas sighed as he rolled a cigarette. "Now you've done it."

The transmission cut out, and we could hear another scream across the yard, this time much closer. Mendoza yelled into his radio.

"Wurzel. Wurzel!" Nothing. He clicked the transmit button again. "All agents, converge on the front office, now! I repeat, converge on the front office immediately!"

Mendoza holstered his radio as he reached behind his back to draw his sidearm. I was familiar with most modern firearms, but the thing in his hand looked nothing like any production pistol I'd ever seen. It was a revolver, that much was clear, but the barrel was even larger than a twelve-gauge shotgun. The ugly, flat-black gun looked as though it only held four rounds in the cylinder, which was similarly over-sized and longer like one of those .410 pistols. Whatever the damned thing was, something told me it could do some real damage.

Case and Grimes were the only agents who had responded to Mendoza's call. They had lined up beside him shoulder-to-shoulder, each armed with a smaller version of Mendoza's pistol. One of the junior agents tossed an object up in the air, something that looked like a coil of thick copper wire. It snapped open over their heads, instantly trans-forming into a stiff wire hoop approximately seven feet in diameter. The hoop landed on the ground, and I heard a "whoomp" sound.

It's a fucking ward circle, one that uses technomagic. Who the hell are these people?

There were more screams and gunshots as the seconds ticked by, each time getting closer and closer to where the three agents waited. I was working on getting out of my cuffs, which were spelled against magical tampering, and craned my neck to see what was going on. I wondered for a moment if I was about to see Maureen in all her kelpie glory, but that's not who walked through the gate to the junkyard.

Nope. It was Jesse, still in human form, but with her eyes glowing green, and her jet-black hair whipping around like Medusa's tresses even though it was a windless morning. She took a few unhurried steps toward us, her lips drawn in a tight line, her fists clenching and unclenching at her sides, each wreathed in black fire. She saw me and stopped in place, maybe twenty feet distant.

"Colin, are you alright?"

"I'm fine, but you need to stand down," I replied.

"Did they hurt you?" she asked.

"No, I'm alright. Just back off, okay?"

"Take her out," Mendoza muttered, and all three agents fired at once.

Three things happened simultaneously. First, I snapped the cuffs open and cast them off me. Second, a wall of earth rose up in front of Jesse. And third, several dozen strange, dart-like projectiles appeared in the earthen wall that stood between the agents and my ex-girlfriend.

Dark, spiny vines grew up from the ground around the edges of the agent's ward circle, each thorn dripping with black sap that I assumed was poison. Something about the vines she'd conjured was *off*, for lack of a better word, but I didn't have time to mull it over. More and more vines sprouted up around the agents, but their magic barrier was keeping Jesse's spell work at bay. The agents were still firing at her, and while neither side was doing much damage at the moment, it was clear that someone would get hurt if the fight were to continue.

I sat up and cut the zip ties from my ankles with my belt knife. Finnegas was already kneeling at my side, grinning like he was enjoying the whole messed up situation.

"So, the girl didn't retain much of the Grove's magic, huh?" he said.

I held my index finger and thumb apart. "I might have underestimated the situation—just a wee bit."

The battle between Jesse and the agents continued to escalate, with the agents shooting continuously as the vines slammed repeatedly against their magic barrier. Mendoza was on his phone calling in reinforcements, and Jesse was floating off the ground. Wherever she floated, the earthen wall shifted to protect her and keep her from getting at the agents, so I figured that was the Oak's doing. Eventually she'd get around it, which meant we needed to end this, fast.

What a clusterfuck, I thought as I turned to Finn.

"Any suggestions on how to keep them from killing each other?" I asked.

He frowned. "Well, if ever there was a time to 'snap your fingers' and stop the clock, this would be it."

"Huh? What do you—oh, right." I looked at the agents and Jesse, doing the calculations in my head. "It won't last long, not if I have to include them all."

"All we need is a minute or so," he replied.

"You sure? Because you told me that I shouldn't—"

"Just do it!" he yelled.

Finnegas almost never yelled, so I figured I'd better comply. I checked to make certain no one would see me release the casting. The three agents were focused on the threat in front of them, and no one else was present to observe. After making a few quick, precise, esoteric gestures, I said the trigger word.

A split-second later, everything froze in a thirty-foot sphere that was just barely large enough to include the agents and Jesse.

Finnegas whistled soft and low. "I see you've been practicing." As he admired my work, the old man walked around the edges of my spell to avoid getting caught in the stasis field.

"Well, there wasn't much else to do when I was stuck in the Void," I muttered, embarrassed at having been caught practicing forbidden magic. "C'mon, we need to get Jesse out of here while the spell is still in effect."

As I sprinted toward Jesse and the earthen barrier, I

snatched one of the now floating projectiles from the air, then handed it to Finnegas. His lip curled as he examined it.

"Flechette rounds—nasty. Plus, it's technomagic, just like that barrier they used. Cold iron laced with silver, poisoned with a paralytic." He frowned and tossed it away. "There's some sort of tracking spell on it as well."

"Shit. Who the hell are these clowns, anyway?"

"I'll explain later. Right now, we need to get you two far, far away from here. I'll get Maureen to mind-wipe these agents—maybe make them think they got into a fight with some rogue Circle operatives." He nodded at Jesse, who'd been struck by a flechette just as she'd become frozen by my stasis spell. "The wound doesn't appear to be deep, but I have a feeling the poison will leave her defenseless for a time. Grab her and let's get out of here."

I grabbed Jesse and carried her out of the range of my stasis spell, then laid her on the ground so I could make sure she was okay. She was unconscious, but otherwise fine. Relieved, I pulled the dart from Jesse's arm, but as I did, the tip broke off and dug itself deeper into her flesh.

"Finnegas, a piece of the flechette came loose, and it's burrowing into her arm."

The old druid turned to look just as the tiny piece of metal wriggled deeper, vanishing completely. "Pfah! I'm not going to be able to extract it, not in the time we have. These technomagic gizmos have a mind of their own, making them much harder to counteract. Best we can do is leave it in for now, and once you're safe you two can work on removing it. Until then, however, Mendoza will be able to track you."

"Great."

Lacking any alternative, I threw Jesse over my shoulder and followed my mentor. Finnegas made a beeline for the

Druid Oak, passing a handful of unconscious agents along the way. As we neared the tree, Maureen dropped from its branches. She took one look at Jesse, and her brow furrowed.

"What's wrong with the lass? I swear, if those eejits hurt her—"

"She's fine, Maureen," Finnegas said. "Just unconscious. She'll recover momentarily, likely as soon as she's back in the Grove."

"What set her off?" I asked.

"Well, we were hidin' in the tree, or the tree were hidin' us, I suppose. I thought we were in the clear, then one o' those thugs pointed his weapon at Rufus. Next thing ya know, the lass drops to the ground and starts waylayin' those agents left an' right."

Finnegas tsked. "Well, what's done is done." He stroked his beard. "Although, I'd be curious to know if it was her decision to protect Rufus, or some residual influence left over from her time as a dryad."

Jesse was starting to stir, so I carefully laid her down at the base of the Oak. "You think the Grove might still be influencing her?"

The old druid shook his head. "I can't be certain, and there's no time to discuss it. Maureen, please see about erasing the recent memories of these government thugs. Colin, get Jesse inside the Grove, and get yourselves as far away from here as you can. Once you're safe, don't contact me. Mendoza isn't stupid, and eventually he'll figure out that someone tampered with his memory. He'll soon put two and two together and start looking for you again."

"But what about you and Maureen?"

The flame-haired half-kelpie patted me on my cheek. "Ya' needn't worry about me, lad. T'wouldn't be the first time the

Gardaí came knocking on my door. I know how not ta' be found. And as fer the Seer, he kin take care o' himself."

"But—"

The old man cut me off. "She's right, we'll be fine. Now, get out of here so we can make sure you aren't followed!"

"Damn it. Alright, but be careful," I admonished.

"Don't tell your grandmother how to suck eggs," Finnegas said with a wink.

"Grandmother? From your lips to my ears, old man."

"Ye'd best not be referrin' ta' me, either of ya'," Maureen warned.

I smiled and grabbed Jesse's hand, then placed a hand on the Oak's trunk and willed us into the Grove.

6

My primary concern was getting Jesse someplace safe and away from Mendoza and his agents. But I also wanted to warn my friends. Anyone who'd helped me recently could be a target, and while Luther and Samson had subordinates and attorneys to look out for them, Hemi and Maki did not.

So, I instructed the Oak to transport us to the Williamson Creek greenbelt near Hemi's apartment. Then, I asked the Grove to look after Jesse while she recovered, and to keep her from leaving, at least until I returned. She'd be safe inside the Grove, but as soon as she left the pocket dimension, Mendoza would know where she was. Once I was certain the Grove and Oak knew what to do, I went Earthside and headed to Hemi's apartment.

Hemi answered the door with his typical broad smile and happy, quiet voice. "Bro, good to see you. I—"

I pushed him inside, closing the door only after I checked to make sure no one had followed me. "Hemi, no time to explain. Can you and Maki leave town for a few days?"

He scratched his head. "Hmm. Bit of a problem, that. Maki is—er, *away*—visiting family. I can get word to her to stay away. But I'm stuck here, aye? No wheels."

"Shit. Okay, I guess you're coming with me." My phone rang, reminding me that I had forgotten to turn it off and remove the SIM card. I was about to do exactly that when I noticed who was calling. "Maureen, what's—?"

"Glad yer too dense to turn off yer phone. Look, more o' those goons showed up at the junkyard afore I could wipe Mendoza's memories. The Seer and I made ourselves scarce afore they saw us, but chances are they'll be on yer tails in no time."

"Crap! Okay, I'm just warning Hemi, then we're taking off."

"While I admire yer loyalty, lad, Hemi is a demigod, and quite capable of taking care o' himself. You worry aboot gettin' that lass away from here, afore those agents find ye agin." She paused, and I heard her conversing with someone in the background. "Oh, and the Seer says ye should cast a small stasis spell on the thingy in Jesse's arm. It'll keep those Cerberus eejits from tracking the girl down."

"I'll do that, Maureen, and thanks for the heads up."

"Fine, then you two be safe. An' turn off yer blasted phone!"

In true Maureen fashion, she'd simultaneously expressed deep concern for my well-being and chewed my ass, almost in the same breath. I chuckled as I snapped the back off my phone, removing the battery and SIM card, which I tossed in my Craneskin Bag. Hopefully I'd be able to find them again, when needed.

"I heard the important bits," Hemi said. "Got the plod after us, aye?"

"If by 'plod' you mean law enforcement, then yes, we do," I replied.

"Thug life it is, then," he said with a bemused grin. "Plan?"

"The plan is to get us the hell out of here. They tagged Jesse with some kind of tracking magic, so we need to take care of that as well." He winced at hearing Jesse's name. "What?"

"Well, it's just that—you know. *Bells.*"

"She told you what happened? Seriously?"

"Not exactly. Called in the middle of the night. Something about 'skank dryads.' Oh, and that you two were through."

I sighed. "This day could not get any worse."

Hemi shook his head. "Bro, no need to jinx."

"You're right. Let's go before shit really goes sideways."

At the precise moment I reached for the doorknob, a very authoritative female voice came booming over a loud-speaker outside. "Mr. McCool, Mr. Waara, this is Lieutenant Carollton from the Austin Police Department. I'm on orders from the Department of Homeland Security to detain you until they arrive. Please come out with your hands held high and in plain view."

I glanced out the door's peephole. There were a number of APD squad cars outside, and about twice the number of uniformed police with guns drawn.

"She's not lying—we're surrounded."

Hemi winced again. "My landlady'll be so pissed off."

"I'll explain it to her later. Is there a back exit?"

He gave me the stink-eye. "Not even. She hates you, cuz. And no, there isn't."

"What do you mean? Your landlady loves me. You've seen the way she looks at me."

"That's the problem, aye? Cougars don't like to be ignored."

I smirked. "So then, why does she love you so much?"

"Watch it," he warned, pushing my head down so he could glance out the peephole. "Any ideas?"

"Besides casting another time magic spell, and yet again risking getting my ass in a sling with who knows what gods for using forbidden magic?"

Hemi arched an eyebrow at me. "Oi, bro—we seriously need to catch up. Yeah, besides that."

"Not a clue, brother. I think I screwed the pooch on this one." I reached into my Bag and pulled out Gunnarson's cloak of invisibility. "I do have this thing, but there's only the one."

"Ah. Wondered what happened to that."

"Wait a minute—maybe we can use this to our advantage. If I create a distraction, do you think you can sneak out a back window and meet me down at the creek?"

"Colin, this is a garage apartment. There is no back window."

"Huh. How did this thing ever pass code when it was built?"

"It's ancient is how. Let's just turn ourselves in, yeah?"

"Sorry, man, can't do that. Here, take the cloak—hopefully it'll work for you—and I'll find a way out on my own. The Druid Oak is parked down by Williamson Creek, in a copse of trees about a quarter-mile east of here."

Hemi took the cloak and held it up to his ear, frowning. "Says it's more than happy to help a demigod—me being worthy of it and all—but man does it hate you."

I rolled my eyes. "Tell me something I don't know."

He looked to the east, which happened to be in the direction of his living room wall. "Think I see the Oak. Strong magic, that. Kinda stands out."

"Which is why we're going to have to stash it somewhere the feds won't look. But we can talk about that later—just head to the Oak and make sure Jesse stays inside."

"She still crazy?"

"Remains to be seen, but I think it comes in fits and spurts. I'll meet you there in fifteen minutes."

"Alright, bro. Be safe."

"People keep telling me that, and honestly, it's not that reassuring."

Hemi chuckled, then slipped on the cloak and disappeared from sight. I opened the door to the garage so he could escape, and stepped out into the open with my hands held high.

One thing nobody tells you when you become a druid is that nature magic is far more powerful than it first appears. Sure, other types of magic are more expedient and flashier, but when you can harness nature's power, the only real limit to what you can do is your imagination. And right now, I needed a pretty big distraction, something to take APD's attention off me so I could escape.

Lightning strike? Hmm, too dangerous. Earthquake? Naw, I doubt I could pull it off. Windstorm? It'll take too long.

"Mr. McCool," the officer said over her patrol car's PA system. I acted like I couldn't hear, because I needed to stall while I came up with a solution to the situation. "Sir, I need you to lay down on your stomach with your hands behind your head. Now!"

I heard another cop talking to the one on the bullhorn, who I figured was Carollton. "You want me to gas him?"

Carollton shook her head. "No, but when he gets closer, taser him."

Gas. Fog. Bingo.

Winters tended to be pretty wet in Austin, and this one had been no exception. Thankfully, I'd become much better at manipulating heat, cold, and the elements while rebuilding the Druid Grove. There was plenty of moisture in the ground and air to work with, so forming a nice thick bank of fog would be a piece of cake.

Officer Carollton continued to bark commands at me, while I acted dumb and mumbled my spells. The first spell heated up the ground within a half-block radius around us, causing moisture to evaporate into the air. I did that by redistributing the radiant heat from the sun being absorbed by the air molecules above us. That lowered the air temperature, and combined with the rapid increase in humidity, I hoped it would produce fog.

Still, I wasn't taking any chances. After casting the spells I stealth-shifted, because I definitely didn't want a repeat of the time my teenage friend Kenny had gotten me tasered. Since I was ignoring the cops, things were starting to get tense. Several more of them were yelling at me now, and they all looked pretty weirded out by the rapidly-falling air temperature. Two of them had their tasers drawn, and they were inching their way toward me while screaming for me to get down on the ground.

C'mon, magic, do your thing. Work, damn it.

Just when I thought things were about to go sideways, the ambient temperature finally reached the dew point and thick mists began to roll up from the ground all around us.

Meanwhile, the earth was still heating up underfoot, forcing every last bit of water it held into the air. This increased the rate at which the air became saturated, and within seconds, the area surrounding Hemi's pad was thick with the type of dense fog you normally only saw in horror movies.

"What the hell?" one of the cops said.

"Where'd he go?" another asked.

"Taser him, now!" the lieutenant ordered.

Too late. See ya, suckas!

I'd already ducked around the side of the garage, headed for the creek out back. The small tributary snaked through this entire neighborhood, its banks bordering many of the homes here, Hemi's included. I followed the spreading fog bank as I made my escape, sneaking past two uniformed officers. Soon, I'd slipped past their cordon, hidden in the dense cloud of water that had been formed by nature magic —my magic.

And I didn't even have to resort to violence. Finnegas would be so proud.

Once past the officers, I took off at a run down the creek toward the spot where I'd left Jesse and the Oak. When I arrived, Jesse was standing next to the tree, screaming at Hemi. He stood in front of her looking bored, tattoos glowing.

"Hemi, I know you don't know me, but I'm warning you— you need to get out of my way, now!" she warned.

The big Maori scratched his nose. He looked calm, but I knew better. "Sorry. Colin said you need to stay here."

"Fine," Jesse replied. "But remember, you asked—"

"Jesse!" I yelled as I came up on them. "For heaven's sakes, settle down already. I got away."

Hemi looked over his shoulder and nodded at me. "See?

Told you the druid had it under control." As he stepped out of the way, the bright blue glow slowly faded from his skin.

Jesse looked relieved, and a little embarrassed. "I just—I thought you were in trouble. The Grove sensed you were in danger, but that's all I got from it, just the feeling. So I freaked out."

I looked at Hemi. "Did you mention that they tagged her?"

"I did. She wouldn't listen."

"Jess, you have to get back in the Grove, now. That agent who came after us earlier shot you with some kind of tracking device. Finnegas told me how to neutralize it, but until we're well away from Austin I think it best you stay hidden. I—"

I was cut off as several flechette rounds hit the Oak's trunk next to me. A quick glance through the trees told me that Mendoza and his goons had located us, and a good number of them were headed our way. Thankfully, both Jesse and Hemi had taken cover with me behind the Oak.

"Alright, boys and girls—looks like it's time to go." I grabbed them each by the wrist and leaned my forehead against the tree.

Get us out of here, now!

The Oak responded with a query, flashing images of several locations in a rapid-fire sequence through my mind.

Yes, that one—go!

The scene around us faded out. A moment later, I was standing in the Druid Grove with Jesse and Hemi by my side.

"Oi, we lose those plods?" Hemi asked.

I wiggled my hand back and forth. "Sort of. We're miles away from them, but they'll be on us in no time flat, now that the tree got tagged." The Oak sent me an image of metal termites burrowing into its bark, and then a fast-forward scene of the sun rising and setting over a forest twice. "It'll be a few days before the Oak gets rid of the trackers, so we'll have to ditch it. I'll have it hop to several locations around town to throw Mendoza off our trail. After that, I'm sending it into the Void to hide while it expels the tracking devices."

Jesse sat heavily on a nearby rock. "Can't we just stay in the Grove until then?"

"Uh-uh, nope," I countered. "For one, I just spent a shit-ton of time locked inside the Grove, in the Void, while it was healing. I have no desire to do a repeat anytime soon. And second, there are dangerous things in the Void. The Oak and Grove can hide from them easily. But without knowing what powers you have, or how well you can control them, I think taking you to the Void would be a mistake. All it'd take is one slip and we'd be swimming in extra-dimensional bad guys. So again, the answer is no."

"Didn't happen just now," she whispered, looking away from me.

"It's not a chance I'm willing to take," I replied.

"So, where'd you take us?" Hemi asked.

"To the nature preserve where the Austin Pack conducts their monthly hunts—among other things. Look, I'm not supposed to bring non-Pack members here, but considering the extenuating circumstances, I figured bending the rules a little wouldn't hurt. But those feds are going to be here within the hour, and the clock starts ticking as soon as we leave the Grove. We need to secure a vehicle, grab some supplies, and be in the wind long before they arrive."

Hemi tilted his head toward Jesse. "Forget something?"

"Ah, hell. Jess, c'mere, so I can deal with that tracker they shot you with. I can't remove it, but I can nullify the magic for a while. Once things settle down, we can get back to Finnegas and have him deal with it."

"Sure, whatever," she said as she stood and pulled up the sleeve of her t-shirt. She pointed to her shoulder, a few inches from the small incision left when the device burrowed into her skin. "I can feel it right about here."

"Alright, hang on. It'll take a few seconds to get this right."

I looked at her arm in the magical spectrum, just to ensure that my stasis spell only affected the foreign object. The last thing I wanted to do was freeze the blood in a major artery and cause her arm to go gangrenous. Once I had a lock on the tracker, I encased it in the smallest stasis field possible.

"Done. Just remember that I'll have to renew the spell every few days, or else it'll wear off and we'll have Mendoza and his team up our butts again."

Jesse nodded, avoiding eye contact as she pulled her sleeve back down. I looked at Hemi, who just shrugged. He was just as clueless as I was when it came to the female species. I cleared my throat, needlessly.

"Alright, so here's the plan. We're about a quarter-mile from the Pack's second clubhouse, which is on private land adjacent to the nature preserve. Once we leave the Grove, I'm sending it on its way—after that, we're on our own. So, we're going to haul ass to the clubhouse, grab some supplies, gear, and spare clothes, and then we're going to borrow a vehicle and get as far away from Austin as possible. Questions?"

Hemi shook his head, while Jesse just hugged herself and looked away. I laid a hand on each of them and willed the Oak to send us Earthside. Once we were standing in the

Balcones Canyonlands National Wildlife Refuge, I told the Oak to go hide in the Void. One minute the tree was there, and the next, nothing.

I wiped imaginary dust from my hands. "Well, let's get moving. And if we run into anyone, let me do the talking."

"Yeah, because the Pack just *loves* you," Hemi quipped.

"To quote Machiavelli, 'it is much safer to be feared than loved,'" I replied as I took off at a jog toward the clubhouse.

"Unless you're feared by an entire pack of werewolves," he muttered, following along and somehow managing to keep the pace in his flip-flops.

No matter how cold it got in Austin, the big Maori always dressed like he was hanging out on Waikiki. I glanced back to check on Jesse, worried she might go all mystic-ballistic again if there were any werewolves nearby. My fears proved to be unfounded—she jogged behind Hemi with her head down and eyes set on the ground in front of her.

As for her sudden withdrawal, I didn't know whether it was guilt, or losing her connection to the Grove, or the fact that she felt out of sorts in her human body. Or maybe it was not having complete control over whatever magic she had left? Obviously, she had to be struggling to cope now that she was human again, but I had no idea how to help her through the readjustment process.

And while I truly did feel sorry for her, the last several months I'd spent dealing with her as "dryad-Jesse" had seriously damaged our relationship. Sure, I still had feelings for her, but right now I felt little desire to rekindle our romantic relationship. I knew it wasn't fair to hold the things she'd done while under the Grove's influence against her, but those wounds were still too fresh to allow me to fully trust her yet.

And then there was the matter of Belladonna. It occurred to me that I hadn't missed her all that much while I was training with Click inside the Bag, and even less so during my time in the Void. I'd spent the Earth equivalent of years apart from her, and rather than absence making the heart grow fonder, it'd had the opposite effect. During all that time I realized that I still cared for Belladonna, but like Jesse, I no longer felt the same intense attraction for her that I once had.

In hindsight, we'd barely gotten past the physical attraction stage. And we rarely got along, except when we were screwing like rabbits. Belladonna was a hard nut to crack. I'd tried and tried to get close to her emotionally, but every time I thought I was making progress, she'd push me away. It was incredibly frustrating.

Bells had been a good friend, that was undeniable. Did I care for her? Of course, and that would never change. But did I love her? I could have, if she'd have let me. But if I was being honest with myself, I certainly didn't now—not any more than I felt romantically inclined toward Jesse. It was time for me to be honest with myself, and with the both of them as well.

Admitting that is such a relief, I reflected with a sigh. *So, what now?*

I knew what I had to do, but I didn't want to deal with it just yet. Besides, it was hardly the time to have a sit-down with Bells, or a heart-to-heart with Jesse. With a mental shrug, I decided I'd deal with everything once we were safely out of Mendoza's reach.

Yeah, right—sure you will.

For a moment, I wished I was back in the Void. Monsters were so much easier to cope with than relationships.

7

A few minutes later, we exited the woods and stepped onto the long gravel drive that led to the Pack's second clubhouse. We were in the middle of the moon cycle, so I doubted anyone would be here. Still, it paid to be careful.

"Try to stay out of sight until I give you guys the all-clear," I whispered.

Jesse glanced around furtively, then trained her eyes on the ground with a nervous nod. She looked scared, but of what I had no idea. I made a mental note to ask her about it when the time was right.

"Um, does Samson know you're borrowing his stuff?" Hemi asked.

"No, and I think it's best we keep it that way. Heck, we'll probably return everything before they even know it's gone."

Hemi scratched his head. "If you say so, bro."

I watched them fade back into the tree line, then jogged in plain sight up the driveway toward the house. Soon the clubhouse came into view, and I cocked an ear as I scanned the area. The place looked empty, and the only sounds were birds chirping, a squirrel chittering in the trees to my right, and the wind rustling leaves in the trees nearby.

Looks like no one's home. Peachy.

Taking the porch steps two at a time, I stopped just before the top step, lifting it up to retrieve the spare key that the Pack kept underneath. The steps were made from heavy slabs of red granite, so only a shifter would be able to lift it. And besides, who'd be stupid enough to break into a place owned by a pack of werewolf bikers?

The only problem was, the key was missing. Someone cleared their throat nearby, and I jumped as I spun toward the sound. Fallyn leaned against the corner of the house, arms crossed as her face split in a wolfish grin. Her hazel, almost yellow eyes sparkled, a good indication that she'd been stalking us since we'd stepped foot on the property.

"Ahem, looking for this?" The she-wolf dangled a house key from her finger.

"Fallyn! Didn't expect to see you out here," I said, bringing the pitch of my voice down a few notches.

"Meh, I was out here checking on some things. Somebody tripped our trespass alarms, but all I found were coyote tracks." Her eyes narrowed, then she arched an eyebrow. "I was about ready to head home until you showed up, Golden Boy. You want to tell me why you're here?"

"We were in the neighborhood, and I just, you know, wanted to drop in for old time's sake."

She snorted. "You are such a sorry liar, Colin. Don't even bother feeding me that line of horse shit, because I already know why you're here. Maureen called to warn us about the raid, and she filled me in on the rest."

"Did she, uh, tell you about Jesse?"

Fallyn pushed off the wall, tossing her chestnut hair over

her shoulder. "The broad strokes. We'd best not waste time—
I don't want those cops showing up here with a warrant. We
have enough trouble keeping Fish and Wildlife off our backs
when we hunt in the refuge." The werewolf nodded toward
the driveway. "C'mon inside. Those two can come along, too."

Hemi stepped out of the woods, waving. "Heya, Fallyn,"
he said with his usual cheerful grin.

"Hi, Hemi." Jesse stepped out from behind Hemi, looking
self-conscious and out of sorts. Fallyn's lips pressed into a
tight line. "Jesse, I take it? C'mon, darlin', let's get you inside. I
think I have some clothes that'll fit you better."

"Thank you," Jesse said softly. She walked up the porch,
avoiding my gaze. Fallyn placed an arm around Jesse and led
her inside. The werewolf's lips were set in a tight frown, and
she slowly shook her head at me as she passed.

I rubbed my chin as I looked at Hemi, and he at me.

"They communicate by telepathy. I'm certain of it,"
he said.

"It's as good an explanation as any," I replied. "We really
don't have much time, so let's go grab some stuff while Fallyn
is getting Jesse squared away."

Lucky for us, the Pack kept this clubhouse well-stocked,
just in case they had to bug out on short notice. Within
minutes, Hemi and I had gathered a pile of camping gear in
the living room, including a tent, some sleeping bags, a
bunch of canned and freeze-dried food, a couple cases of
bottled water, three backpacks, and a few other odds
and ends.

Fallyn joined us while we were sorting and packing our
loot. "Jesse's trying on some clothes. The stuff she had on was
practically falling off her."

"They're Maureen's, I think," I said, preoccupied with packing.

Fallyn grabbed me by my shoulders and spun me around to face her. She might have been smaller than me, but she was damned strong—and if she gripped my shoulders hard enough to leave bruises, I sure as hell wasn't going to mention it. Once I stood facing her, the female 'thrope released me, pressing her lips into a tight frown as she crossed her arms.

"What?" I shrugged.

"You're completely clueless, aren't you?" she asked.

"You know me well enough to know the answer to that question. So, I'm not even going to argue," I sighed. "Just tell me what I did wrong so I can apologize."

Hemi let out a low whistle as he occupied himself with needlessly rearranging our food supplies.

"I'm not asking for an apology from you, dipshit." She pointed toward the bedrooms, lowering her voice. "She's the one who deserves an apology, not to mention a little reassurance right about now."

I scratched my head and scowled. "What? I mean, I've been looking after her, haven't I? Heck, if it wasn't for her we wouldn't be in this mess in the first place."

"You just don't get it—but I suppose I can't blame you. It's hard to understand what it's like to leave your old life behind, if you've never had to do it."

"I'm not tracking," I said, meaning it.

Fallyn lowered her head. "For someone with such a noble heart, you sure are self-absorbed at times. Colin, consider what she's going through right now. She was a spirit, a ghost, for over two years. In all that time, she never left you. Think about that for a moment. Then, she tried to make it back to you—at great risk to herself, I might add—and ended up locked inside an alien body, and insane to boot."

"I—"

Fallyn held her hand up, her eyes hard as she interrupted me. "Let me finish. Now, because of circumstances beyond her control—"

"Meddling gods," Hemi interjected.

"—she's destroyed any relationship she ever had with the only man she's ever loved. And, even though she's alive and human once more, she has *no one*. No family, because how will she explain coming back from the dead? No friends, because same thing, plus they've all moved on by now. No home, because all that and then some."

"But I didn't—"

"'You didn't think,' is right. As usual, you're too busy being Mr. Big Shit to consider what the people around you are going through."

"Now, where have I heard that before?" I muttered.

"Surprised you don't hear it more often, Golden Boy. You can only get by on good looks and a smart-assed attitude for so long. Now, listen." Fallyn poked me in the chest to emphasize her every word. "She. Has. Nothing. So, you need to either find it in your heart to forgive her, or you damned well better fake an Oscar-winning performance and convince her that all is forgiven."

I slumped down on a couch nearby, exhaling heavily. "Ah, shit. I guess I'm just no good at picking up on emotional cues. Seriously, I didn't mean to be such a dick."

Fallyn sat down next to me, patting me on the knee. "You never do, but somehow you always manage to fuck up royal anyway. I know you mean well—"

"I second that," Hemi said with a nod.

"—but someone has to call you on your bullshit. Don't worry, I still have hope for you. Now, I'd better go pack if I'm going to come along and keep you three out of trouble."

Fallyn strolled off to the back rooms, leaving Hemi and me to stare at each other again.

"Um, did she say she was coming with?" I asked.

"Uh-huh. You got dropped in it with that girl, aye?"

"No comment."

While we were waiting for Fallyn and Jesse, I hopped on the Pack's computer to do a little research into Cerberus on the dark web. I used a VPN, plus warded the machine against magical surveillance, so I figured I was safe. My search turned up diddly-squat on Cerberus, but I found a crap-load of articles and discussion threads claiming the government was doing secret supernatural research.

The conspiracy claims ran the gamut—top-secret islands where they supposedly did Dr. Moreau shit, gene-splicing, super soldiers, the works. Most of it sounded like crazy talk, so it was hard to determine what to believe. Still, my own experiences had taught me there was always a thread of truth hidden within urban legends. I tucked the info away and made a mental note to revisit the topic at a later date.

A few minutes later, Fallyn emerged sans Jesse, motioning for us to follow. She led us to a grey mid-nineties Land Cruiser parked behind the house. The thing was immaculate, and when she cranked it over it ran like a top—no surprise, considering all the gearheads motorcycle clubs tended to attract. Except for a faded Sturgis bumper sticker on the rear window, it looked like some soccer mom's daily driver, albeit an older one.

The 'thrope turned the engine off, and I followed her as she walked around and opened up the hatch. I looked the SUV over again and chuckled.

"This thing's kind of tame for a bunch of outlaw biker shifters, dont'cha think?"

Fallyn shrugged as she tossed her gear into the back. "Do you want to blend in, or not?"

"Good point," I replied. She tossed me the keys. "I guess I'm driving, then?"

"Since you haven't told us where we're going, yeah," she said.

"I call shotgun!" Hemi shouted.

Jesse stood off to the side, staring at the dirt and looking for all the world like your typical basic bitch in yoga pants, boots, a long-sleeve thermal shirt, and a puffy vest. She even wore one of those watch caps with a fuzzy ball on top—all she needed was a pumpkin spice latte to complete the ensemble. To tell the truth, though, she looked kind of cute. She also looked completely lost, and I had no idea how to remedy that situation.

Fallyn nudged me with an elbow. "You really don't do peopling very well, do you?"

"Who, me?" I said with a lopsided grin. Fallyn's forehead crinkled, and my smile faded. "Ah, hell. Truth is, I've screwed up about every decent relationship I've had over the last few years. Give me a monster to stab, smash, burn, or banish, and I'm fine. But ask me to navigate the vagaries of interpersonal relationships, and I'm as directionless as a deaf bat in daylight."

"So I've noticed," she observed drily. "Don't worry, Druid. I'll look after her until you get your head out of your ass."

"Um, thanks, I guess?"

My she-wolf friend ignored me as she slammed the hatch closed, then she walked over and asked Jesse which window she wanted. They both climbed in the back seat, where the two immediately began conversing quietly.

"This is going to be a long trip," I whispered.

Hemi stuck his head out the passenger window. "Oi, you coming?"

I waved a reply as I pulled a dry-erase marker from my Bag. I then began marking see-me-not and "go away, look away" runes and glyphs all over the truck, muttering under my breath about the treacherous nature of relationships and unfathomable mysteries of the opposite sex. Moments later, I slid into the front seat of the SUV and exhaled heavily.

Hemi arched an eyebrow at me. "You alright?"

I sucked air through my teeth with a grimace, and nodded. "Yeah. Just, uh, eager to get on the road."

Fallyn leaned forward and handed me a phone. "Throwaway, programmed with burner numbers for Pack members who can quickly get messages to Samson, Luther, Maureen, and Finnegas. Don't use it unless it's an emergency."

I took the phone and tucked it in my pocket. "Does your dad know you're going with me?"

"He knows. He doesn't like it, but he knows. Someday, Dad'll get used to having a second who doesn't jump when he says frog. Right now, he just blames it all on you—but eventually he'll face facts and realize I'm not his little girl anymore."

Just what I needed—to be a thorn in Samson's side. "After having Sonny around all those years, I figured he'd be used to having a second who didn't listen," I said.

"Not really. Sonny was a good lap dog, right up until he wasn't." She leaned over me to hit the trip button on the odometer. "Gotta track mileage for tax purposes. Now, are you going to tell us where we're headed?"

"Big Bend National Park. Perfect place to hide out. It's well away from Austin, nobody knows us there, and we'll have four hundred eighty-six square miles of mountain and desert to get lost in."

Fallyn flopped back into her seat. "Good hunting grounds. There's a local pack that hunts Santa Elena Canyon south of the border, but they should leave us alone. I approve."

I turned to look at Hemi and Jesse in turn. "Any objections? I mean, if anyone has any better ideas, I'm all ears."

"Nah, bro, I'm good." Hemi crossed his arms, leaned his head against the window, and shut his eyes. "Wake me up when we get there."

Jesse briefly made eye contact, then she stared out the window. "I can't think of any alternatives, and I obviously don't have any plans at the moment. I'm good."

Yeah, this is definitely going to be a long trip. I sincerely hope the feds give up and go home soon.

"Alright, let's get this show on the road. It's about a seven-hour drive. Let me know if anyone—"

Hemi was already snoring, while Fallyn and Jesse were quietly chatting in the back, leaning close like a couple of teenage girls on a school trip. I sighed and plugged my phone into the stereo input jack so I could listen to some tunes, then shifted the Toyota into gear and headed out.

After we left the Austin area, the trip was uneventful. We had a brief, tense episode on our departure, when Fallyn spotted black helicopters circling the nature preserve adjacent to the Pack clubhouse. Thankfully, the runes and wards I'd put on the vehicle were enough to keep prying eyes off us, and we soon crossed the county line without further incident.

Roughly nine hours later, we made it to the Chisos Basin visitor center on the west side of the park. It was dark, so rather than drawing attention to ourselves by heading out in the middle of the night, we grabbed a few hours of fitful sleep in the truck until the first rays of dawn peeked up over the mountain.

Yawning and irritable, we each disembarked in search of hot food and hopefully clean restrooms. It was mid-week so there were fewer visitors, and while we didn't exactly have the place to ourselves, it was close. Fallyn paid for our camping permit with cash using a false ID, then we headed off to find a secluded spot to camp.

Hours later, we'd selected a remote location several miles west of the Chisos Basin campgrounds as our home base. Our chosen campsite was near a little-used trail, on a hidden plateau above a canyon. Mundane humans would have difficulty accessing the area, and with any luck, we'd remain undisturbed for the remainder of our stay.

Fingers crossed.

Hemi and I set up camp while the girls hiked back to the visitor center in order to avail themselves of the luxuries of civilization—namely, the restaurant and showers. On the hike out, Jesse's new body proved to be made of much sturdier stuff than that of the average human. For each of us, the five miles or so of rough, inhospitable terrain made for an easy thirty-minute jog in each direction. Being of supernatural origins did have its perks, after all.

Once our chores were done, Hemi and I kicked back with a couple of beers, admiring the view. We were just about to crack another beer when the smell of greasy hamburgers caught my attention.

"Company," I said in a conversational tone.

"The girls?" he asked.

"Yes, it's us," Fallyn's voice replied as she and Jesse rounded a boulder twenty yards to the east of our camp. "Who else would be hiking up here? Damned cliffs are a long fall waiting to happen."

She tossed Hemi a grease-stained bag, which he tore open with his meaty hands. "Thanks, Fallyn."

"Just be sure Golden Boy burns the bag and wrappers," she replied. "There's a mama black bear roaming these parts, and I don't want to have to scare her off."

The big guy tossed me a couple burgers wrapped in white paper. They were barely warm, but I didn't care. As we scarfed down the burgers, Fallyn and Jesse stood off to the side, looking uncomfortable.

"Are you going to tell him?" Jesse asked.

"Tell me what?" I echoed, knowing that "him" must've meant "me."

Fallyn briefly glanced my direction. "I guess, but you know how this is going to turn out. Once he gets involved, you can bet the house that things are going to go sideways in a hurry."

"Um, 'he' is sitting right here," I said between bites of delicious, greasy cheeseburger, only to be completely ignored.

"Did you ever consider that maybe that's why we're here?" Jesse said to Fallyn. "I don't think that trouble follows Colin—I think he's somehow attracted to it."

Fallyn scowled. "Like it's his destiny to trip over his dick and fall into the pig sty every time he turns around? Naw, he's just a world-class shit magnet is all. A lovable one, mind you, but a shit magnet just the same."

Hemi guffawed and spat chunks of hamburger. "She's got your number, bloke."

"Still sitting right here," I protested under my breath as I took another bite. I chewed it slowly, wincing as I swallowed. Despite the hunger I'd felt moments earlier, I was beginning to lose my appetite. I wrapped the remainder in the paper and tossed it to Hemi's waiting hands.

"Not hungry?" I shook my head. "More for me, then," he said as he wolfed the rest of my burger down.

Meanwhile, Jesse and Fallyn were still engaged in a heated discussion about me, and they were still acting as if I wasn't seated right next to them. I heard something about "ghosts," "children," and "magic." I cleared my throat rather loudly. Both girls looked at me like I'd grown a third eye, then continued what was fast becoming a full-fledged argument.

"They're everywhere, Fallyn. Tell him!"

"Girl, that boy may have a heart of gold, but his ability to kick up shit is legendary. Once he gets involved, you can forget about us flying under the radar."

Finally, I'd had enough. Taking a page from the Finnegas playbook, I infused my vocal chords with power as I formed a magical connection with a storm cloud off near the horizon. After I released a small pulse of magic through that link, I counted the seconds in my head.

One-one-thousand, two-one-thousand, three-one-thousand...

A distant rumble of thunder reached us as I stood to my feet and shouted, my voice booming off the canyon walls below.

"Would you stop arguing and tell me what the hell is going on?"

For a split-second, the girls stopped arguing as they looked at me. Then, they each busted out in hysterical laughter.

"Oh, Colin," Jesse tittered. "It's scary when Finn does it, but when you do that booming voice thing you just look silly."

Fallyn grabbed her sides as she split a gut. "Aw, he wants our attention—that's so fucking cute!"

I hung my head and waited for their laughter to subside. "Har-har, you've had your laugh. Now, would you two please fill me in?"

Fallyn wiped tears from her eyes, although she was still laughing between sentences as she replied. "Oh crap, Dad's going to get a kick out of this. Okay, okay—I give in. Go ahead, Jesse, tell him."

Jesse was still chuckling as well, although the look she gave me was not an unkind one. "Colin, while we were at the restaurant we heard one of the park rangers say that a couple of kids, a brother and sister, went missing down by the river."

"And that's not all," Fallyn said as she finished wiping her eyes. She looked at Jesse, her expression suddenly serious. "You want to tell him the other part?"

Jesse shook her head, and her smile vanished.

I looked back and forth between them and shrugged. "I suppose we can help with the search. What's the big deal?"

The werewolf frowned. "The big deal is, there's something in this park that isn't human. I picked up its scent when we were headed back from the visitor center, and from what I could tell it was headed south, toward the river."

8

I nodded, realizing why Fallyn had been hesitant to fill me in about the lost siblings. We *were* supposed to be laying low, after all. But with two kids missing, and the possibility that a supernatural creature was involved, well—I couldn't just turn a blind eye.

"Any idea what it was?" I asked.

Fallyn's nose crinkled slightly—'thropes did that sometimes when they experienced sensory recall. "No idea. Something feline, but not a were. Whatever it was, it smelled like witchcraft."

"That could be bad," I replied, scratching my head as I considered our options. "Alright, let's see if we can pick up that trail and follow where it leads us. And if we don't turn anything up, we'll search the area where they were last seen. Did you get a description, by chance?"

My werewolf friend tsked. "Hello, I was raised by an alpha —of course I got a description. Two Mexican-American kids, siblings by the names of Robert and Lydia Guerra. The boy is seven and his sister is eight. Little brother was last seen wearing jeans and a blue puffy jacket. The sister was wearing jeans and a canvas rancher's coat."

"I should never have doubted you," I said, shading my eyes as I looked at the sun overhead. "We'd best get going. On the odd chance they're simply lost, another night of exposure to the elements could do them in just as easily as a supe. Lead the way, oh mighty pack second extraordinaire."

"Smart ass," she replied, grabbing a light backpack as she trotted off toward the campground with Jesse on her heels.

Shit, the last thing I need is Jesse running around drawing attention to us.

Hemi gauged my reaction, then grabbed another beer from the cooler and sat down. With a face that was suspiciously devoid of emotion, the Maori warrior quietly sipped his beer as he observed the scene that was about to play out.

Thanks for nothing, I mouthed at him, only to receive a "who, me?" look in reply. Hemi was notorious for holding the neutral ground when those around him were at odds. I cleared my throat loudly to get Jesse's and Fallyn's attention.

"Hey, um—Jess? Don't you think it's best that you stay here, with Hemi?"

Fallyn pulled to a stop at the edge of camp, while Jesse spun around to face me, shoulders squared and her mouth set in a thin line.

"What are you getting at?" she said in low tones. "Go ahead, spit it out."

I took time to choose my words carefully. "It's just that, well—we're mostly here to hide you from the authorities, remember?"

"I'm not a child, Colin," she hissed. "And I don't need your protection."

I raised my hands defensively. "Look, I'm just saying—"

Jesse placed her hands on her hips. "What, you're afraid I'll lose control? Go batshit crazy?" She waved her hands in the air next to her head, pantomiming a person in distress. "'Ooh, look out, everyone, it's that nutty girl who came back from the dead—no telling what she might do!'"

"Jesse, I don't think you're crazy," I said softly. "But right now, we don't really know the extent of your magic, or how well you can control it."

"I can control my magic just fine!" she protested, shoulders set and fists balled at her sides. The ground trembled slightly as a nearby mesquite tree began to shake and sway menacingly. Desert grasses at Jesse's feet began to grow and curl together, intertwining into thin ropes that darted to and fro like snakes looking for something to attack, even as they withered from green to brown, before turning nearly black. I shook my head as I pointed at the effects her magic was exerting on her surroundings.

"That's exactly what I'm talking about. What if someone saw that? Or worse, what if somebody got hurt because you couldn't control your magic?"

She glared at me, and I thought for sure we were about to go at it. Then, one of the grass snakes brushed against her leg, causing her to look down. As she saw the plant life she'd inadvertently influenced with her magic, her shoulders sagged and the tension drained from her body. Along with it went the magic she'd been holding. Slowly, the grasses reverted to their natural state, and the mesquite tree settled and grew still.

My ex hung her head, deflated. I couldn't recall her ever looking so tired, or so sad. "I—you're right," she whispered. "I'll wait here with Hemi."

I walked over to her and gently laid a hand on her shoulder. "Jesse, I promise you we'll sort this out. Once things have settled down, I'll help you figure out your powers, and Finnegas will show you how to control them."

"Yeah, whatever you say." Eyes downcast, she shrugged my hand off and headed toward the seat I'd vacated. Plopping down next to Hemi with her hands in her lap, she stared at a spot in the dirt a few yards away, tight-lipped and withdrawn.

I was about to say something else when I felt a hand on my shoulder. "Leave her alone for a while," Fallyn said. "She just needs time to process everything that's happened. C'mon, we're losing daylight."

The 'thrope nodded toward a game trail, then took off at a jog toward the campgrounds. With one last look at Jesse, I sighed and headed after her.

Once we'd scrambled down the cliffs to the canyon trail, we jogged east about a mile before Fallyn picked up the creature's scent. She knelt to examine barely-visible prints in the dirt at our feet.

"Whatever it is, it's big, but it moves like a much lighter animal. See the size of these prints? Something that large should leave deeper depressions with each footfall, but these tracks are hardly noticeable."

"Magic?" I asked.

"Can't you smell it? The trail reeks of witchcraft."

Using my druid senses, I did pick up something odd, a magical signature that was unlike any I'd experienced before. The scent carried the distinct bouquet of witchcraft, but it had a feral quality to it that set my nerves on edge.

"Could it be a skinwalker?"

Fallyn cocked her head. "Maybe. I've heard of skinwalkers taking the form of mountain lions, but these prints don't look like any mountain lion I've ever seen. They're definitely feline —but not made by a cougar, and certainly not by a bobcat."

"Well, let's follow it and see if we can find out what this thing is—before it hurts anyone."

Without comment, she rose to her full height and began stripping off clothing.

"Um, what are you doing?" I asked.

"I'm getting undressed, what's it look like I'm doing?" she said with an amused grin as I averted my eyes. "Oh, get over yourself. It's not like you haven't seen it before. Trust me, it'll be easier to follow the trail if I shift into my full wolf form."

"Say what? I've never seen a 'thrope go full-on wolf."

"Usually only very old 'thropes can, because they're more in tune with their wolf. Most younger 'thropes can only achieve a form that's in-between the two. I've been able to do both, ever since I was little. Freaked Dad out the first time I did it." She paused for a second, and her voice grew serious. "Don't tell anyone you saw me do this, okay? The only Pack members who know I have this ability are my dad, Sledge, and Trina."

"Sure, I can keep a secret. But why all the secrecy?"

Fallyn chuckled humorlessly. "Bad enough that Samson made his daughter his second. Imagine the trouble there'd be if word got out I was different. Emotionally speaking, the Pack is still recovering from that whole Sonny situation. I'd rather not make things worse."

"Okay, but what if someone sees me hiking with a wolf?"

"You know as well as anyone people see what they want to see, and believe what they want to believe. They'll just think I'm a dog." I heard her stuffing her clothes into her backpack, and when she tossed it at me I caught it without looking. "Now, be quiet and let me concentrate."

Moments later, I heard a whiny yip. I turned just in time to see a hundred-ten-pound wolf trotting south away from me. Her coat was a mix of auburn red on her legs, haunches, and sides, fading into a white blaze on her chest and throat, with charcoal tips on the fur that covered most of her back, neck and head, and tail.

Fallyn paused and fixed her yellow wolf eyes on me as if to say, "Keep up if you can." Then, she loped off into the brush.

We traveled for miles on almost non-existent game trails that led through the rough terrain. Fallyn easily navigated the vegetation and landscape, while I found myself fighting it at turns along the way. Finally, I simply began barreling through the undergrowth, stealth-shifting to spare my skin from the many scratches, scrapes, and thorns I'd have had to endure otherwise. My clothing suffered, but at least I wasn't slowing Fallyn down anymore.

Turning southwest, we continued at that pace for hours, finally following the trail down the dry riverbed that ran through Smuggler's Canyon. We exited into the Rio Grande river bottoms, in an area wooded with acacia, willows, and the odd cottonwood tree. Soon, we could hear the river lapping at its banks in the distance, and the sound of a woman softly crying that carried on the wind.

Fallyn growled a warning, hunkering low as she began to stalk through the undergrowth. I did my best to follow her lead, slowing my pace and taking time to quietly pick a path through the trees and brush. When we neared the river, the crying grew louder. As it did, the woman's voice took on an ethereal quality that made it seem distant and yet close all at once.

The she-wolf paused at the edge of the woods, hiding among some shrubs as she scanned the riverbank ahead. As I settled in next to her, being sure to keep myself hidden, I noticed that she'd zeroed in on something down by the river. I followed her gaze, and there ahead of us in waist-deep water was a woman holding two young children. She cried over them, weeping hysterically as they hung lifeless from her arms.

"*¡Ay, mis hijos!*" she wailed, over and over again.

Were we too late? Was this Mrs. Guerra, mother of the missing siblings? Had she found her children here, drowned in the shallow waters of the Rio Grande? Or was it a family caught in tragedy, one of the many thousands who crossed the border each month, desperately seeking a new life north of the river?

Distantly, in the recesses of my mind, a warning bell sounded.

Something about this isn't right.

Yet within seconds my instincts had been suppressed, replaced by a sadness that settled on me like a familiar, threadbare blanket. Despair crept over me then, a despondent melancholy of a type I hadn't felt since Jesse died. Within moments, I felt the sort of deep and abiding sorrow that said nothing and no one would ever be right in my world ever again.

What's the point of looking for these kids? I thought. *They're probably already dead, anyway. I should just head back to camp instead of wasting my time out here.*

I looked up at the woman, crying over her children as she stood holding their heads just above the water.

Yes, that's them. Dead, of course. Like everything in this world, their passing was like a wisp of smoke on the wind. Pointless. Senseless. Transient. And no one will remember them when they're gone.

I glanced at the river's waters. Green, peaceful, calmly flowing to the sea. Beckoning me.

Maybe I'll wade out there, too. Just walk out to the middle, and let myself drift to the bottom. It'd be nothing to let the air seep out of my lungs as the water filled them back up again, and then I could drift off and finally be rid of this—

A sharp pain in my left arm brought me back to my senses. I glanced down to see that Fallyn had her jaws clamped on my forearm. She growled and worried at it like an attack dog working a training dummy, her eyes locked on mine. Momentarily, the feelings of sadness and despair I'd felt subsided, and soon I was thinking clearly again.

Bitch must be using magic that fucks with your emotions.

"Thanks for that," I whispered.

Shaking off the last bit of fuzziness, I peered out of our hiding place to get a good look at the witch, or whatever the hell she was. Her back was turned to us, and although I couldn't see her face, she had straight black hair down to her waist that glistened wet in the afternoon sun. The woman was tall and thin, but she came off as being graceful rather than gangly. She was dressed all in black, with a black shawl over her shoulders to match, and her lacy black dress billowed out as it floated on the surface of the water around her.

Her wailing intensified as she gently lowered the children

into the water, hanging on to their wet clothing to prevent them from drifting away. The river was high due to recent rains, and it didn't help matters that she had taken the children to the deepest part of the channel. I could guess what was coming next, and in that moment I knew who—or rather, what—this evil thing was.

La Llorona.

I shrugged off Fallyn's backpack as I reached into my Bag, digging around as I nudged Fallyn with my knee. "As soon as I attack, you get the kids and run." She looked up at me with those yellow eyes and whined. "Just do it, and don't look back!"

My hand found what I'd been looking for, one of the few things I hadn't used to feed the Grove during its recovery. Against lesser creatures of the Void, I'd found it to be too useful. Plus, it was great on tomatoes, and the Grove could grow one hell of a beefsteak tomato.

I ran from cover while pulling a fistful of rock salt from my Bag, muttering a spell to infuse the salt with kinetic energy. Sprinting down the river bank, I yelled at the spirit while building up the enchantment in order to achieve the maximum effect. I might only get one shot at her, and I wanted to make sure I did some damage.

"Hey, bitch—leave those kids alone!"

It wasn't the finest example of a witticism I'd ever uttered, but the idea was simply for her to turn her head. I figured a face-full of enchanted rock salt might get her to release the children, then Fallyn could grab them and run. Time seemed to slow as *La Llorona* responded to the sound of my voice while I closed the distance between us.

What the fuck is up with her face?

When the specter turned to look at me, her face simply

wasn't there. In its place was an unbroken expanse of dusky skin vaguely formed in the shape of a woman's facial features. Yet she had no eyes, or lips—or eyebrows, for that matter. I wondered for a moment how she could cry without a mouth to form words, and eyes to form tears.

That's when I learned the bitch could scream.

"*¡No puedes tener mis hijos, hombre!*"

The ghost's voice was a piercing wail that drove daggers of pain into my skull, driving me to my knees as I skidded to a halt on the muddy bank of the river. I vaguely heard Fallyn cry out somewhere behind me. Her hearing was much more sensitive than mine, and if I was in this much agony, I couldn't imagine what she must be experiencing.

I covered my ears with my fists, not wanting to release the only weapon I had that might do some damage against an ethereal creature. Forcing myself to open my eyes, I took stock of the situation as the pounding in my head subsided. *La Llorona* was already back at her gruesome task, a child in each hand as she submerged them under the water.

No you don't, bitch!

"*Scaoil!*" I shouted, releasing the spell as I tossed the rock salt at her back.

The pebble-sized granules took off like buckshot from the barrel of a shotgun, forming a tight pattern as they struck *La Llorona* cleanly between her shoulder blades. She screamed again, but this time the effect was greatly diminished. Instantly, her corporeal form disintegrated into a cloud of dark mist, but not before she turned that faceless mien on me one last time.

"*El hombre oscuro viene, druid. ¡Él viene!*" she wailed. Then, her voice trailed off in the distance as the mists faded from sight.

The kids!

I saw a hand bob to the surface, just for a moment, then a flash of cloth in the water a few feet away, but both disappeared just as quickly. I leapt from where I was, using my Fomorian strength to dive into the waters where I thought the two children might be.

9

When I dove into the river, I lucked out by snagging a child's coat in my hands almost immediately. I swam to the surface, lifting the kid's head above the water—it was Robert. Thrashing about frantically, I tried desperately to locate his sister in the murky depths, but with no luck. Soon, Fallyn was there with me, diving under to help me search as we both drifted downstream.

I'd almost lost hope when Fallyn finally surfaced, now in her human form, holding the young girl in her arms. We scrambled for shore, me with the boy and she with his sister. Neither was breathing as we lay them down on the muddy bank. I checked the boy's pulse—it was weak, but there. Fallyn did the same for the girl, but she shook her head.

I thought back to my first aid training, trying to recall vital information that would tell me what needed to be done. The problem with treating drowning victims was two-fold—water in the lungs, and laryngospasm. Both conditions had the same result, keeping the lungs from perfusing oxygen and carbon dioxide.

One problem at a time, Colin.

I uttered a spell, making it up on the fly. All that time I'd spent fixing the Grove had given me much greater control of the elements, and I used those newfound talents to draw the water from each child's airway. As soon as the boy's lungs were clear, he took a sputtering breath, coughing out the last drops of water as his inspiratory drive kicked in. As long as his vocal cords didn't spasm, and so long as he didn't develop complications from drowning, he'd be fine.

His sister was not as fortunate, and she still wasn't breathing. Despite the fact that werewolves rarely required first aid —they healed like Wolverine, after all—Fallyn began performing textbook CPR on Lydia Guerra. She tilted her head, cleared the airway, and then attempted to perform rescue breathing.

"I can't get any air in," she stated. She repositioned the girl's airway by tilting her head back, then she tried again. "Still nothing—shit!"

"Her throat is probably spasming," I said, as a potential solution occurred to me. "I think I might be able to help. Open her mouth and make sure her tongue isn't blocking her airway."

Fallyn looked at me like I was nuts, but she did it just the same. I closed my eyes, using my druid senses to feel the air that sat in her mouth and larynx. I gave it a gentle push, attempting to force air into her lungs without success.

In severe cases of airway obstruction, paramedics would either intubate or perform an emergency cricothyrotomy, if they couldn't place an artificial airway. I'd once performed just such a procedure on Fallyn using the barrel of a marker as an airway tube, but now I lacked anything I could use in similar fashion.

Time to improvise.

I focused on the air in Lydia's throat, compressing it into a sort of wedge. Then, I envisioned her vocal cords in my mind, and ever-so-gently I pressed the tip of that wedge into the spot where her vocal cords met. I felt some resistance at first, then the muscles in her throat slowly parted, allowing air to escape with a strident hiss.

Slowing my own breathing, I went into a meditative state to maintain focus as I kept her airway open. Then, I held her vocal cords apart using druid magic while Fallyn did chest compressions. Soon the girl's heart began to beat on its own, and she began breathing again as well. However, her throat was still in spasm, so I had to magically maintain her airway to keep her alive. Meanwhile, Fallyn retrieved her clothes from her backpack and got dressed.

It was a hell of a thing, maintaining that sort of control over air molecules in such delicate manner, and I soon lost track of time. Before I knew it, the whump-whump-whump of helicopter rotors appeared overhead, and Fallyn's voice echoed in the distance as she guided the paramedics over to me and the children.

"The boy is breathing on his own, but the girl, um—she's wheezing really bad. My friend seemed to think her throat had closed up."

"What's he doing? Praying over her?" a male voice asked.

"Yeah, well—CPR wasn't working, so what were we supposed to do?" Fallyn replied with irritation in her voice.

Soon I was pushed out of the way, and the paramedics began to work on Lydia. "Her vocal cords are spasming—she needs to be intubated," I said.

"We'll take it from here, sir. Now please, let us work."

Satisfied that they knew their business, I stumbled to my

feet, exhausted from the effort it had taken to keep the girl alive. Vaguely, I heard the paramedics marvel at the fact that Lydia was still alive. They chalked it up to the mammalian diving reflex and luck, but Fallyn and I knew better.

The life flight helicopter was soon en route to the nearest hospital, some eighty miles distant. Park authorities showed up shortly before they left, and we were detained while they asked us a few questions. Once they verified our story with the paramedics by radio, we were allowed to leave, with the admonition that the park rangers and local authorities might want to question us again at a later date.

Of course, we gave them false names and showed false IDs, so we wouldn't be answering any questions anytime soon. The less the authorities bothered us at the moment, the better. We were offered a ride back to our campground, which we declined. It earned us some quizzical looks, but we really didn't care.

Neither of us spoke until we were halfway back to camp.

"Colin, what was that thing, anyway?"

"A folktale—'La Llorona,' The Crying Lady. As the story goes, a poor young woman fell in love with a charming, aristocratic young man. They had children and were happy for a time, but the man had to keep their affair a secret from his parents. Eventually, he was forced to marry someone of his own station, although he swore he'd still look after the woman he loved, and their children."

"Something tells me I'm not going to like how this story ends," Fallyn said.

"Nope, you won't. The woman attended her lover's wedding, dressed in all black. After witnessing the man she loved marrying another woman, she went off the deep end. Maybe it was post-partum depression—I mean, who knew about that stuff back then? When she got home, she took their children to the river and drowned them, then killed herself as well."

Fallyn sighed. "And now she haunts rivers and steals kids so she can drown them, just like she did her own children."

"So the story goes," I replied solemnly.

"Think she'll be back?"

"Considering the fact that I didn't kill her because I don't know how, and that we robbed her of her intended targets— yes, I do."

"Well, hell." She paused for the span of several footfalls. "Do I need to say I told you so?"

"No. No, you do not."

"Shit magnet."

"Bitch."

"I was born this way—what's your excuse?" she countered coyly.

"The same, Fallyn. The same." I made an "s" and an "m" by contorting my fingers in a ridiculous imitation of a gang sign. "Shit magnet for life, yo."

Fallyn punched me in the shoulder. "You are such a nerd."

It was almost dark and we were halfway back to camp when Fallyn whispered to me, barely loud enough for my sensitive ears to hear.

"We're being followed."

"Human, or other?" I asked.

"Other, maybe. Smallish animal, moves like a predator. Might be a coyote."

"Skinwalker?"

She shrugged. "It's been following us for two miles. Would have attacked by now if it was. They're fairly territorial."

"Just in case, let's set up an ambush before we get to camp."

As soon as we rounded the next bend, each of us found a hiding spot in the brush on either side. Crouched and coiled for action, I waited until our stalker came into sight. Despite the fading light, I could make out the shape of a dog-like animal as it quietly and furtively padded down the trail toward our hiding spots.

It was thin, rangy, and nearly hairless, with pale grey skin, red glowing eyes, pointed canine ears, and a mouthful of sharp teeth that projected past its lips at odd angles. At roughly fifty pounds or so, it was maybe the size of a large coyote or a coy-wolf. Yet it was clearly no coyote.

Even more strange, the thing was singing to itself. Sort of.

"Let the bodies hit the floor, let the bodies hit the floor, let the bodies hit the floor," it chanted, over and over again in a near whisper. Then, it started making the most horrible noises. "Doo-doo-ding, dingle-lang-a-lang! Doo-doo-ding, dingle-lang-a-lang!"

At first I thought it was in distress, then I realized it was beat-boxing the guitar riff from a Drowning Pool song. From across the trail, Fallyn gave me a quizzical look as she drew a finger across her throat.

Should I kill it? she mouthed.

I shook my head "no" and motioned for her to hold tight. Then, just as the thing passed us I sprang, landing on its back and rolling it on its side. I pinned it with my hands at its throat and my knees straddling its torso. The weird creature snapped at me, out of instinct more than anything it seemed, because when it saw my face it calmed down and gave a sheepish grin.

"Oh, hiya there. Guess you knew I was following you, eh?" The creature had a sort of Brooklyn accent, and his voice reminded me a lot of Steve Buscemi's. He looked down at my hands with his glowing ruby eyes and cleared his throat. "Can you, uh, ease up a bit? I got sensitive skin, and all this chafing is really gonna play hell with my eczema."

"That depends on whether or not I decide to snap your neck," I replied through clenched teeth. "It's been a rough day—hell, a rough month—and I don't have the patience for playing games right now."

The creature's eyes darted to Fallyn, undressing her as he looked her up and down. "Does, uh, she have time for games? Because I could think of at least a half-dozen I could play with her."

I squeezed harder.

"Oh-kay," he wheezed. "Ease up, already. I meant no harm."

"Why were you following us?" Fallyn asked, barely keeping a smirk off her face.

The thing smacked his lips nervously. "Well, I, uh, saw what you did down at the river. Not that I was spying or anything. I just happened to stroll by while you two were dealing with the lady in black. After I saw how you handled it, and when I realized you two were more than just your average backpackers out for a hike, I got curious. So, I followed you."

"Curious, huh?" I said. "Fallyn, are you buying any of this?"

"He seems pretty harmless." She looked the creature in the eye. "What are you, anyway?"

The thing puffed up his chest, despite the fact that I was crushing it with my weight. "Larry the Chupacabra, at your service."

"Come again?" I replied. "The bloodsucking monster? Seriously?"

Larry's eyelids fluttered. "Hey now, that bloodsucking thing is just a myth. I'm vegan. How do you think I maintain this svelte figure?"

I looked up at Fallyn. "What's your gut telling you, partner?"

She bit her lip and chortled. "I dunno. Is that even what a chupacabra is supposed to look like? I thought they were more... what's the word I'm looking for?"

"Anthropomorphic?" I asked.

She snapped her fingers and pointed at me. "Exactly! Sort of like an imp, but green and scaly."

Larry's voice took on a sarcastic tone. "As if. I can assure you, any artist's depictions you've seen on shows like *Destination Truth* have been greatly exaggerated. I mean, you know they just act like they're seeing things, right? Like, Josh Gates goes, 'Oh, I think I just saw something move in the bushes,' and then they run around doing the shaky camera thing to make you think it's for real. Lame!" He winked at Fallyn. "Humans are such suckers—amirite, beautiful, or what?"

Fallyn examined her fingernails. "Right on both counts, but don't get too familiar. I haven't decided if I'm going to rip your head off yet or not."

I smirked at Fallyn. "He does have a point. Still, I'm with you—this is definitely not what a chupacabra is supposed to look like."

"What, you've never seen a chupacabra before?" Larry protested. "C'mon, my mug's all over the internet! They got pictures of me, video, the whole bit. I'm famous—or internet famous, at least."

He babbled on about how many followers he had on social media, while Fallyn and I ignored him.

"What do you think we should do with him?"

"Well, he smells like Quorn, so he wasn't lying about that." She scratched her nose. "I dunno. Let him go, I guess. Like I said, he seems harmless."

I looked Larry in the eye. "If I release you, are you just going to follow us back to camp?"

"Of course. You guys are the most excitement we've had here in—well, forever. And I can't wait to see what happens when you two run into that dickhead of a skinwalker—"

Fallyn and I did a double-take.

"What skinwalker?" we practically yelled in unison.

I soon discovered that threatening Larry the Chupacabra was pointless. As it turned out, he'd been cursed by the skinwalker, and thus considered himself to be beyond death's grasp so long as the curse remained. The logic escaped me, but Larry consistently maintained that he was un-killable due to the effects of the curse. Once we were back at camp, we bribed him with junk food and a few cans of PBR to get him to spill the beans.

"Alright, Larry—tell us what you know about this skinwalker," I demanded.

Larry had his snout buried in a bag of Funyuns, busily licking up every last crumb. "Like I said, this asshole cursed me a few years back. I've been trailing him ever since and waiting for an opportunity to trick him into removing the curse."

Fallyn leaned over to whisper in my ear. "Pfft. I have a feeling Brainiac here would have a hard time tricking a third-grader out of their lunch money."

"Why'd the skinwalker curse you?" Hemi asked. He'd become fascinated with Larry as soon as he'd heard the word "chupacabra." The big guy was deep into conspiracy theories, a hobby he justified on grounds of professional curiosity. He didn't necessarily believe them, but instead thought most such rumors were started to cover up events that spilled over into the mundane world from the World Beneath.

"I stole a bunch of corn and squash from his garden," he said as he shook the bag off his snout. He looked up, realizing that everyone was staring at him. "Oh, so now I'm the weird one? Have you kids taken a look in the mirror lately? Let's see here, we got a druid, a demigod, a werewolf, and whatever yuppie Wednesday Addams over there is—nope, that's not strange at all. Anyway, you try being a vegan when you don't have hands. Ever open a can of green beans with your teeth? It ain't pretty, lemme tell you."

Fallyn squinted and cocked her head to the side. "Wait a minute—I'm confused. Did the skinwalker turn you into a chupacabra?"

Larry's mangy ears twitched. "Huh? No, he cursed me so I couldn't shift into my human form. Duh."

Jesse piped up from where she sat sulking a few yards distant. "But you just said you don't have hands, which was why you stole produce from the skinwalker's garden. Are you saying he cursed you before you stole the vegetables?"

"No, after. Look, I can only transform into a human under

the light of a full moon. So, that's when I normally get all my shopping done and do food prep for the month. I put everything in zip-lock bags—easy to rip open with your teeth."

Fallyn frowned as she massaged her temples. "This is giving me a headache."

"Let's get back on task," I interjected. "Why is the skinwalker here, Larry?"

"Oh, that's easy," Larry said as he slurped PBR from a bowl. "His son called and told him you were headed this way."

Now *I* was getting a headache. "His son?"

"Yeah, what's that kid's name? Stu? Steven?"

"Stanley?" I ventured.

"Yup, that's it," the chupacabra nodded. "Stanley Bylilly. The kid's sort of a pushover, but his dad is a real piece of work, believe me. Half-Hopi, but they cast him out on suspicion of using black magic. He's, uh, kind of bitter about it—about life in general, really."

"I thought skinwalkers were a Navajo thing?" Hemi asked.

I shook my head. "Most of the Native American tribes of the Southwest have their own version of the legend. The Navajo term for them is *yee naaldlooshii*, which roughly translates into 'with it, he goes on all fours,' referencing their use of magic or a focus object to shift. Hopi and Utes also have their own versions of skinwalkers, while Mesoamerican tribes have a different term for a practitioner of magic who can slip their skin—*nagual*, which more or less means a magician."

Larry's rat-like tail twitched. "No matter what language you say it in, that old man is bad news. And let me tell you, he is seriously invested in tracking you down."

"Any idea why this witch is looking for you?" Fallyn asked.

I sighed. "No idea. Then again, Stanley and I have had a couple of run-ins. I'm definitely not his favorite person. Maybe the old man wants to take revenge on me for embarrassing his son?"

"Oh, hell," Jesse exclaimed as she stood up quickly. "Larry, what's the father's name?"

Larry licked the bowl clean of beer foam and belched loudly. "Stanley's dad goes by Ernie around white people, but I once heard a Hopi call him *Istaqa*. I'm told it means 'coyote man.' Fitting."

Jesse smacked her forehead. "Colin, think back to the time when I first started haunting you. Doesn't that name ring a bell?"

I scratched my head. "Hmm, Ernie, Ernest... Ernesto! That's the old man who helped us find the peyote for that potion Finn cooked up, the one that allowed us to—ahem, *communicate* while you were a..."

I paused, unwilling to say it.

"When I was a ghost, Colin," Jesse said. "It's okay to talk about it. I got over that whole thing a long time ago. Besides, if this skinwalker is coming to collect on the debt you owe, I think we have bigger issues."

Larry looked back and forth between us. "Man, and I thought my relationship with that zombie corgi was bizarre," he said under his breath. Everyone turned to stare at the chupacabra, causing him to grin sheepishly. "Oops—did I say that out loud?"

10

"C'mon, Jess—do you really think this guy would bother to track me down, way the hell out here? All he did was give us some psychedelic cacti. Heck, I even offered to pay him for it, but he said he'd rather trade out, favor for favor, at a later date."

Jesse frowned. "Colin, there had to be a good reason why he insisted on that particular form of payment. He likely sensed or saw something in you that made him think it'd be worth it to have you indebted to him."

"You mean, like my Fomorian alter-ego?" I asked.

"Exactly," Jesse replied. "And chances are good he's going to ask you to do something you won't like—something he either can't or doesn't want to do on his own."

"Plus, you made a fool out of his kid, twice," Fallyn interjected. "Don't forget that part, shit magnet."

I winced. "That's really starting to hurt, you know."

She rolled her eyes. "Oh, cry me a river." She began peeling off layers of clothing. "I'm bored and hungry, so I'm going to go hunt. If this skinwalker shows up, give him my regards."

Larry pushed himself up on his front paws, obviously very much interested in what Fallyn was doing.

"Eyes front, Caladryl," Fallyn growled.

Larry kept looking until Hemi grabbed him by the scruff and held him over the side of the cliff. "You might not be able to die, but I reckon a fall from this height would hurt. Speaking from experience."

"Alright, alright already," the chupacabra groused. "Sheesh, can't a cryptid have a little fun every once in a while?"

Hemi set Larry down, just in time for him to catch a look at Fallyn's half-wolf form retreating into the fading dusk. He continued to stare long after she'd gone.

"Wowza, what a canine," the chupacabra muttered.

Ignoring them both, I pulled out the burner Fallyn had given me. I turned it on and walked around camp, trying to get a signal.

"Aren't those for emergencies only?" Hemi asked, stroking his chin.

"So she said, but I need to make a call." I turned the phone off with a growl. "I'm going to head back to the campgrounds, see if I can get a decent signal. If not, I think I saw some pay phones there."

Hemi shook his head. "I don't think that's a good idea—"

"C'mon, Hemi—lighten up. You think the federal government is monitoring every single phone in the nation with voice recognition software, just waiting for me to make a call?"

"Yes," he stated, crossing his arms over his chest. "Ever

hear of a little NSA project known as Boundless Informant? Or PRISM? Carnivore? MYSTIC? Stuff is real, Colin."

"I have a computer surveillance chip inside my skull," Larry said to no one in particular.

I tsked, ignoring the chupacabra. "You spend way too much time in those conspiracy groups, dude."

Hemi arched an eyebrow. "Honestly, Colin, I don't think—"

Jesse rolled her eyes at me. "Don't bother. You know he always has to find things out the hard way."

"Yeah, but you figure a bloke'd learn his lesson, eventually," Hemi replied.

"I can hear you!" I said as I exited the camp.

"We know!" my friends said in unison.

I was halfway to the visitor's center when I was startled by a voice that spoke up right next to me.

"Don't suppose you have any trail mix on you, do you?"

I jumped five feet sideways, landing just off the trail with my Glock in one hand and a fireball in the other. "Holy shit— you scared the hell out of me! And how in the hell did you sneak up on me like that?"

"Magic. Duh." The chupacabra yawned. "So, no trail mix?"

I holstered my pistol and extinguished the fireball. "Sorry, all out." Feigning nonchalance, I headed toward the welcome center with the chupacabra padding along beside me. "Larry, why are you following me?"

"Would you believe it's because you're the most interesting one of the bunch? Besides that sexy-ass shifter. Hubba, hubba," he said, somehow managing to waggle his nearly bald, dog-ish eyebrows.

"I'm not buying it. Try again."

"Well, druid, it might be because you're my ticket to getting this curse removed. Not that I mind being in my natural form, mind you—it's just that it's kind of hard to shop for eczema cream when you look like a coyote with alopecia."

"Speaking of which," I said as I picked up the pace, "what exactly are you? As far as I know, the legend of the chupacabra is a fairly recent addition to world folklore. I've never seen or heard of a creature quite like you before—"

"Thank you," Larry replied.

"Um, that wasn't a compliment. As I was saying, I've never seen anything like you before, and it makes me wonder how you came to be."

"You really want to know?" he asked in a quiet voice.

"Yes, I do. Considering that you seem to have latched onto me and my—er, crew—it seems only fair that I should know more about you and where you came from."

I let that statement hang in the air, waiting to see how Larry would react.

"Plum Island, New York. That's where."

My ears perked up when I heard that name—several of the conspiracy sites I'd recently looked at had mentioned it. "I've heard rumors about that place. That's where the U.S. government studies animal diseases."

Larry snickered. "Among other things. I mean, if the public only knew what the feds are cooking up there. Stuff that makes me look like a Happy Hugs Build-a-Bear."

"You were created in a lab?"

"Yup. The military has been researching the genetics of cryptids and supernatural creatures for decades. And before that, they attempted to interbreed various species. Wasn't until the human genome project was completed that they experienced a breakthrough, though. That's when they figured out how to combine human and 'thrope DNA."

I pulled up short, hands on hips. "Come again?"

"Oh, that surprises you? I mean, look at me, for cripes' sakes. My kind were one of their early failures—and believe me, there are more. The Mothman, the Lizardman of Scrape Ore Swamp, the Skunk Ape, the Shunka Warakin—I could go on and on."

"Huh. Okay, I'll bite. How'd they make you?"

Larry sat on his haunches so he could scratch his ear. "They were trying to create Wargs. Can you believe it? The government wanted to create giant war dogs that would obey their every command. So, they decided to mix the DNA of normal dogs with werewolf and kitsune DNA, and bam! They got me."

"Kitsune—explains how you're so sneaky, anyway."

He nodded exuberantly. "Oh yeah, kitsune are good at that stuff. Magical ninjas, almost." His voice dropped to a whisper. "I can see ghosts, too. Shitty talent, really, cuz once a ghost figures out that you can talk to them, they'll never leave you alone. There's a bunch hanging out at your camp, by the way. Kinda weird, since I never—"

I cut him off mid-ramble. "Any idea why the government would engineer that trait into your DNA?"

"None. Probably a mistake. Now, if only they'd been able to genetically engineer some hair on me. I—" Larry stopped mid-sentence, sitting up like a prairie dog with his front paws in the air. His ears swiveled left and right, and he let out a low whine. "Aw shit, we gotta hide!"

"Hide? From what?"

"Skinwalkers," he said, his voice trailing off as he disappeared from view.

Great.

Before Larry had faded off into the night, I had Dyrnwyn out and a lightning spell readied in my other hand. Faint crackles of electricity jumped between my fingers and they ran up and down my forearm, lighting the area around me with an eerie blue-white glow. I didn't need the light to see, of course, both due to my naturally-heightened senses and because I was already stealth-shifting. Enhanced senses were part of the Fomorian package, after all.

Two shadowy shapes loped out of the darkness, just to the edge of the pool of light. The pair looked somewhat like transformed werewolves, half-human and half-animal, but twisted and distorted in a way that made my stomach churn. Their bodies were long, lean, and covered in short, grey fur that faded to tan and white in places, mostly on their under-sides and chests. They moved on all fours in a manner that was both graceful and disconcerting at the same time, as if their limbs were popping in and out of joint with their every stride, in contrast to the quicksilver smoothness of their gait.

But strangest of all were their faces. They looked much more human than animal, muzzles only slightly elongated with most of their human features still in place. The lead skinwalker's eyes flashed red as my spell flared slightly, while the one trailing had gold-yellow irises that shone in the night. That one scowled at the sight of me, while the apparent leader maintained a poker face that betrayed little in the way of emotion or intent.

Since they'd shown no aggression, I decided to keep Dyrnwyn's blade extinguished. Besides, I wanted to surprise them if worse came to worst. As they came to a halt they shifted, morphing out of that twisted, four-legged form that tied my stomach in knots. The pair rose on their hind legs, their spines straightening as their hair, teeth, and claws receded, giving way to burnished bronze skin and lean muscle. When the transformation was complete they were each naked, save for the coyote skins draped over their shoulders.

I raised my chin, half in greeting, and half in challenge. "Ernesto, Stanley. Fancy meeting you two here. To what do I owe the pleasure?"

Stanley spoke up first, his eyes flashing gold in the dark. "We still have business, druid. I—"

"*Sowi'ngwa*, quiet!" the old man barked over his shoulder, instantly silencing his son. "As I told you earlier, you may settle your quarrel with him later—after he repays his debt to me." Ernesto turned to stare me in the eye. "You've not forgotten our agreement, have you, druid?"

He hadn't changed much since I'd last seen him, save for a few more scars and wrinkles. Wispy tendrils of shoulder-length white hair blew in the faint breeze, in stark contrast to his weathered brown skin and the thick gray-brown hair on the pelt that rested across his shoulders. The old man was lean and wiry, with just a hint of fat and loose skin around his midsection, but not so much that you'd mistake him for being soft. His ropy muscles and calloused hands spoke otherwise.

But it was the cold and uncaring look in his eyes that gave him away. This was no harmless old man, no fragile retiree content to collect pension checks and watch reruns on television. No, this man was a killer, and age had only tempered and hardened him in that regard. Unlike his son, Ernesto Bylilly was not a man to be trifled with.

"I remember, and I wondered when you'd come to collect. Kind of strange timing though, tracking me down while I'm on vacation. Speaking of which, how'd you find me?"

Ernesto remained taciturn, his face an inscrutable mask. "As it turns out, my son isn't a complete fool after all. Stanley guessed you'd go to the wolves for assistance. When you showed up at their hideout, he placed a tracking spell on their vehicles."

"Impossible—I would have noticed," I said.

Stanley snickered. "Nobody ever checks the tires."

I will now, I thought as I turned my eyes on the old man. "This is all fine and dandy—I mean, really, it's a pleasure to see you both—but I'm kind of in the middle of something. Is there any chance this could wait until I get back to Austin?"

The old skinwalker clucked his tongue. "No, druid, it cannot. The gods smile on me, because your path and that of my prey have converged."

"Huh. And I take it the way I'm supposed to repay you has to do with this 'prey'?"

Ernesto's eyes flashed red again, and by some trick of the shadows his face took on a skeletal appearance. *Creepy.* "Indeed. There's a creature here that I wish you to find and bring to me. The Mexicans call it *La Onza.*"

"Whoa, whoa, whoa—you do realize that I'm a druid, right? We're not exactly into trophy hunting."

The skinwalker's son snorted. "I told you he'd go back on his word."

His father shushed him with a hiss before turning his gaze to me again. "This is no ordinary animal, druid, and you'd be doing the people of this area a favor by hunting it down. La Onza is a supernatural creature, a predatory cat that has been known to hunt livestock, pets, and even small children on occasion. Many times, when mountain lions have been blamed for the deaths of humans in this area, it was La Onza who did it. Is that not reason enough to kill her?"

I released my spell—it was starting to make my hand itch. "You speak of this animal as if it were a person. No offense, but I find it hard to believe you're concerned by the loss of a few human lives. Why do you want this La Onza dead?"

"I won't deny that it is purely for selfish reasons. I want her pelt for a ritual."

I sniffed and scratched my nose with a knuckle. "Would this ritual happen to allow you to take on La Onza's form?"

He nodded. "It would."

"So, obviously this creature must have some power you lack."

"And that is why I'm asking for your help in hunting her down. La Onza is sly and able to blend in with her surroundings, much like a chameleon. And she can move more silently than any mountain lion, while leaving very little trace of her passing. Pfah! I'm too old to be chasing a dangerous animal through the mountains, which is why I need you to do it for me."

"Why not get Stanley here to do it? He's young and spry."

The old man pursed his lips. "He is not capable of hunting such a creature. La Onza would feast on his entrails."

Stanley sulked in the background, averting his eyes in shame at his father's assessment. I almost felt sorry for him, and based on how I'd seen his dad treat him over the last several minutes, I could see why he was such a dick.

I rubbed the back of my head. "I dunno, Ernesto. I figured

when you called that chip in, it'd be to ask me to help you grow bigger tomatoes or something. Didn't expect you'd ask me to track down some animal and kill it."

"Again, druid, this is no mere animal. It's a dangerous creature, a man-killer. It deserves to be brought down."

I exhaled heavily. "Give me some time to think about it. Once I have more information, I'll make a decision and get back to you."

Ernesto scowled. "I'll give you twenty-four hours, and then I *will* come for your answer. But listen, druid—if you go back on your promise, you'll be under my curse. And my magic is not to be taken lightly."

Instantly, he transformed, flowing like oil into his alien, half-coyote form before he bounded off into the night. Stanley glared at me for a moment, then he followed suit. After they were long gone, Larry reappeared beside me.

"Oh geez, this is bad—really bad!"

"Which part? The part where I committed to doing a favor for a very nasty person, and now those chickens are coming home to roost at the worst possible time? Or the part where I don't want to do what Ernesto is asking, so I'll likely have him for an enemy by this time tomorrow?"

Larry sighed and wiped his head with his forepaw. "Phew. I thought for sure you were going to take him up on it. La Onza is more than just some cryptid. She's an old-school *bruja*—another magical shapeshifter."

I rubbed my chin. "She's human, eh? That could change things. Tell me what you know about her."

Larry paced back and forth as he spoke. "I don't really know if she's fully human. If she was once, she hasn't been in a long time. From what I've heard, she's been around for a few centuries, and she protects the people who live along the Mexican border."

"So she doesn't eat babies, wilt crops, and spoil milk? Shocking."

"Not even. In fact, Ernie and her have been going at it for years. That wily old skinwalker got a little too crafty for his own good. After the tribes ran him off, he had to find a new hunting ground. Well, he made the mistake of encroaching on land that La Onza considered under her protection, and the two have been enemies ever since."

"I get the feeling there's more to this than a little trespassing." I rubbed my neck and rolled my head side to side to work the kinks out. It had been a long day. "Explain what you mean by 'encroach.'"

"You know that skinwalkers who follow the witchery way almost exclusively deal in death magic, right?"

"Yes, I'm aware," I said, thinking back to my initial encounter with Stanley. He might not have been the brightest bulb, but those death magic spells he'd thrown around were no joke.

"Well, I think it started with some grave robbery. La Onza was worried if she didn't step in, Ernesto would be emboldened enough to do worse."

"Smart of her." I nodded. "And would he do worse, Larry?"

The dog-like creature stopped pacing and cocked his head at me. "He cursed me for stealing a few vegetables from his garden. Think about that for a moment. He locked me in this form over some produce, druid. What do you think a guy like that is capable of?"

I ran my fingers through my hair. "Something tells me I don't want to find out."

Once we made it to the visitor center, Larry took off to rummage around in the dumpsters behind the restaurant. I warned him that they were probably bear-proof, but he just gave me a snaggletooth grin and loped off into the darkness.

I checked the cell reception on my burner, then thought better of it and found a payphone. Before I even picked up the receiver, I graffitied the thing to ward it against surveillance. Not that I'd admit doing so to Jesse and Hemi, but it paid to be careful.

After looking up the person I needed to call using the burner, I searched my pockets for loose change. *Empty.* A cantrip tricked the phone into thinking I'd dumped a few bucks worth of quarters into it, and I dialed the number.

"*Bueno?*," an older woman's voice answered as she picked up the phone.

"Hello, Doña Leticia," I replied.

"*Ah, El Mago. Como estas, Colin?*"

"I'm well, thank you." I respected Doña Leticia a great

deal, both for her skill as a *curandera* and for the quality of her character. Plus, I owed her, which was all the more reason to treat her with deference instead of my typical impatience. Out of courtesy, I waited for her to initiate the remainder of the conversation.

A short silence ensued, followed by a low sigh. "I'd hoped this might be a social call, but no such luck, eh, *mijo*?"

"I'm afraid not, Doña. My apologies," I added, meaning it.

"The skinwalker has called in his favor, *¿verdad?* And you want my opinion on whether you should do as he asks?"

"He wants me to hunt down a creature, but I think this being is more than just a magical beast. I've been told it's a *bruja* in animal form."

"*Nagual*," she said.

"God bless you," I responded, eliciting a chuckle from Leticia.

"*Cállate, chiflado.* You know what I mean. This *bruja* travels in animal form. She's not a true shifter, not like *los hombres lobos*. But she has power if she is a *nahuālli*—and that is very old magic." She clucked her tongue. "Is she evil?"

I shrugged, even though I knew she couldn't see me. "Honestly, I don't know yet. I only have one source of info on her, and I'm not sure if I can trust that person's opinion. But he seems to think she practices white magic."

She tsked. "White magic, black magic—you know better than to use those *gringo* words, *Mago*. Magic is a tool and nothing more. It's the user that makes it evil, not the tool itself."

She spoke the truth—even necromancy could be used to do good, under certain conditions. "You're right, of course," I agreed. "Suffice it to say that my source claims she's been protecting the locals from Ernesto."

More silence. "Then you know what to do, *mijo*. You should let an old woman rest, rather than waking her in the middle of the night to ask her for answers you already know."

Her tone was good-natured, despite her chiding words. "I'm sorry to have disturbed you, Doña Leticia. *Gracias por tu tiempo.*"

She made a sound halfway between a hiss and shush. "Ay, Mago! Your Spanish is as bad as your healing magic. When this mess is done, come see me and we'll work on both."

"I will, Doña. Good night."

"*Cuídate, mijo.* The skinwalker is a dangerous enemy to have."

She hung up before I could respond. I placed the phone back on the receiver, considering her warning. Based on what I'd gathered, I was dealing two very powerful witches, and both were likely much more skilled at magic than me. Combine that with our current situation with the feds, and I was up to my ears in trouble as usual.

No way I'm doing that skinwalker's dirty work, though. I guess I'd better find this La Onza, if only to warn her. Maybe she'll have an idea about how to deal with Ernesto.

I was deep in thought when my druid senses warned me of someone approaching. I turned, half-dropping into a crouch until I recognized their gait. Not many people could move that silently in human form, and it was a dead giveaway who it was.

"Penny for your thoughts?" Fallyn said as she strolled out of the night, naked as the day she was born.

I focused very hard on maintaining eye contact, and being nonchalant about it. "How much of that conversation did you hear?"

"Enough. Well, all of it. I picked up your trail earlier, and

followed you here after I caught a whiff of the skinwalkers."
She wrinkled her nose. "Phew, coyote and death, not a
pleasant smell."

I winked at her. "Why, Fallyn, I had no idea you cared so
much about my well-being."

Her expression soured slightly, but she couldn't help but
grin at my tease. "How's Jesse doing?"

"She's fine, I guess. She and Hemi were giving me hell
right before I left."

Fallyn crinkled her nose. "I'd say her upbeat mood is
mostly an act, and done for your sake. We talked a lot on the
way down, and emotionally, she's a mess. Go easy on her."

"I am, Fallyn, I am. But what I don't get is how you can
give me the full court press while still expressing concern for
Jesse. Am I missing something here?"

The she-wolf stalked up to me, invading my space until
we were nearly chest to chest. Clearly she was flaunting her
current state of undress, and she smelled like musk and the
desert night. She looked up at me, her hungry, almost-yellow
eyes flashing in the light of the sodium lamp above.

"You know how I feel about you, Colin. I've made it plain,
and my sympathy for Jesse doesn't change that." She ran a
finger from the hollow of my collarbone down my chest to
my sternum, where she poked me with a razor-sharp nail.
"You want my advice? Neither of them are right for you,
because they both want something you can't give."

"And you, Fallyn? What do you want?"

"Me? You know what I want, and you also know that I
accept you for who you are, without reservations or conditions. Can you say the same for the others?"

"It's more complicated than that, Fallyn. You know that."

She chuffed and shook her head. "It always is with you,

Golden Boy. I'm patient, druid, but even a she-wolf's patience has its limits. Suss out your feelings for the dryad and the serpenthrope, before it's too late."

Fallyn leaned in on tiptoe, but instead of kissing me, she nuzzled my neck. Then she was gone, melding like liquid shadow into the dark once more. I looked down, noticing that she'd left a small scratch over my heart, marked by a tiny bloodstain.

I do want her, and I'm always at ease when we're together. She's loyal, and there's a soft heart under that rough exterior. And unlike Belladonna, Fallyn doesn't go off at the drop of a hat. If that's the case, why do I feel so guilty about entertaining the possibility of a relationship between Fallyn and me?

Larry spoke from my immediate left, startling me out of my reverie. "Don't worry, druid. If you break her heart, old Larry'll be there to pick up the pieces."

We were a few miles from camp when my druid senses alerted me that something *else* wasn't right this night. I stopped, not checking to see if Larry followed suit, and I extended my awareness out into our surroundings. The desert was surprisingly alive with activity, especially at night, and it was relatively easy to use the surrounding fauna to zero in on the anomaly.

A few miles to our north, animals were fleeing some sort of disturbance. Using druid magic, I found an animal I could commune with—a female desert cottontail that had seen some years. She was wily and knew the desert well, and whatever had disturbed her was absolutely foreign to the lands she called home.

I gently merged my own thoughts with hers to sift through her mind. Rabbits interpreted much of their world through their senses of hearing and smell, which meant I had to search for more than just her recent visual memories. Immediately, three scent-images stood out amidst her slightly chaotic rabbit thought-stream.

Death!

Blood!

Human!

It was all I needed to get me moving in that direction. Stealth-shifting on the fly, my legs ate up the desert ground with long, powerful strides. Larry was still with me, albeit barely visible to the naked eye. Although he seemingly had the ability to become functionally invisible when sitting still, he couldn't cloak himself as well when he was moving at speed.

"You're obviously geared up for a fight. Care to tell me where we're going?" he asked, just loud enough for my sensitive ears to pick up.

"Not sure. Something has the local animal life riled up, and I want to see what it is."

"Um, just so you know—chupacabras aren't very good in a rumble. We're more the 'hit and run and hide' type, you know?"

"If there's trouble, I'll handle it. Just stay out of the way."

"You don't need to tell me twice," he muttered.

Five miles to the north, we crossed a park road, after which Larry disappeared completely. I continued on, and a mile or so past the road I discovered what had the wildlife so stirred up. An RV was parked at one of the primitive campgrounds, its side door hanging from a single hinge and creaking back and forth in the night wind. I circled it at a distance to get the lay of the land.

"Uh, druid? I see a couple of ghosts wandering around," Larry warned. "They look fresh, too."

There were bullet holes in the windshield, and one of the side windows had been shattered outward. How I'd not heard the gunshots was a mystery to me, but as I continued around the vehicle to the downwind side, I knew why the shots had been fired. I smelled human blood, fresh and lots of it, as well as a scent I'd recognize anywhere.

Revenant! What the hell is it doing out here?

Months in the Hellpocalypse had provided me with senses finely tuned for detecting the undead. Revenants were a sort of cross between vampires and ghouls, the result of a human who'd been infected by a vamp but only partially turned. They had most of the speed and strength of a higher vamp, along with razor-sharp teeth and claw-like nails, but their bodies tended to decay like the lower undead. Moreover, they were mean as all hell, with a wily, feral intelligence that made them incredibly deadly predators.

I'd lost count of the revs I'd put down back there. They were fast, sneaky, and aggressive, and unlike deaders and ghouls, they preferred flesh and blood, not brains. So, they often left their victims alive once done with them—and, of course, those victims would turn once they succumbed to their injuries.

In the Hellpocalypse that wasn't an issue, because there were deaders everywhere anyway. It wasn't like one more zombie or ghoul would make much of a difference. But here? A single rev could spread the vyrus to dozens of people, causing an undead outbreak that would quickly get out of control.

So, I'd have to put it down.

I listened carefully for signs that the rev was still around. The night wind carried the distinctive sounds of a hemovore feeding, loud lapping and slurping noises punctuated by the occasional sound of ripping flesh. I soon determined the noises were coming from within the RV, so I stayed down-wind and stalked toward the vehicle.

My plan was to enter from the side door, surprising and hopefully trapping the creature at either end of the camper. I had no doubts that I could run a revenant down in the open desert, but really didn't want to risk letting the creature get away. I also had no idea if there might be survivors hiding within the vehicle or out in the surrounding desert.

Should have checked for that—sloppy. Best to just corner it and end it quickly, then I can look for survivors. And figure out where this thing came from.

Using every bit of stealth I could muster, I crept up to the entryway of the vehicle. The door continued to creak as it swayed back and forth in the breeze, banging every so often against the side of the camper. That all served to cover the sounds of my approach, but it also masked other noises that carried on the night.

For example, the second revenant that perched on the camper's roof above. I caught a flash of movement overhead, then Larry blurted a warning from behind me.

"Look out, druid! There's one on the roof!"

Larry's warning came a dollar short and a day late. The second revenant had already landed on my back, and it was making short work of my jacket and shirt. I reached back and grabbed the rev by the arm, yanking it over my shoulder as I tossed it through the open door of the RV. Those vehicles looked solid enough, but the new ones were about as sturdy as a papier-mâché dollhouse. I must've tossed it a bit too hard, because the rev went straight through the opposite wall.

"Shit! Larry, keep an eye on that thing and make sure it doesn't get away," I hollered.

"On it!" the chupacabra replied. "But you're going to owe me a broccoli pizza and some brewskis for this."

"Whatever," I muttered as I entered the RV.

Now that there were two ready-made exits, I didn't want to let the first rev escape. The creature wasn't going anywhere, intent as it was on its current meal. It was in the middle of the galley area, crouched over the body of a sixty-something male retiree.

The revenant looked to have been in her late forties when she died. She was dressed in mom jeans, an expensive technical windbreaker, hiking boots, and flannels over a long-sleeved thermal baselayer. Two small bullet holes punctuated the dark black veins that stretched across her face—one in her forehead, the other just under her left eye. She screeched at me as she hovered over her meal, warning me away from her kill.

Huh. Looks like she got turned here in the park. Something tells me finding patient zero is going to be a bitch.

As for the old man, his chest had been ripped open, ribs splayed out and his innards on full display like a scene from *Aliens*. Blood soaked his shredded white t-shirt and tan Member's Only jacket, while his dead eyes remained fixed on a spot far above the roof of the RV. Oddly enough, his reading glasses were still perched on his nose, even after the struggle that had apparently taken place when he'd first been attacked. Plates, cups, and silverware were strewn all over the floor, and his right hand still clutched a suppressed .22 caliber pistol.

Hard to get a license for those—and expensive, too. Silenced .22 doesn't make much noise and wouldn't draw attention in an R.V. park, which was probably why he had it. Bad choice for killing revs, though. Poor old dude never had a chance.

I didn't have time to screw around with this rev. As far as I knew, its partner was the original carrier, so I needed to track it down, and quick. I pulled out Dyrnwyn, lit it up, and calmly walked toward the revenant. As expected, she leapt at me, either to protect her kill or to add me to the menu. Without much room to maneuver, I stepped slightly to the left and bladed my body, all while removing her head from her shoulders with an upward forehand slash.

Her head went rolling out the door, while her body landed in a heap near the back bedroom. Not wanting to take any chances on someone getting infected, I torched the cabin with a fireball on my way out the door. Once the thing was up in flames, I tossed the revenant's head inside, then took off at a jog after its partner.

This one was smart, but picking up the trail was fairly easy. Rather than stick around, it had turned tail and run toward the Christmas Mountains, off park land. The last thing I wanted was for it to reach that rough country, because it'd be harder to track there, and there were occupied ranches and homesteads out that way as well. I took off at a sprint, determined to catch it before it holed up at sunrise.

After I'd run for a mile or so, I heard snarls and growling in the distance. I pressed on, worried that the revenant had stumbled across more campers. As I came over a small rise, my fears were quelled.

On the other side of the rise, Larry was harassing the creature in an obvious effort to keep him from running off—and he was doing a surprisingly good job of it. The chupacabra would disappear and then reappear behind the rev, snapping at its heels to get the thing's attention. Enraged, the rev would lunge at him, only to have its arms close on empty air because Larry had already gone invisible and slipped away.

The thing hadn't noticed me yet, so I took a moment to study it. It had been an adult male, also late forties, and was dressed in similar fashion to the female I'd taken out back at the RV. Expensive hiking boots, technical jacket, thermals, the works. It was quite possible the two had been a couple and turned at the same time. Which meant the carrier was still at large.

Of course, there was another possibility, one I didn't care to consider.

One thing at a time, Colin.

I wasn't about to chase this thing another step, so I pulled my Glock from my Bag and switched out the magazine for silver ammo. Then, I carefully drew a bead on the back of the rev's head and squeezed off a single round. Call it luck, but I hit it right at the brain stem, cutting its strings like a marionette. After snagging the shell casing from the ground, I dropped it and the pistol back into my Craneskin Bag.

Larry literally appeared at my side, tongue lolling through his crazy snaggled teeth. "Hell of a shot, druid, hell of a shot. You ever think of hunting monsters for a living?"

"No, that never occurred to me, Larry," I deadpanned.

After checking the area to make sure we had no witnesses, I approached the body and squatted down next to it. Based on the skin color and level of decomposition, it was clear this man had been turned at roughly the same time as the female. I stood and began walking back to camp, absently tossing a fireball back at the corpse to set it alight.

Shit. Hunted by the feds, backed into a corner by the skinwalkers, and now I have to deal with an undead outbreak.

Or perhaps not. Maybe it was far worse than a random undead outbreak. Maybe someone was out here, killing people and raising the dead.

"You look worried, druid," Larry said as he loped along beside me.

"I am."

I broke into a jog and made a beeline for our campsite.

12

As I ran to tell the others about the revenants, the sun came up behind the mountains to the east, painting the morning skies in pastel brilliance. Sadly, I was too occupied with worry about what I'd witnessed to fully appreciate the natural beauty around me. My sole consolation was that Larry had disappeared miles back, leaving me alone with my thoughts for a few blessed moments.

Voices echoed off the canyon walls as I neared camp. I bounded up the virtually impassable game trail leading to the plateau we'd claimed, curious as to what the fuss was about. There were three female voices, laughing and chatting. Fallyn, Jesse, and—

What the actual fuck? Bells?

The girls were gathered around the campfire, sitting on camp chairs sipping coffee. Hemi sat off to the side, the obvious odd man out in their little kaffeeklatsch. His shoulders were tense, and he gripped a steaming mug like it was his only lifeline. Our eyes met, and he mouthed a silent "sorry" that spoke volumes.

"Well, look what the cat dragged in," Fallyn quipped as she hid a smile behind a cup of coffee cradled in both hands. "And from the looks of it, shit magnet found more trouble on his way back from the visitor center. I swear, Colin, we can't take you anywhere."

Belladonna's expression was neutral, if somewhat bemused. Despite the hard stare she gave at first, a smile teased the corners of her mouth as she looked me up and down. "You look like shit, and you smell like death."

Jesse sat slightly behind the other girls, observing them with a long face as she sipped her coffee. She glanced at me and shrugged. "You do look pretty rough, slugger."

Danger, Will Robinson! Danger!

I decided that showing weakness at this juncture would be a mistake. Desperately in need of a power move to assert my dominance, I sauntered into their midst and poured myself a cup of coffee from the brew pot that sat on a cooking grate over the fire. The pot was hot enough to sizzle as it touched my skin, but I pretended not to notice.

"Hmm... something tells me you've all been talking about me behind my back," I observed drily, still holding the pot out of sheer stubbornness.

Fallyn cleared her throat. "I'm the one who called this little pow-wow, so don't blame them. After I filled Belladonna in on Jesse's unique situation, these ladies have decided to raise the white flag."

"I see," I said, not really seeing anything clearly at all. "Uh, Bells, that whole thing you saw, uh, the other night—"

"She knows, Colin," Jesse said. "I tricked you while I was under the influence of the Grove's magic. You had no idea what you were doing."

"And while I'm not happy about it"—Belladonna paused

to flash Jesse a halfhearted scowl—"we were broken up at the time, and actually neither of you knew what you were doing. How could I hold it against you? After all, you thought you were sleeping with me, *pendejo*."

Fallyn chuckled, and even Jesse broke out of her funk to crack an embarrassed grin. The she-wolf cleared her throat before interrupting.

"As I was saying, these two have decided to call a truce. And seeing as how you've been so conflicted where they're involved, they've decided to *un-conflict* you."

Jesse suddenly found something to stare at in the distance, while Belladonna's eyes met mine with defiance. The serpenthrope nodded once as if to agree with Fallyn's assessment. "It had to be done. You're too kind to make a decision that might hurt someone, and too dumb to realize such a thing is necessary."

"Hey, now—" I objected, only to be cut off by Jesse.

"She's right, Colin. You're too nice for your own good, and way too much of a people-pleaser. You've always been able to make the hard calls when it came to violence and bloodshed, but when it comes to relationships, you're a huge wimp."

"*Encerio!*" Belladonna agreed.

"Preach it, sister," Fallyn exclaimed.

I set the coffee pot back on the grill, as my hand had been burned to the point where I feared it would be permanently attached to the pot handle. It hurt like hell, so I shoved that hand in my pocket, stealth-shifting to speed up the healing process. Needing a moment to process what was happening, I took a sip of coffee and promptly burned my tongue. Undaunted, I swallowed that hot slug of coffee, nearly choking on it as it went down.

Belladonna cleared her throat as she sat up straighter in

her chair. "So, we've decided to make peace and cut you loose. After all, it's not Jesse's fault that she died while you two were madly in love."

"And it's not Belladonna's fault that you fell for her while you were still mourning my death," Jesse said quietly.

"Plus, I think everyone is in agreement that Golden Boy here is bound and determined to step in huge piles of horse shit every time he turns around," Fallyn said as she looked at the other two women before turning her eyes on me. "Now, it's not your fault that you got saddled with carrying on the druid legacy, nor is it your fault that you attract trouble like a turd attracts flies."

"I'm starting to resent all the scatological references," I muttered.

Fallyn frowned. "Are you done? As I was saying, your life is complicated, and that complicates things for anyone who gets involved with you. That's a fact. Also—and this is purely my own observation..." She glanced at the other two women in turn. "Whoever chooses to become romantically involved with you needs to be willing to accept the entire package, which includes your tendency to try to rescue the world and fix everyone else's problems. And it's unfair to expect you to change, just because those tendencies are inconvenient to your significant other."

Jesse looked at Fallyn, brows furrowed, but she remained silent. On the other hand, Belladonna's mouth was set in a hard line as she turned to Fallyn to object.

"Girl, you know it's true," Fallyn said calmly. "You've been expecting him to change and focus all his attentions on you, simply because you fell in love with him."

"I'm not in love with him," the huntress objected in a flat voice.

"Whatever you say," Fallyn replied, "but it ain't fair to expect Colin to change to suit you."

Bells chewed her lip, eyes downcast and thoughtful. "Yes, I suppose you're right."

Fallyn looked at Jesse. "And you came back expecting to just pick up where you left off. 'Cept you came back plum crazy, and he was already involved with another woman. Can you blame him for being more than a little gun shy now?"

Jesse held her gaze for several seconds, first with hard eyes, but gradually her expression softened as she turned her eyes to me. "No, I suppose I can't blame him at all."

I stood there with a burned hand, a scalded tongue, and my jaw on the floor. Meanwhile, the girls shared a collective sigh.

Fallyn looked at the other ladies with the barest hint of sympathy. Then, she turned those hazel predator's eyes at me. "Now, that's settled. Do you have anything to add?"

The girls each looked at me, waiting for me to respond.

"Take your time," Fallyn said. "I know it's a lot to take in."

Frustrated, I poured my coffee on the ground. While at first blush it might seem like this turn of events would simplify things, in fact it would only made things harder. Now, pulling that thorn was going to be twice as painful, because it was going to look like I was using this as an excuse to be let off the hook.

Plus, I definitely resented that certain—*decisions*—had been made without my input. Never mind that Fallyn had obviously orchestrated this entire thing to force my hand. Or that I'd come to similar conclusions on my own.

Celibacy is looking really good about now.

"Do I have a say in any of this?"

"No!" they all shouted in unison.

"Alright, then I'm going to bed," I said as I stumbled off toward one of the tents. "By the way, there might be a necromancer roaming around the park, and I think it could be Ernesto Bylilly. Whoever it is, they're raising revenants and turning them loose on local campers. Wake me up if you need me to kill anything." I gave a two-fingered wave over my shoulder as I entered the tent. "'Night, all."

There was a long silence punctuated only by branches crackling in the fire.

Finally, Hemi cleared his throat. "Um... that went well, don't you think?"

After four hours of fitful sleep, I emerged from the tent bleary-eyed and in serious need of caffeine and calories. While the girls were nowhere to be seen, Hemi was sitting next to the fire, futzing with the coffee pot and looking like he needed something to do. He nodded at me, and I nodded back as I sat down cater-corner to him with my back to the sun.

"Heard you stirring, so I put some of the black stuff on. Never done it this way though, so—"

"Not to worry, I'll filter the grounds out with my teeth," I yawned, looking around. "Where are the girls?"

He glanced sideways at me beneath arched eyebrows. "You sure you want to know, after they ambushed you like that?"

"Speaking of which, thanks for stepping in on my behalf."

Hemi held his hands up defensively. "Far be it from me to get involved in your harem issues. Anyway, they're out looking for whoever's raising the dead."

"Ah," I said, before the first part of his answer registered. "My 'harem'? Like those trashy fantasy novels? That's gross, dude."

He chuckled. "You kinda have one, ya know. A harem, that is."

"Stop it, already." He poured me a cup of coffee and I took it, taking time to blow on it before I had a sip. "That's actually not too bad."

"Bells brought you some of Luther's special blend. Said you probably needed a taste of home, although she also said you didn't deserve it."

I quietly sipped my coffee while taking a moment to reflect on my so-called *harem issues*. "They're all too good for me, you know."

He sat back, legs outstretched and ankles crossed, hands over his belly. "Poor you," he replied sarcastically.

"Ouch. Can't a guy engage in a little modest self-pity once in a while?"

"Naw. If I let you, you'd be at it all the time." He closed his eyes and leaned his head back. "So—Fallyn, aye?"

"After that stunt she pulled, arranging that ambush? Maybe not," I chuckled.

"It's clear she's keen on you. You feel the same?"

"Not sure. We did sort of bond on that trip to New Orleans."

"I'd say she bonded to you way before that."

"Although I didn't see it." I rubbed my eyes before taking another sip of coffee. "Gotta say, she's easy to be around. Fallyn doesn't expect me to be something I'm not, you know? I can't just stop being the Junkyard Druid, and I can't call up the fae and all the gods I've pissed off and say, 'Hey, let's call it even and go our separate ways.' They're always going to keep coming at me, and I'm always going to stand in their way when they fuck with humanity. Fallyn gets that, but Bells? Not so much."

Hemi scratched his upper lip. "You sure about this?"

"Nope." I sipped my coffee, reveling in the thick black warmth, despite having no sugar or cream. "But I'm sick of trying to figure out what Bells wants from me all the time. She's hot and cold, and it's like I'm always breaking the rules with her, but I never know what the rules are. Belladonna is"—I searched for the right word—"exhausting."

"She did know what she was getting when she took up with you," he said, nodding sagely. "And Jesse?"

"Whole other can of worms, buddy. I still love her, just not romantically."

"Does she know that?" he asked.

"I—we—I guess there hasn't been much time to talk, since she came back."

"Now that she's sane, you mean." He interlaced his fingers behind his head. "And that doesn't change things?"

I worked a few kinks out of my neck as I considered his question. "Nah, it doesn't. It's been a couple of years since she —well, since I killed her."

"Since 'it' killed her," he interjected. "That wasn't you."

"It was a part of me, enough to take responsibility. Anyway, even though it was only a few years ago, it seems like forever. We were just a couple of high school kids back then. I'll always hold a flame for her, but those days are gone, Hemi."

He sighed. "I hope that never happens with me and Maki."

I patted his shoulder and gave it a squeeze. "Me too, brother, me too."

A voice that was becoming increasingly familiar chimed in, singing an old Nazareth song off-key. "'Love is like a flame, it burns you when it's hot'—right, fellas?"

Larry appeared out of thin air across the fire from us, stretching out with his head resting over crossed forepaws. Hemi practically jumped out of his chair. I was getting used to these unexpected entrances, so I was only mildly startled.

"Bloody hell—sneaking up on a bloke like that!" Hemi shook a fist at the creature as he stood up. "You wanna hiding, you mangy mutt?"

"Relax, bro," I said. "He's annoying, but I don't think he means any harm."

Hemi glared at the chupacabra, who seemed altogether unimpressed at the demigod's display. Finally, my friend sat back down. "How d'ya do that, anyway?"

"Magic," Larry replied. "Not really sure how it works. I just think about fading out, and I do."

"Like that cloak you nicked from Gunnarson," Hemi said to me with a grudging nod. "Thing like that comes in handy, I reckon."

"Larry here seems to get by alright," I replied. I looked at the chupacabra. "There's no food, by the way—if that's why you're here."

He raised his head and cocked it as he considered my question. "I'd take some if you had it, but naw, that's not why I came."

The chupacabra dropped his head back to rest on his paws. Hemi and I looked at each other, then at the mangy cryptid.

"What?" he asked.

"Why'd ya come here, then?" Hemi asked through gritted teeth.

"Oh, yeah. That hot-ass werewolf chick sent me to get you. She says another kid is missing, and they spotted La Llorona along the river."

Unfortunately, we were too late this time. EMS and the park authorities were already loading up a half-empty body bag on a stretcher by the time Hemi and I caught up to the girls. La Llorona had killed another victim, a young life snuffed out way too soon in the most senseless way imaginable.

After the authorities left, we spent hours searching for the deadly specter, up and down the river banks, to no avail. Finally, dejected, depressed, and exhausted, we gave up and headed back to camp.

It was dark by the time we arrived, yet there was a fire going when we walked into camp. Ernesto crouched by the fire, sipping a cup of coffee as he stared into the flames. I supposed it was either that or look up at the stars, and the skinwalker didn't seem like the type to admire the beauty of nature.

"You're wasting your time here, Bylilly," I said as I approached him, the others at my back. "I'm not going to do your dirty work, so you'll just have to come up with another way for me to repay you."

He glared at me and set down his coffee mug. Well, our coffee mug, but after his lips had been on it, it may as well have been his. "You sure about this, druid? Breaking your promise to a *brujo* has consequences. And I'm certainly not one to be crossed."

"You're trespassing on my territory, walker," Fallyn said, stepping in front of me. "And it's time for you to leave."

Ernesto scowled. "This doesn't involve you, whelp, nor the Austin Pack. Tell me, does your father know you're making enemies for the Pack on his behalf?"

Jesse tsked. "I think you're barking up the wrong tree. She kind of does what she pleases." Her hair began to fan out around her, and her hands burst into black flames as eyes started to glow a pale green. "Now, I don't like that you're threatening my friend, so I'm seconding Fallyn's suggestion. Leave, or one of us is going to throw you over the cliff."

Ernesto's eyes widened at Jesse's display. "Amazing," he whispered to himself. "I wouldn't believe it if I hadn't seen it—"

"I'll do it," Hemi said, cutting Ernesto off by smacking his war club in his palm. "And I'll toss him real high first, so he has an extra ways to fall."

"I approve of that plan," Bells said as she sighted down the barrel of her Desert Eagle at Ernesto. "And I bet I can empty a magazine in him before he hits the ground."

I held my hands up and looked around at my companions. "Seems as though you're outnumbered, Ernesto. We've all had a long day, so get lost before this gets ugly."

Ernesto stopped staring at Jesse long enough to glare at me for a few seconds. Then he stood, and as he did, his shadow stretched and lengthened behind him. It might have been a trick of the light, but I could have sworn his shadow looked more beast than human. It was altogether creepy, and a reminder that I really had no idea about the limits of Ernesto's powers, or what he might do if attacked.

"So be it, druid," the skinwalker hissed as he backed away from the fire. "Just remember that I gave you a chance to repay your debt. What happens next is on you."

I summoned a fireball and let it hover over my

outstretched hand. "I'm getting bored of this conversation, Bylilly. Leave, and that's the last time I'll say it."

He threw something at the fire, and the flames roared fifteen feet or more in an instant, blinding me until they died down a second later. By that time, Ernesto was gone.

"Don't think we've seen the last of him," Hemi remarked.

"Not by a long shot," I replied. I looked around at the others. They all looked depressed and worn thin. "It's been a shit day. I'll set up some wards around camp—that way, we can all get some sleep."

"Don't have to tell me twice," Fallyn said, heading off toward one of the tents.

Jesse flashed me a weak, inscrutable smile. "Goodnight, Colin."

She turned toward the tents, and I called out after her. "Jess? What was Ernesto so freaked out about?"

Jesse's eyes were sad, but otherwise her expression betrayed little. "It's nothing, Colin. Don't worry about it."

"Look, I know you're tired—we all are. So I guess we can talk about it later." I rubbed the back of my neck. "Oh, and thanks for having my back just now."

"I always have, and I always will," she said without looking back as she entered her tent.

While the other girls had gone to bed, Belladonna just kind of stood there looking lost. For lack of any better options, I pointed at my tent. "You can take mine, Bells. I plan to stay up a while anyway, to set up the wards."

She gave a nearly imperceptible shake of her head. "Actually, I'm staying at the lodge tonight, then I'm heading back to Austin in the morning." She glanced at the tents where Fallyn and Jesse had retreated for the night. "It's a little crowded around here. And despite the current situation, I think you have things covered."

An uncomfortable silence followed. I decided to break it, against my better judgement. "I never meant to hurt you, Bells."

She nodded once, blank-faced, although her voice was tight with emotion. "*Yo lo sé, pero no duele menos.* Take care, Colin." Without giving me time to respond, she bounded off into the night.

"You too," I whispered.

I stared after her for a long time, until Hemi cleared his throat. Feeling slightly embarrassed, I turned around to face him. "You stuck around for that?"

"You two were between me and my tent. Been a bit awkward to interrupt that exchange, aye?"

I exhaled heavily. "You think Ernesto will be back tonight?" I asked.

Hemi looked at the surrounding dark with a frown on his face. "Mebbe. He seemed awful interested in Jesse. Question is, you really going to trust your wards with that creep running around out there?"

"Not on your life. I'll take first watch."

13

I got up early the next morning and took off alone to find some answers. We had two skinwalkers traipsing around the park, revenants popping up out of nowhere, a specter killing kids, and no idea what was going on. Clearly, I needed to get to the bottom of it all, and currently I had only one lead. La Onza was the one missing piece of the puzzle—something told me that if I found her, I'd also find out how everything was connected.

Larry showed up beside me about fifteen minutes after I left camp, just like I knew he would. "What's the plan, chief?"

"Well Larry, it's like this." In the blink of an eye, I'd snagged the mangy rat-dog by his scruff, holding him up in front of me. "I need to find La Onza, and something tells me you know where to find her."

"Me? How would I know—"

I formed a fireball in my other hand. "I wonder how long you'd last if I shoved this down your throat—curse be damned."

"Alright, alright. I might know where she has a hideout. Set me down and I'll show you."

I extinguished the fireball, then I pulled out a magic marker and drew a symbol on his rump. "That rune is a tracking spell. Disappear, and I will find you and end you."

"C'mon, druid, you know I wouldn't ditch you. I need you to kill Ernesto so I can be rid of this curse. Think about it—I got a vested interest in seeing you succeed."

I rolled my eyes. "Whatever. Just lead me to La Onza."

"Follow me, then."

Larry headed southwest toward the Rio Grande and Santa Elena canyon. When we reached the river, we took the canyon trail—a path that led to nowhere, according to park maps.

"Larry, this trail doesn't go anywhere. It's a dead end."

"Ah, you only think it's a dead end. But you'll see."

Just when I thought we'd reached the end of the trail, Larry showed me a cleverly-hidden set of handholds and steps in the cliffs that led to a ledge above. Once we'd made the climb—me in the conventional manner, and Larry by jumping goat-like from handhold to handhold—we followed the ledge to a slot canyon that had been artfully obscured by illusory magic. The obfuscation spell was old, and had been reinforced many times over the years. From what I could tell, the caster had been keeping this area a secret for decades, or perhaps even centuries.

Larry nodded toward the entrance to the canyon before sitting down in the shade of a rocky overhang. "Her cave's in there. La Onza's not, though, I can tell you that. She don't get found unless she wants to be found. But you want to poke around in her stuff, have at it. I'm staying out here."

"Fine," I said, heading into the wide cleft in the cliffs.

A short ways into the canyon, the path inclined steeply upwards, and soon I was easily a hundred feet above where we'd started on the banks of the river. Fifty yards in, the canyon dead-ended at a cliff wall, underneath an overhang that jutted from the cliff face thirty feet above. I scaled up to the overhang, where I found a ledge maybe ten feet wide in front of a small cave that had been hidden from view below.

Place is warded nine ways to Sunday. Someone really doesn't want to be bothered.

A closer look at the wards told me they were old, layered, and dangerous. Whoever cast them was very good with protective magic, and I doubted I could unravel the spellwork. But I thought I might be able to send a probe past them, just to see what was back there.

I found a smooth, round pebble and rolled it between my palms, infusing it with magic and attuning it to my druid senses. Then, I looked for a gap in La Onza's wards—all I needed was a small hole to toss the stone through. I soon found what I was looking for, and flicked the pebble from my open palm through the hole.

The stone popped past the wards with nary a fizzle of magic, landing in the dirt beyond. I sat down cross-legged, closed my eyes, and focused on the pebble. Seconds later, the stone began to roll away from me.

This was one of the first spells I'd learned, a primitive method of using sound waves to scout an area before entering. Although I couldn't see it, I could sense where it was going, connected as it was to me through my magic. My magic also conveyed every single sound the stone made as it skittered around the circumference of the cave ahead. It was crude, but effective.

Unfortunately, something else had detected those sounds as well. Although there'd been nothing there before, I suddenly sensed a presence—something old, dark, and powerful.

A guardian spirit. Should be alright on this side of the wards—

Before I could complete the thought, a large clawed hand reached out of the cave entrance, snatching me and pulling me through the wards.

Strangely, I didn't set the wards off when I passed through them. Instead, it felt more like I'd passed through a magic portal. And indeed, the other side of the magical barrier looked quite different from what I'd seen just moments before.

I was in the same cave, but it wasn't *exactly* the same. This place was ill-lit, gloomy, and oppressive, and no light filtered in from outside the entrance. Shadows gathered in the far corners of the cave like thick black spider webs, and the darkness seemed to press in on me from all sides.

Momentarily, I had a flashback to the time when Maeve abandoned me in a lightless cave deep underground. It had been without a doubt one of the worst experiences of my life. A lump formed in the pit of my stomach as cold, stark fear began to grip me. I shook the memory off by reminding myself this was an entirely different situation. Once I'd regained a bit of mental calm, I slowed my breathing and focused on dealing with my current predicament.

Panic time is over, Colin—time to figure this shit out.

It was entirely possible that my presence had triggered a darkness spell when I was pulled through La Onza's wards.

To test that theory, I cast a light spell and tossed it at the cavern ceiling above. Instead of floating up and illuminating the area around me, it rose a few feet and then fizzled out.

Well, that's different.

Even more peculiar was the silence. The ambient nature sounds that had been present just moments before were now gone. I no longer heard the waters of the Rio Grande rushing through the canyon, the wind whistling past the cave entrance, birds chirping as they flew overhead—it had all been replaced by an almost palpable absence of background noise.

I kept my eyes on the shadows deeper within the cavern, and hollered over my shoulder. "Hey, Larry? You still out there?"

Nothing. Shit.

I took a good look around me, finally coming to grips with the situation. This place was a darker, fucked up version of the cave I'd seen through La Onza's wards, and it was pretty easy to determine that I definitely was not in Kansas anymore. When I'd been dragged through the wards, apparently I'd been transported to some dark, parallel dimension —an alternate version of La Onza's cave on another plane of existence.

It wasn't uncommon for powerful magic-users to capture, coax, or enslave supernatural entities to guard their homes and treasures. The presence I'd felt must've been some sort of guardian spirit, and it was a good bet that thing had transported me here. Where "here" was, I had no clue—not really. But the fact that this creature could portal me to another dimension told me it was probably not to be trifled with.

It has to still be here. Is it watching me? Studying me, maybe, before it attacks?

I didn't want to think about the alternative, which was that it had pulled me into this shadowy, alternate dimension only to leave me here. Reaching out with my senses, I probed the area beyond to see if I was truly alone.

"Interesting. It possesses more than one kind of magic," something said in a voice that sounded like nails being dragged across a chalkboard—high and reedy, and altogether unsettling.

"It does," I answered. "Care to tell me where I am?"

"The shadow dimension," it replied. "Think of it as a parallel universe, just beneath the skin of your own reality."

The words echoed off the walls of the cave a few times before being eaten up by the unnatural silence. I probed further, but instead of finding a life form in the darkness beyond, I sensed a large area that was barren of any living presence. At first I thought nothing of it, then that large dead spot began moving closer.

Curious.

I took a deep whiff of the stale air in the cavern. The odor that met my nostrils was a scent I'd become intimately familiar with during my time in the Hellpocalypse. I could recognize that combination of decaying flesh, clotted blood, and grave dirt anywhere.

"I wonder," the reedy voice said. "Does it do tricks?"

"It does, vampire. Come any closer, and you'll find out just what my magic can do."

If I can get a spell to work here, that is.

The thing made a dry, wheezing noise that sounded like a carnival organ on its last legs.

"Little wizard, you speak with no mere vampire. Does a puddle call itself an ocean? Does the firefly compare itself to the moon? You stand in the presence of something much older and greater than those anemia-stricken corpses who call themselves vampires." The thing wheezed another short laugh. "No, I am no vampire."

"Fine, so you're not a vampire," I replied. "Whatever you are, it looks to me like you were captured and placed here to guard La Onza's lair. That tells me you're not quite as high and mighty as you let on."

Shadows gathered around the dead spot, a column of night ten feet across and easily fifteen feet high. "Careful now, mortal. I've not had a meal in some time, and my curiosity is easily overcome by my hunger. Choose your words carefully, because every stray syllable may shorten your already meager lifespan."

"Yeah, yeah," I said. "So far, all I've seen from you is a lot of boasting and bluster, and frankly, I think you're bluffing. So, let's just move this whole thing along and get to the point where you try to eat me so I can split your skull open, alright?"

That got its attention.

It was still dark as hell inside the cave, but I'd started stealth-shifting so my enhanced vision was kicking in. Shadows receded as something with considerable bulk dropped from the cavern ceiling ahead. The shadowy figure was perhaps nine to ten feet tall—not quite as big as the *caddaja* demon I'd fought recently in Austin, mind you, but still the size of a fucking truck.

Huh. I was going to save the full Fomorian monty for a surprise—looks like I should've started that party from the get-go.

At first, the thing looked like a giant, dark-gray cocoon. As it unfurled itself, I realized that the "cocoon" was a pair of huge, leathery wings. The creature had an enormous wingspan, easily twenty feet across, with each wingtip touching the cavern walls to either side.

As the last wisps of shadow disappeared, my captor was finally revealed. The thing's charcoal-skinned body was shaped like that of a giant, heavily muscled man. Its clawed feet ended in long, articulated toes that looked like they could grip or slash with equal ease. By contrast, its hands were much more human, but equipped with equally wicked claws.

Yet easily the most bizarre feature was its grotesque face. From the neck up, the creature looked exactly like a giant bat —complete with the beady eyes, a squished up nose, huge ears, and sharp teeth. Honestly, the damned thing was one of the most hideous monsters I'd ever seen, and I'd seen a few.

Speaking of which, he did remind me of a certain someone...

Damn, he's like a bigger, buffer version of Rafael.

Rafael was an ancient nosferatu I'd tangled with a few years back. He'd pretty much tossed me around like a rag doll. Considering its size, if this creature had powers that were similar to Rafael's, I was in deep shit.

"And just what the hell are you?" I asked, fishing for clues as to its nature and powers.

The creature puffed out its chest, snapped its wings taut, and drew itself to its full height. "Behold your demise, mortal. I am the night—"

This again? Yeah, he and Rafael are definitely related.

I held my hands up, waving them back and forth. "Whoa,

whoa, whoa—hold it right the fuck there. 'I am the night'? You're really going to lead with that?"

"You dare to interrupt me?"

"Yeah, I dare. That line is kind of taken."

The bat-like creature's wings drooped slightly. "By who?"

"By Batman, duh," I replied.

"I'm the Bat-Man," the beast responded with a self-assured nod. "And I have always been the night."

"No, dude, I'm telling you. You are definitely *not* Batman. Batman is a comic book character, and one of the most iconic superheroes in modern culture."

"There is nothing comical about being the night!" the creature shrieked, nostrils flaring. "And I am the night!"

"Not anymore. Everyone in my world thinks that Batman is the night."

"The people of Aztlan worshipped me as a god," the beast fumed, glaring at me. "I will not allow a human hero to usurp my title."

"Well don't blame me," I replied. "You can blame Bob Kane—he's the guy who created the character."

"Bob Kane is Batman?" the giant man-bat asked.

"No, no, no—'Batman' is a fictional character. Bob Kane made him, and then other people brought him to life in the comics and movies."

"What are these comics you speak of?"

I thought about it for a moment. "They're pictures people draw to tell stories."

The man-bat's ears twitched. "If they memorialize the deeds of this 'Batman' in pictures, he must be mighty indeed. Perhaps he is one of my offspring, then. Yes, I will definitely kill him."

"But you can't kill him—he's not real."

"Liar!" the creature shouted, flecks of spittle flying from his thin chiropteran lips. "Do not attempt to fool me, little wizard. You just said Bob Kane and his followers brought this 'Batman' to life!"

I grabbed great handfuls of my hair in my fists. "Argh! You don't understand. Bob Kane made Batman up."

"Ah, this Bob Kane is a shaman. He uses magic to create creatures that do his will. I will kill Bob Kane then, and take back my title. Then all will know and fear Camazotz once more."

Camazotz—this is starting to make sense.

Camazotz was the ancient Mayan bat god. He was closely associated with darkness, night, and death. No wonder the damned thing's identity was tied up with being "the night"— he'd been worshipped as a being synonymous with things nocturnal for centuries.

"Camazotz?" I asked. "As in *the* Camazotz? Not just an avatar?"

Camazotz frowned, an expression that made his already ugly face considerably uglier. "I am no avatar. Pfah! The other gods fear to appear on the mortal plane, so they send facsimiles to placate their worshippers. Camazotz has no such fears. I am the night—I am death! Where I roam, there is Camazotz. No other like me exists."

"Except Batman," I muttered under my breath.

He bristled. "What did you say?"

I tensed, slipping a hand inside my Bag in case I needed to draw Dyrnwyn. "I said, 'Exactly, man.'"

"*Bat*-Man," Camazotz groused. "And your validation is inconsequential. I *am* the night, after all."

"Oh, for sure."

My acquiescence seemed to deflate the bat god's anger, and I breathed a sigh of relief. Demi-gods and avatars were one thing, but I definitely did not want to tangle with a full-fledged deity. I needed to defuse this situation and get back to my own plane of existence, pronto.

And in the process, maybe I could gain a little advantage should things go sideways with Ernesto. He'd looped me in when I was over a barrel—why not take a page from a bad guy's book?

Time for a little fast-talking.

"I see it clearly now," I said. "Without a doubt, mighty Cama-zotz, you are the greatest and only Bat-Man, ever."

The bat god's ears swiveled in my direction. "Yes, everyone knows this. What is your point?"

"Indeed, you are the Bat-Man. However, the current situa-tion does pose a—no, I shouldn't speak out of turn," I demurred with a wave of my hands.

Camazotz swiveled his weird giant bat head and turned those beady eyes on me. "What?"

"Oh, it's nothing. I shouldn't have mentioned it, now that I know in whose unmatched glory I currently bask."

Camazotz closed the space between us in an eye-blink. He gripped me by the throat with one massive hand and lifted me off the floor effortlessly. This was in of spite the fact that I currently weighed better than 300 pounds in my stealth-shifted state. The bat god pulled me in close, his rank, metallic breath washing over me as he hissed with low menace.

"Speak, mortal! You were about to say something, yet now you deny your intentions. State what is on your mind, blood bag, or I will drain you immediately, instead slowly savoring your lifeblood over the course of several decades as I had originally planned."

Yeah, let's not.

I clucked my tongue. "Well—and I mean no offense by pointing this out—if you're going to kill Bob Kane, and reassert to the world that you are, indeed, 'the night'—"

"I am," he interjected, with only a hint of uncertainty in his voice.

"If that's your intention, you sure can't kill the guy from here."

Conflicting emotions played across the bat god's wrinkled, blunted face. First, his eyes narrowed, then his nose twitched as his lips drooped in a frown, and finally his expression softened completely. Resignedly, Camazotz dropped me to the floor, then he sat on a nearby boulder, curling his wings in as he propped his chin on one massive fist. It was almost comical—dude looked like a Guillermo del Toro version of *The Thinker*.

"Drat! You are correct, tiny wizard. I cannot kill the shaman known as Bob Kane while I am trapped here."

"And how exactly did that happen—if you don't mind my asking?"

"I'd—I'd rather not say."

I snapped my fingers. "Treachery! I knew it."

Camazotz nodded sagely. "You have the gist of it. I was tricked, although I am loath to admit it. The nahuālli is no match for me in a fair fight, powerful though she might be. But like most witches, she is both cunning and deceitful.

Thus, she lured me to her lair with promises she never intended to keep, and then trapped me in this place."

"What promises? Again, I don't mean to pry, but—"

"We were to have intercourse."

Alrighty, no beating around the bush then.

"My apologies. I didn't mean to inquire into your personal matters."

The giant bat-man shrugged. "It is a natural act, and Camazotz takes what he wishes. There is no shame in it. In times past, I would simply bring a loyal priestess into my cave to satisfy my urges. But after a long sleep, I awoke to find that all my followers were gone, and that I had been—"

He struggled to finish that last sentence, so I stepped in to rescue him. "No need to say it—it's happened to many gods over the centuries."

The bat god's shoulders slumped. "The witch promised me offspring, minions by which I could rebuild my temples and draw followers to me once more."

"But it was all a lie," I remarked with a slow, sad shake of my head. "That hussy!"

"Thus, it was not my libido that was my downfall, but hubris. The witch knew my desires, and played upon them to entrap me. When I entered her lair, the spell-traps had already been set, and I walked right into them. I'd been weakened by my long rest, and had not fully restored my strength, so—"

"Ah—she knew you'd have enough power to pull anything that wandered into her cave across to this side, but not enough juice to free yourself. And that's how she ended up getting a god to guard her shit."

"If by 'shit' you mean her possessions, then yes. And here I have remained, for the better part of two centuries." With a snarl, he smashed a huge fist into a nearby rock wall, sending splinters and shards of rock flying. "Since then, I've fed on every single wayward animal and human who wandered close to La Onza's cave. Yet none have increased my strength enough to allow me to escape."

"And by the time another creature or human comes along, you're weakened again."

"Indeed. I could feed on you—you look strong enough to sustain me for a few decades, at least. But there's no guarantee I'd get another meal before the sustenance wore off."

Camazotz sighed and kicked a football-sized stone across the cave as if it were a pebble. The sound of it echoed once, twice, and then all was still again.

Gah, but this place is creepy. I definitely don't want to be stuck here—or to become a Scooby snack for bat-boy here. Time to reel him in.

"Huh," I said, tapping a finger on my chin.

"What? You have insight that mighty Camazotz has not yet considered?"

"Maybe—and don't take this the wrong way, but I've known a few gods in my time. If there's one thing you folks are bad at, it's asking for help. Being immortal and mighty and all, you often discount the ability of mortals to further your cause—beyond worship and sacrifice, that is."

Camazotz scowled. "What are you getting at, little wizard?"

"Well, La Onza trapped you from the other side—from our world. Doesn't it make sense that another skilled magic-user could free you from the other side, as well?"

The bat god's ears perked up, and if it wasn't so damned dark I'd have said there was a twinkle in his eye that hadn't been there a moment before.

"It does. Camazotz has considered this, but what reason would a human wizard have to help Camazotz?"

Fish. Hooked.

"Camazotz, I would have every reason to help you if I knew you'd return the favor at a later date. Now, here's what I propose..."

14

Long after the sun had set, I popped back into my own plane of existence on the other side of La Onza's wards. There, a short, stout, dark-skinned woman sat with her legs pulled beneath her on the other side of a small campfire that had been built in the middle of the ledge. She pointed to the opposite side of the fire with a stick, which I took as an invitation to sit.

As I approached, I gathered what little information I could from her mannerisms and appearance. Her features were typical of the *mestizos* of the region, with brown, almond eyes, a wide face, high cheek bones, a hawk-like nose, and strong jawline. Regarding her age, it was indeterminate—she might have been thirty or sixty, as her skin was smooth, but she had the rugged look of someone who spent a lot of time outdoors. Her long dark hair was parted in the middle and pulled back in a ponytail, and I noted that it was flecked here and there with the occasional strand of gray. She wore primitive, handmade sandals, a flowing, ankle-length skirt, and a worn ringer t-shirt with a faded picture of Snoopy and Wood-stock on the front.

"Not many people survive a meeting with Camazotz," she remarked drily, in only slightly-accented English. "I hope the deal you made was worth it."

"La Onza, I presume."

She barely hitched one shoulder. "So they call me. And you are the druid the skinwalker sent to kill me."

I sat on the other side of the fire, cross-legged. "I refused. I only came here to seek you out so I could get some answers."

"Answers about why the dead roam the park? Why La Llorona ranges so far south, haunting and hunting the Rio Grande instead of the Rio Colorado? Answers to why a skin-walker wants me dead?"

I inclined my head. "Yes. And how to stop it."

She tilted her head back and laughed. "Hah! You're the reason for it, druid. Leave, and these troubles leave with you. But you will not. You will choose to face him here, in this remote area, and me and mine will suffer for it."

"I don't understand."

The witch pulled a stick from the fire, pointing the glowing end at me. "Do you know what I protect here—what Ernesto Bylilly really wants?"

"No, I don't," I said, squirming just a little beneath her cold, hard stare.

"Some would call it a *kiva*, but it's more than that. It's not just a ceremonial structure, but an actual gateway that leads to the underworld. The skinwalker wants to use it to draw spirits to himself, evil spirits that will increase his power. I can't let that happen."

I scratched my head. "Now I'm confused. He said he wanted your pelt, so he could steal your powers."

"That's simply the way Ernesto works. He made a deal with the one who seeks you, that if he helped capture you, that one would get me out of the way so the skinwalker could gain access this cave. But Ernesto is clever. If he could get you to go after me, he wouldn't have to put himself at risk. When you and I fought, you would win, but the cost to you would be high. Ernesto planned to capture you after you'd been weakened by the battle. Then, he'd have what he wanted, and he could sell you to the other for a high price."

"Who is this 'other' person that you keep referring to?" I asked.

"You know of whom I speak. La Llorona even warned you of him, although you didn't listen. Who do you know that hates you, who also has the power to raise the dead?"

Shit.

"The Dark Druid."

La Onza nodded. "Yes. From what I understand, he engaged the younger skinwalker's services after you bested him in your most recent battle. Stanley was supposed to keep an eye on you and keep the Dark One updated as to your whereabouts. When he heard you were forced to leave Austin, he sent the skinwalker after you."

"Huh," I sagely observed. "And how'd Ernesto get involved?"

"Stanley let slip that he was working a job involving a certain druid, and that piqued the old man's interest. He made his son arrange a meeting with the Dark One, and then Ernesto convinced him he could deliver you in exchange for assistance in dealing with me. But, as I said, the elder skinwalker would betray his own mother if he thought it would gain him some small advantage. So, he tried to pit us against each other."

I chuckled humorlessly. "If Ernesto thinks he can double-cross the Fear Doirich and get away with it, he has another thing coming."

La Onza stirred the coals with her stick. "It doesn't matter, now that you've refused to help him. As he sees it, you've broken your agreement, and he'll do whatever he can to help the Dark One gain his revenge on you."

"Speaking of which, how do you know all this?"

Larry appeared on the other side of the fire next to La Onza. "I, uh, might have been spying on Ernesto for her. Sorry, bud, but we didn't know if you could be trusted."

La Onza absently scratched Larry behind the ears as she stared at the flames. "This one came to me for help in breaking the curse Ernesto placed on him. I told him the only way to break the curse would be to kill the caster."

I chewed my thumbnail, out of habit as much as a desire to make things a bit clearer. Old Fionn's magic did still have its uses, after all. "And that's a task you're either incapable of or unwilling to take on. Otherwise, you'd have gotten rid of Ernesto yourself a long time ago."

"You speak the truth of things," she said as she threw another branch on the fire. "We are evenly matched, in both skill and power. I am older and more knowledgeable, but the path he follows allows one to gain much power quickly—but at a terrible cost."

"Death magic and necromancy always come with a high price, at least from what I've seen," I replied. "It did a hell of a number on the Dark Druid."

"But you are the cause for his current condition." A branch in the fire crackled, sending sparks and motes of ash into the sky. "Because of that, the Dark One's hatred for you runs deep, and he'll do anything to get revenge. But what he wants most now is to escape from his rapidly-decaying body. And you may have brought him the means to do so."

"I don't understand," I said. "He's locked in that body for good now—no more jumping to a new host for him. Finnegas and I made sure of that."

"Unless he had access to magic that could reverse the effects of the spell you cast on him. He'd need a source of power that could both give life and reach across into the realm of the dead." She locked eyes with me across the fire. "There is one who came with you who has such talents, is there not?"

"Jesse—you're telling me he's after Jesse?"

La Onza nodded. "The girl is unique in that she somehow can use both life magic and death magic at once. If he siphons off her power, he'll have the means of breaking the spell that locks him inside his current host."

"I have to get back to camp and warn them." I stood up quickly, already stealth-shifting on the fly. "Will you help us, La Onza? The enemy of my enemy, and all that?"

She shook her head. "It's not my fight, druid. This is a white man's war, and it has nothing to do with me. Besides, my responsibility is to protect the gateway from *brujos* like Ernesto Bylilly. And if you've made the deal with my guardian that I think you have, I'll need to stick close to this place—just in case you fail to defeat the Dark One."

"Well, I can't say I blame you, and thanks for the warning." I looked at the mangy rat-dog sitting beside her. "Larry, you coming?"

"I think I'll stay right here, druid—no offense," he replied.

"Thing is, if you win, I'm free. If not, then I don't want to give Ernesto a reason to curse me twice. Sorry, but a chupacabra has to look out for himself."

"Again, I can't blame you. Good luck, Larry," I said as I leapt off the cliff to the canyon below.

"Same to you, druid," he yelled. "And not just because I want that curse lifted!"

I took off at a dead run, wishing for about the millionth time that I had the ability to magically gate myself from place to place. I'd been gone for hours, and there was no telling what had happened since I'd left earlier that morning. For all I knew, the Dark Druid had shown up and snatched Jesse, and it was twenty miles to camp across some of the roughest country in the state. Even at an all-out sprint in my full Hyde-side form, it'd take me well over an hour to get back and warn the others.

Or, maybe not.

It'd been a few days since we'd parted ways with the Druid Oak—surely that was enough time for it to heal and rid itself of the tracking devices? Besides, time worked differently in the Grove and the Void, so maybe it was already up to snuff and just waiting on my signal to return.

But could I call the Grove from here, if it was floating somewhere in the Void? I had no idea how my connection to the Grove worked across distances, as I'd never tried to communicate with it when I wasn't in its immediate presence.

No time like the present to find out.

As I sprinted through the desert, I tested my connection to the Grove and Druid Oak. At first I got nothing, but then I thought I sensed just the barest tickle of the Grove's presence in my mind. It was there, but distant and ever so faint. I tried to grab onto that tiny thread between us, but just when I thought I had a handle on it, the connection would slip away.

C'mon, c'mon!

Running wasn't helping my concentration any, so I came to a stop and sat down on a nearby boulder. I took several deep breaths to calm myself, slowing my breathing so I could focus on reaching the Grove. Again, I searched for the connection. When I found it, rather than snatching at it, I simply relaxed my mind and let it come to me. Soon, I felt the bond between us getting stronger of its own accord.

That must be the secret—trying too hard just screws things up. I have to work with the natural flow of our bond, and not against it, just like everything else in druidic magic.

The process of strengthening the connection took several minutes, and I had to resist the urge to jump up and start running back to camp again. But my patience was soon rewarded, as I had a somewhat weak but serviceable link to the Druid Oak and Grove. I sent it a simple query, not wishing to strain the connection between us.

Have you rid yourself of the tracking devices?

The images it returned were faint—dead leaves falling off a tree, metal bugs being squashed by falling branches, and the like. I took it to mean that the Oak had done as I asked.

Good, then I need you here, now. My friends are in trouble, and I—

Before I finished that thought, I felt the Oak's presence beside me. I opened my eyes, and there in the moonlight stood a fifty-foot tall oak tree, looking for all the world like the most anomalous thing that had ever grown in the Big Bend desert basin.

"Man, it's good to see you," I said aloud, meaning it. Images of warm spring days and sunshine washed over me, making me chuckle in spite of the dire situation. "I need to get somewhere, fast. Can you take me there?"

I sent the Oak an image of the plateau where we'd made our camp. An instant later, I felt the distinct sensation of being magically transported into the sentient pocket dimension I'd come to know as the Grove. Before I could even get my bearings inside the Grove, I was outside of it again, standing next to the Druid Oak on top of our campsite plateau.

Hemi was sitting next to the fire when I arrived, keeping watch. The sudden appearance of the Druid Oak startled him, at least until he noticed me standing beside it.

"Damned invisibility and portal magic," he complained. "I'll never get used to people popping in and out all the time."

I took a quick visual survey of the campsite. Everything seemed to be in place, except Fallyn and Bells were nowhere to be found. Thankfully, Jesse was sleeping soundly in a sleeping bag, not far from the fire.

"Hemi, we've got serious trouble—"

"Since when do we not?"

"Er, right. First off, where are the others?"

"Fallyn is off hunting, as usual. We saw Bells at the visitor center, while she was packing up to head home. Said she had better things to do than babysit you."

"Huh," I remarked with my usual astuteness. "I guess she really is cutting me loose."

"You think?" he said, lowering his voice so as to avoid waking Jesse. "Once Fallyn got those two to agree that it wasn't worth it to fight over you, it became a matter of pride for Belladonna to wait and see which one you'd pick."

"Which one? Huh? Who says I was going to pick either of them?"

"Sshh! You want that one to hear?" Hemi said, inclining his head at Jesse's supine form.

I looked more closely at her, and it occurred to me that something was off. For starters, Jesse had always been a light sleeper—it was part of the whole druid training thing. Finnegas had taught us that heavy sleepers tended to wake up in the afterlife, so we'd both learned to sleep with one eye open.

And second, she wasn't breathing.

"Shit!"

I ran over to try to rouse her, but when I touched her shoulder my hand passed right through.

"Fucking illusion!" I tuned my vision into the magical spectrum to get a signature on the spell. The magic was dark and shadowy in nature—definitely not something Jesse would cast, even if she knew how.

"Hemi, tell me everything that happened before I got here."

The big guy rubbed a hand over his face. "Aw, lemme think. Belladonna left before it got dark, then Fallyn took off as soon as the sun went down. I heated some food, but Jesse said she wasn't hungry, and she wanted to be alone. She went to go sit by herself, I went to take a piss, and when I came back she was in her bag, asleep."

"Where was she sitting when you last saw her—awake, I mean?"

"Over here," he said, leading me to a large flat rock next to the cliffs. "She sat right there on that rock."

I cast a cantrip to enhance my senses, searching the area around the rock. It didn't take long to find large, semi-canid footprints, as well as some sort of powder that I couldn't identify. I pinched a bit between my fingers, and my fingertips immediately went numb where the powder made contact.

"Skinwalkers?" Hemi asked.

I nodded. "I'm certain of it. I think they snuck up on Jesse, drugged her, and left the way they came, over the cliffs. See this powdery substance? I've heard tell that some *brujos* use a paralyzing poison, similar to the stuff Haitian bokors use. They use pufferfish toxin and other ingredients, and it's said to be so potent it makes it look like their victims died of natural causes."

"Aw, Colin—this ain't good. But why'd they take her?"

"That's what I came here to tell you. I finally found La Onza, and she turned out to be a font of information. According to the witch, Ernesto and Stanley are working for the Fear Doirich. He's looking for revenge against me for all the shit I've done to him, and he thinks he can use Jesse to help him do it."

The big Maori's brow furrowed. "How's he think he'll do that?"

"By siphoning off her magic. Finnegas and I noticed something different about her this time around. She still retains a bit of the Oak's nature magic, and has a sort of connection to the Grove as well—just much, much weaker. But all that time she spent roaming around as a ghost affected her too. She's alive, but she has a definite connection to the world of the dead."

"Death magic?" he asked.

"Either that or a form of necromancy. Think about that— life magic and death magic, all in one package. If it's ever happened before, I've never heard of it. And La Onza thinks the Dark Druid plans to siphon that magic off so he can use it to break the curse Finnegas and I placed on him."

"Colin, if that's the case—"

"Yup—he'll be able to take another crack at jumping into my body. And here's the kicker. Last time I had Balor's Eye stashed inside my skull, and that made me mostly immune to necromancy. But now? I have no idea if any of that resistance remains."

"Bugger all, cuz—we need to find that girl, and fast, before they hand her over to the Dark Druid."

"Way ahead of you. I'm going to partially shift and sniff around, figure out which way they went. You scratch out a note for Fallyn to let her know what's up. Then, we're going skinwalker hunting."

15

The trail wasn't hard to find, since Jesse's scent was familiar to me and unmistakable. I wasn't as good a tracker as Fallyn, but she hadn't returned yet, so we took off without her. Hemi and I followed the skinwalkers' trail for the better part of an hour, to the mountainous area below the South Rim.

I lost the trail for a time, until I realized they'd obscured their scent and signs of passing with magic. After that, it was just a matter of following the magic instead of trail-sign, and that led us up an impossibly steep slope to a cleft in the ridge-line that was partially hidden by vegetation. Illusory magic had been cast to further obscure the approach, but it was hastily placed and easy to dispel. Finally, we came to yet another cave entrance, one that was suspiciously left unguarded.

"You reckon they took her in there?" Hemi asked.

I knelt to examine the ground in front of the cave. The surface beneath our feet here was rocky and barren, but I could just make out a few faint scuff marks on the rocks. It was doubtful that Ernesto or Stanley would have left any physical sign of their passing, unless they were carrying a heavy load.

"Someone came through here, possibly carrying a body. Besides, I'm pretty sure that crappy obfuscation spell cinches it," I replied, standing up and scanning the area around the cave. "Weird that there are no wards protecting the cave entrance, though."

About that time, I heard shuffling footsteps coming from within the cavern, accompanied by the odd groan or growl. Even without having spent months in the Hellpocalypse, I'd have known what was coming by the smell. Animated rotting corpses tended to throw off putrescence like cheap perfume at a Mary Kay convention—and man, did we get a lungful. A wave of foul air washed over us, just as several dozen ghouls and a handful of revenants came rushing out of the cave.

I backed up a few steps, getting enough space to draw Dyrnwyn. Hemi didn't bother backing away. He just reached behind him and pulled his massive, axe-shaped club out of thin air. In the same motion, he spun and swung the heavy end at a couple of unlucky ghouls. The club impacted with a loud, sickening crunch, and the pair of them went sailing off the cliff.

It'd been a minute since I'd seen my friend in fighting form, and it was still a sight to behold. His tattoos glowed a pale blue, and his war club left a faint after-image of blue light as he spun and swung it around. Although the long, tapered weapon was almost as tall as I was, and as big around as my upper arm at the thick end, Hemi spun and twirled it like a drum major leading a marching band. All the while, he chanted and stomped and made faces at his enemies, working a haka into his dance of death and destruction.

"Neat trick, pulling that stick out of thin air," I shouted, jumping into the fray with Drynwyn's blade lit up like a Roman candle on the Fourth of July. I chopped the arms off a ghoul, kicked another in the chest, and took the head off a revenant as an afterthought. "You'll need to show me that sometime."

Hemi paused and took a two-handed grip on the weapon, which he used to shove a half-dozen ghouls back like a cop on crowd control duty. The lot of them went tumbling, tripping up those behind them. A revenant jumped over the crowd at him, and the big guy smacked it across the face, spinning its head and twisting its neck around at an unnatural angle. The rev dropped to the ground, where it twitched once before going limp.

Hemi grinned ear to ear as he hollered over his shoulder at me. "You got that Bag, aye? I think you're good, mate!"

"Fine, be that way," I said, ducking under a ghoul's lunging grasp as I stuck Dyrnwyn's blade through the underside of its jaw and out the top of the thing's head. "Keep your secrets—but I'll remember that the next time you need a ride to the grocery store."

"Eh, Maki takes care of that stuff now," he replied, spinning and striking with his club in dizzying patterns. Each time the club changed direction it hit something, caving in skulls, snapping bones, and sending ghouls flying. "Can't hold that one over me."

"See how you are?" I said as I dropped into a spinning sweep kick to take a revenant's legs out from under it. I followed through with a backhand slice of my blade as it fell, severing its torso just below the rib cage. "You get a girlfriend and suddenly you're all, 'I don't need you anymore, Colin.' What ever happened to bros before—"

"Watch it!" he warned, with a dangerous look in his eye. "Manners, and all that."

"Okay, okay," I pouted as I finished the still-squirming corpse off by separating its head from its shoulders. "Sheesh."

Although Hemi and I had mowed down the first wave, there were still more revs and ghouls coming out of the cave. "Hemi, we don't have time for this shit! Move back so I can cut loose on them."

Hemi swung for the fences, tossing a few limp ghoul corpses toward the advancing crowd. Then he skipped aside, surprisingly quick on his feet despite his size. Once he was clear, I muttered a spell and launched a fireball into the midst of the undead. It bowled a few over, torching through flesh and charring bone along the way. But that wasn't the effect I was looking to achieve.

"*Pléascann!*" I shouted, uttering the trigger word in badly-accented Gaelic.

The fireball exploded in an expanding ball of super-heated gas that enveloped everything inside the mouth of the cave. Most of the undead were consumed by the flames, but the blast also sent goop and body parts flying everywhere, and I caught a lump of steaming slime in the face. Meanwhile, Hemi had ducked around the side of the cave entrance, managing to avoid the worst of it.

I wiped cooked ghoul muck off and slung it to the ground as Hemi applauded my performance. "Well done—in more ways than one, aye?"

"Let's just go rescue Jesse, and let's also agree not speak of this again. Ever."

Hemi chuckled softly. "Oh, slim chance of that, mate," he said, snapping a picture of me with the burner phone Fallyn had given him. "This is going on Faebook."

Inside, the cave narrowed before opening up into a wider tunnel that led on into the darkness ahead. Hemi couldn't see as well as I could in the dark, so I conjured a small globe of light that bobbed above us, just beneath the ceiling some fifteen feet overhead. Despite that, the shadows seemed to push the cold white light cast by the orb back toward us. And every so often, I'd see shades flitting past out of the corner of my eye.

"See that, mate?" Hemi whispered.

I glanced around, checking my flanks instinctively for an attack. "We're definitely not alone. Let's keep moving, but be ready for anything."

Hemi took up the rear guard, walking backwards at times while I took the lead and pushed ahead. As we went deeper into the cave, the darkness grew until it became unnaturally thick, and the pool of illumination cast by my light spell receded with every step. I'd seen this sort of thing before, when I'd fought against a *nachtkrapp* that had been abducting children in Fredericksburg. Certain creatures of the dark had a knack for manipulating shadow, intensifying it and even creating constructs from the darkness that were substantial enough to do real physical harm.

Low, chattering voices began to echo from the dark around us, accompanied by evil, tittering laughter. Glowing orbs appeared in the darkness—grapefruit-sized balls of eerie red, orange, and yellow light that faded in and out of existence as they floated around us, always just out of reach. They began swooping in closer as we moved ahead, blinking in and out in patterns that made it difficult to gauge their location and bearing.

"Don't let those orbs touch you," I said in a low voice. "I'm pretty sure they're lost souls, the kind that feed on living energy."

"You don't need to tell me," Hemi said. "Seen similar stuff in the underworld."

Not wanting to swing a blade with Hemi in such close quarters, I slipped Drynwyn into my Bag, reaching for my war club instead. It had proven time and again to be effective against all things fae, and while these orbs weren't made of fae magic, they definitely had the same alien presence about them.

More orbs flashed and swooped around us, edging closer and closer by the second. I took a tentative swing at a yellow orb that came too close for comfort, but it changed course on a dime, flitting away before it disappeared. This seemed to embolden the others, and soon we were ducking orbs and swatting at them as they passed, to little effect.

One brushed against my shoulder, numbing it instantly. The orb that touched me brightened after making contact, while I felt weakened and slightly diminished. Another skimmed past Hemi's leg, barely touching him. The Maori warrior stumbled, clutching his leg where it had struck.

"Leg's numb. Damned things pack a wallop."

"Can you walk?" I asked.

"Yup, but if we get swarmed we're goners."

Plan B time.

"Hang on, I have an idea."

If I was right about the nature of the orbs—that they were lost souls under Ernesto's control—then they'd have the same weaknesses as ghosts. I could use my remaining rock salt to pour a ward circle around us, but then we'd be stuck here. Obviously, that wouldn't do us or Jesse much good.

What I need is a ward that can move with us.

An orb swooped in, catching Hemi in the upper arm.

"Gah, bloody things!" he exclaimed, grabbing his arm, which now hung a bit slacker than it had before.

Another came in low at my ankles, and I just barely moved out of the way in time to avoid it. The others began to circle us, like sharks coming in for the kill.

Or piranhas.

"Keep them away from me while I come up with something to fend them off, alright?"

"I'll do my best!" Hemi said. "But be quick!"

I sat down cross-legged with my war club in my lap, chewing my thumbnail. Hemi stood over me, spinning and twirling his own club while chanting to activate his runes. I heard and felt the stick spinning and whirring, acting a temporary shield to protect us, but only for so long.

If only he could spin that thing in all directions at once.

I tried to relax while Fionn's magic did its thing. The magic allowed me to see the big picture, and while I was under its spell, connecting the dots to solve a given problem came easy to me. Despite its utility, I tended to avoid using it, more out of pride than anything. But now wasn't the time for foolish pride.

Hemi's stick whistled past my face, just inches away as it did the work of shielding us from the orbs.

"Any time now, Colin!" he shouted. "These little shits are getting cheeky!"

Shield... spinning... bingo! You suckers are gonna love this.

I focused on the air around us, grabbing it and forcing it into a vortex that created a sort of dust devil in a vertical column that was just a foot or so wider than Hemi's reach with that club. Once I had the air rotating fast enough to support it, I reached inside my Bag for a handful of rock salt, infusing it with just enough of my magic to make it obey my will.

Then, I tossed the salt in the air.

Immediately, the churning air currents picked it up, spreading it throughout the spinning column. Undaunted, one of the orbs attempted to fly through my "salt-devil," with disastrous consequences. As soon as the orb made contact with the salt, it burst like a balloon in a flash of sickly green light. Then there was a loud, shrieking wail that trailed off into the distance until it was gone.

I kept the salt vortex moving, focusing my intentions and magic so it picked up speed. Another orb attempted to pass through the barrier, only to meet with a similar fate. When a third orb failed as well, the rest began winking out, one by one, until the only glowing globe left was that of my original light spell.

"Well, that was darned impressive," the Maori remarked.

As I released the spell, the salt dropped to the ground in a neat circle around us. I scooped up as much as I could, tossing it back in the jar in my Bag.

"C'mon, they'll be back if we hang around. Let's go get Jesse."

Hauling ass out of that chamber, we rounded a corner into a tunnel that led straight ahead for a good thirty yards. A glance over my shoulder told me those orb thingies weren't coming back for another go around, so I set my eyes on what might lie ahead.

Through the opening at the end of the tunnel I saw a

large, flat boulder that had been crudely carved into the shape of an altar. Necromantic runes and symbols had been painted all over it in what was most certainly fresh human blood. As I watched, the runes began to emanate a dark energy that appeared to eat the light around them, casting the chamber in reverse exposure as the magic increased in intensity. The cavern shook, causing dust and pebbles to drop from the ceiling all around, and dark, wispy shadow-creatures began to flit and fly about inside the chamber.

I knew bad portents when I saw them, and this was an eleven on the ten-scale of "pretty fucked up." But worst of all, a limp, unconscious form lay on top of the altar.

Jesse!

The Dark Druid stood behind her, chanting incantations and waving his arms around with an exultant look on his face. As he wove his spell, tendrils of dark magic wrapped around and enveloped Jess, lifting her off the table like an audience volunteer in a Vaudeville magic act. Then, a black and green mist began to flow out of Jesse's body, coalescing in a tight whirlwind pattern that the necromancer sucked into himself.

It looked as if he were breathing in her life force. And for all I knew, he was.

"Damn it, he's already started the ritual!" I said, taking off at a sprint with Dyrnwyn in hand.

"Right behind you, bro," Hemi said, his much heavier footfalls first echoing mine step for step, and then falling back as I poured on the speed.

In my human form, I could run a hundred yards in under eleven seconds—not fast enough for a spot on the Olympic team, but still enough to beat most humans on foot. But in my stealth-shifted form, I was easily the equal of any normal 'thrope or baby vamp in speed, strength, and reflexes. Ten seconds in the 100 meters might be the benchmark for an Olympic-level sprinter, but for a supe? Try six seconds, which is about the time it takes for a cheetah to run the same distance.

So, when I hit the magical barrier, I was doing close to fifty miles per hour with no intention of slowing down. It was a rookie mistake. The Fear Doirich wasn't just any magic-user. He was among the world's preeminent practitioners of the craft, having studied and perfected the druidic and dark arts for millennia. And to say he had a nasty mean streak, well—that would be an understatement.

The instant my body made contact with the Dark Druid's enchantment, three things happened. First, the barrier lit me up with about 100,000 volts of electricity via a full-fledged lightning strike delivered straight to my chest. Second, the electrical discharge superheated the air around me, resulting in a flash burn over the entire front half of my body. And third, the barrier exerted a concussive counterforce that was many times greater than the impact my body made when I triggered the trap, crunching my bones like peanut brittle.

Thankfully, Hemi was about a dozen yards behind me at the time, otherwise I'd have had nothing to break my fall when I went flying backward at highway speeds. I bowled him over, earning a few more broken bones in the process as I came into contact with his wards, and we landed in a heap twenty yards or so from the barrier. The entire episode had left me semi-conscious, but I had the wherewithal to attempt rolling over so I could see how Jesse fared.

An agonizing shriek filled the tunnel, and at first I thought it might be Jess, screaming out in pain at what the Dark Druid was doing to her. Then I realized it was me, a reaction to having my shattered radius and ulna forced through the skin and flesh of my forearm. It shouldn't have been such a shock, but it hadn't occurred to me how badly I might be injured, at least not until I tried to make my body respond to simple commands.

Hemi gingerly attempted to extricate himself from under me, but every move he made caused my broken bones to grind together in multiple places. My reaction was more screaming and cursing. Between the agony of my Fomorian healing factor attempting to realign and put me back together, the burns to my chest, torso, and face, and Hemi jostling me around, I was not having a very good day.

"Sorry, bro!" Hemi exclaimed.

"Just... help... Jesse," I wheezed, realizing at that moment that I had a rib sticking out of my chest on the left side of my rib cage.

"But, Colin—"

"Go!" I said, rolling myself off him with a primal scream of rage and pain, accompanied by the sound of multiple broken and splintered bones grinding and rubbing together. I passed out for a moment, only to come back to my senses when my Fomorian blood decided it was time for my Hyde-side to come out.

An extended, unintelligible groan was the only sound I could get out of my mouth as dozens of shattered bones realigned all at once, knitting together as they simultaneously lengthened, thickened, and healed. I'd thought that shifting rapidly was a nearly unbearable agony when I'd started the process whole and well, but no—this was an entirely new level of suffering. Despite my Hyde-side being in the driver's seat, I nearly blacked out again.

Groggily, I started coming to my senses when I heard a thunderous hammering nearby.

Boom. Boom. BOOM!

If a hill giant had decided to bang out a rhythm on a giant hollowed out oak tree, it might have sounded like that. Chanting and growls accompanied the noise, in a language and voice I recognized.

It's Hemi—he's trying to break through the barrier.

Tuning it all out, I concentrated only on speeding up the healing process so I could be ready to help Jesse and deal with the Fear Doirich when his wards fell.

16

F inally, I was whole enough to move. Thankfully, pain
tolerance wasn't really a thing for Fomorians—they
thrived on it. Pushing myself up on one massive, overly-
muscular arm, I snapped the other arm out with a whipping
motion, forcing the still broken bones in my forearm to
realign all at once so they could mend completely.

Why's it so quiet all of a sudden?

I sat up and rolled up to one knee in a single, somewhat
smooth motion. My right leg hadn't completely healed yet,
and as I stood bones and connective tissues were still being
knit back in place. Despite that, I rose to my feet, turning to
see what had become of Hemi and Jess.

My Maori friend stood framed by the tunnel exit, back
turned to me, his war club dangling from one hand. I was
much larger than him in this form, yet I still couldn't see past
him as his bulk blocked my view of the cavern beyond.

"Hemi, what happened?" I demanded, stumbling toward
him with increasingly confident strides. "Where's Jesse?"

He looked back at me. "She's there, Colin, but—"

I shoved him out of the way, squeezing past so I could get to Jess. She was there, alright, right where the Dark Druid had left her after he was done with her. Her hair had turned completely grey, her skin had wrinkled and turned translucent, and her plum-red lips had gone ashen and gray.

In an instant I was next to her, lifting her limp body off the makeshift altar and cradling her in my arms. Her head lolled to the side, eyes dead and fixed and her mouth slack. She looked as though she'd aged eighty years, sucked dry of every last bit of life she'd possessed.

I looked over my shoulder at a very stunned and traumatized Hemi. His wide eyes welled up with tears, voice quivering as he spoke.

"Colin, mate—I couldn't break through in time."

"What happened? Tell me what you saw."

He staggered to the nearest wall, reaching out to shore himself up. "I saw you were healing, and figured I'd better break that barrier. Give you a clear shot once you came 'round, aye? I beat on it and beat on it, and felt it weakening. But the Dark Druid—he was well into that spell, you know?"

Hemi heaved a shuddering sigh as he choked up.

"I watched her, the whole time. He just—sucked the life right out of her, magic and all. It was awful. I'm so sorry, bro."

My head and shoulders drooped, eyes hot and wet with huge tears that plopped like raindrops all over Jesse's face and chest.

Hell of a thing, this. Never knew Fomorians could cry.

I slumped down and sat against the rock, crying and rocking her back and forth. Apparently, the Fomorian physiology was incompatible with grief, and soon my body began the transformation back to my human self. Hemi came and sat next to me on the rock, clapping a hand on my shoulder as he muttered apologies and words of comfort and support.

At some point Fallyn arrived, maybe minutes or hours after Jesse's passing. It was hard to say how long it took for her to find us, as the only light in the cave came from torches that were close to burning out by the time she showed up. Hearing her familiar footfalls echo down the tunnel, I wiped my eyes and looked up to greet her when she walked in.

"She's gone, Fallyn. I failed her, again."

A large, strong hand squeezed my shoulder. "Now there, mate—don't blame yourself. It was that evil bastard what did this, not you."

"What happened?" Fallyn said. "I went to hunt, and when I got back all I found was Hemi's note."

As I brought her up to speed, Fallyn's eyes grew hard, her mouth went taut, and her hands balled up at her sides. As I finished the story, she slammed a fist against the wall of the cave, sending bits of stone flying in all directions. Then, she exhaled slowly before walking over to gently brush a stray lock of hair from Jesse's face.

Fallyn craned her neck, arching her back as she pointed her face to the ceiling to let out a long, high, keening howl that seemed to go on forever. It struck a chord deep within me when she did it, nascent Pack bonds exerting whatever meager effect they could on a misfit Pack member like me. Her howl was like a note plucked on a guitar string inside my chest, vibrating in tune to my own pain, letting me know I was not alone.

Then, something curious happened. At a distance far removed from where I mourned my recent loss, a stronger, deeper voice joined in, harmonizing with Fallyn's howl. It wasn't anything I could hear normally, but instead it resonated inside me in a tone that was clear as a bell to my inner beast. Soon, dozens of other voices joined in, crying a soulful, longing chorus that sang of loss and love, of family and pain, of mates lost and children gone, and of bonds that even death could not break or erase.

Hemi couldn't hear it, but based on the astonished look on his face, I knew that he felt the mourning song of the Pack wash over him as well. The bond between us was deep enough for him to sense the Pack's presence, not because of a bond of blood, but one of brotherly love. I was glad to have him by my side at such a dark and terrible time.

Finally, the beast within me answered the call of the Pack in the only way it could. Fomorians were never creatures of family, hearth, or home. Neither were they prone to sentiment, mercy, or frailty. Cú Chulainn's curse, a remnant of interbreeding between Tuath Dé, Fomori, and humans, made that side of me incapable of experiencing such emotions. So, the beast inside me could not cry with what my human side felt—the deep, remorseful pain of love and loss and death.

No, that part of me—my other, darker half—could only cry out for one thing.

Blood.

I answered the Pack with a battle cry, a roar of primal rage that echoed off the cave walls, down the tunnels, and out into the basin below. It reverberated through the Pack bonds, bridging the distance between us in a heartbeat. And their answer was clear. Despite our differences, the Pack would back my play.

Because I was going to war with the Dark Druid.

We buried Jesse inside the Grove, in a small meadow that appeared of its own accord when I showed up with Jesse's corpse. Hemi and Fallyn were there, but that was the extent of the funeral party, as I couldn't safely return to the junkyard or even Éire Imports to fetch Maureen and Finnegas.

At the moment, the last thing I wanted was for Mendoza and his goons to show up in the park. Still, I thought they might be of use to me yet, so I dug the tracker out of Jesse's arm before we buried her. The damned thing had gone deep, so it was messy and felt like a desecration, and the experience was way too reminiscent of when my Hyde-side had killed her. When I finished, I tucked the tracker in my Bag for safe-keeping and tried not to think about what I'd just done.

Each of us said a few words, then we laid her to rest. The Grove gently swallowed her up at my command, but first it sent me a series of images in response. A seed planted in the ground, a sprout poking up through moist earth, and flowers spreading out over rich, dark soil in all directions.

Sure, some flowers would be nice. I think she'd like that.

The Grove sent me an image of a rock, but I didn't know what to make of that. Maybe it wanted to leave a grave marker or something. It seemed an unnecessary gesture, so I decided to leave it to its own devices.

Fallyn wrapped her arm in mine, leaning close as we silently stood over the grave.

"You think Samson will let Finn and Maureen know?" I asked.

"Probably, although with the whole Pack heading here, he might want to keep things on the down-low until this Dark Druid issue is resolved." She squeezed my arm a little tighter. "You do have a plan for that, right? The Pack is behind you, one-hundred percent—we owe you that much after what you did during the whole Sonny thing. But these people have families, Colin. I don't want to lead them into a death trap."

"I have a plan, and when it comes to it I'll be facing him down alone," I replied, grim determination in my voice. "He killed my dad, he nearly killed Bells, and now Jesse..." My voice cracked, and I struggled to keep my emotions in check.

Deep breath, Colin.

"Fallyn, thousands of people died in Austin because of him. And why? Because of a vendetta between his family and ours that goes back thousands of years. It has to stop."

Hemi cleared his throat. "If you don't mind me asking, what are the particulars of this feud? You never have told me the full story."

"I never told you two all this?"

Both shook their heads.

"Okay, then—back when Finnegas was still young, the Fear Doirich was infatuated by Sadhbh, daughter of Bodb Derg. When she refused his advances, he turned her into a doe. Fionn MacCumhaill found her, somehow they broke the spell, and the two fell in love. The Fear Doirich never forgave either of them, and he later turned her back into a deer when Fionn wasn't around. MacCumhaill's son Oisín was found wandering in the forest years later, but Fionn never reunited with his wife."

"That's harsh," Hemi remarked.

"And not the end of it," I said. "Later on, Fionn—with Finnegas' guidance—put an end to the horrific reign of the Avartagh, the Dark Druid's son. The Avartagh was a vampiric dwarf, and a powerful magician to boot, trained by his dad. Supposedly he died young, so the Fear Doirich learned necromancy to raise his son from the dead, which is how he became an undead menace in the first place.

Anyway, Fionn was more than happy to smite his ass, and that deepened the enmity between him and the Dark Druid."

"And you're related to Fionn, right?" Fallyn asked.

"Yup, direct lineage, in fact. Somewhere along the way, Cú Chulainn's line got mixed in, but I've never been clear on how that happened. Anyway, after Fionn died, the Dark Druid couldn't take revenge on him anymore, so he decided to take his beef up with Fionn's offspring."

"Your fam," Hemi remarked.

"Yes," I said, scratching my head. "You sure I never told you guys this story?"

"Nope," they said in unison.

"Okay, sorry. Well, since Fionn died, the Dark Druid has been using necromancy to steal the bodies of Fionn's descendants."

The Maori warrior snapped his fingers. "The body snatching thing."

"Right," I replied. "He tried it on my dad, but pops wouldn't let him. I think he killed himself before the Dark Druid could complete the ritual. Anyway, he tried the same thing with me, but I had Balor's Eye in my skull at the time and it made me more or less immune to necromantic magic. So, Finnegas and I put the whammy on him, the Dark Druid got trapped in a decaying corpse of a body, and he's been pissed at me ever since."

"Are you still immune to necromancy?" Fallyn asked. "That's a trick that could come in handy, considering who you're going up against."

I shrugged. "Finnegas seems to think so, and hopefully it hasn't worn off yet. Guess I'll find out if I still have that superpower when I face him."

Fallyn pulled me around to face her. "Colin, if he's not locked in that body anymore—he'll be after yours, right?"

"Affirmative," I nodded.

"Then isn't it kind of a suicide mission for you to face him?"

"Only if the Eye's effects have worn off."

Hemi grunted. "This guy is ancient, right? And he probably thinks like a god, which means he plays the long game."

"So?" I asked.

Hemi arched an eyebrow. "What if the magic he stole from Jesse lets him trump your immunity to necromancy?"

I rubbed a hand across my face before I responded. "Well, then I guess I might be fucked. That being said, I have a contingency plan—a sort of 'break glass in case of emergency' thing."

Fallyn's lips curled into a half-frown. "Ri-i-ight. Because your plans *always* work out the way you intend."

Back at camp, I sat under the Oak on top of the plateau, meditating while I sorted things out in my head.

Everything in my life always seemed to be spiraling out of my control. No matter how much I tried to contain it, constant chaos and trouble had become my new normal. It started with the attack on my hometown by the Avartagh, when I'd asked Jesse to help me take him out. After that, she and I had lived a few short years of relative happiness, training under Finnegas and killing the occasional supernastical creature.

Then, my ríastrad had surfaced and Jesse died—the first time around—at my hands. Following that tragedy, I'd dropped out of the hunter life until Maeve had dragged me back in, and boy did she ever. Everything after that had been one big shit storm—the battle at the graveyard, Sonny trying to take over the Pack, Underhill, Gunnarson, Hideie tricking me out of the Eye, and then the disaster in Austin—with no breaks and no end in sight.

And now this. Oh, Jesse, I wish I'd never asked you to come with me that day.

As for the shit storm, I had no idea how to escape it. According to Finnegas, the gods of the Celtic pantheon had taken notice of me, and not in a good way. I'd also made enemies of gods from other realms and regions by killing their offspring and avatars. Obviously, that hadn't improved my standing with the Tuatha Dé Danann at all, as it made me appear more of a threat than a nuisance.

Sure, I had a few Celtic gods on my side. The Dagda for one, Lugh on a good day, and maybe Niamh—also known as Maeve, Austin's faery queen. Although I *had* pissed her off but good when I'd screwed up all the gateways to Underhill, so that was no sure bet. And the problem with having the Tuath Dé for allies was they were so damned fickle. One minute they'd be doing you favors; the next, they'd be cheering your impending doom.

But there was one thing I thought I could get right, and that was taking care of the Dark Druid for good. It wouldn't be easy, that was for sure. This was the guy the Tuatha Dé Danann had once tapped as their very own druid, after all. Sheesh, if ever there was proof that the Tuath Dé were a fucked-up bunch of immortals, it was that. But it also spoke to just how damned dangerous the guy could be.

He'd been weakened at our last meeting, stuck in that decaying body. Plus, he'd been relying on the Eye to do his heavy lifting. No way he'd let me get the drop on him this time, no sir. If Hemi's hunch was right, he'd be coming at me with both barrels blazing from the get-go, aiming to take me out so he could jump from his old busted body into mine.

And then he'd have my powers, too—Fomorian abilities. Combine that with the Fear Doirich's druid magic and necromancy, and he'd be a force that would likely make some of the lesser gods shit their pants. He had to be stopped.

After that? I was going to take a break, far away from the junkyard where I couldn't be found. Maybe I'd focus on my magical studies under Finnegas, or get some sword lessons from Hideie, or learn to play slide guitar. Or, I could always finish my training with Click and head back to the Hellpocalypse for a while. At least there, things were simpler—if not crazy as fuck.

Hell, I had no idea what I planned to do after this was done. All I did know was that I was going to end the Fear Doirich at any cost, and then I'd take a nice, long vacation. If I was still alive, that was.

Either way, I had to locate the bastard first. And to do that, I needed some very specific help. If there was one person who knew everything that went on in this park, it was La Onza. I'd learned that much from my meeting with her, although the other revelations she'd shared had been a dollar short and a day late.

For holding out on me until it was too late, I figured she owed me—and I intended to collect. I opened my mental link to the Druid Oak.

Take me to La Onza's hideout.

We arrived at the hidden slot canyon instantly, the Oak somehow fitting its massive bulk between the canyon's walls. But when I exited the Grove and climbed up to the cave entrance, no one was there. Heck, there wasn't even a trace of the fire from the night before.

She keeps a tidy house, that's for sure. I looked around, just to be certain she wasn't hiding in cat form on a ledge above me. *Alright, let's draw her out.*

"La Onza! I know you're keeping an eye on this place. Show yourself, damn it!"

Nothing.

"Fine," I yelled. "Since you won't come talk to me, I'm going to let Camazotz loose. Then you'll be good and fucked," I said, turning in a slow circle. "I'd like to see you deal with Ernesto then—"

As I completed a full circle, the diminutive bruja stood at the mouth of her cave, right where she hadn't been standing a moment before.

"Um, hey."

She glared at me. "So much power, in one so young and foolish. Speak, then."

"Okay, I'll get right to it. I'm looking for a showdown with the Dark Druid, and you know where to find him."

"I suppose you want my help fighting him, too," she said, crossing her arms over her chest.

"Think about this for a minute. If I lose, the Dark Druid is going to help Ernesto take you out, either by direct intervention or magical assistance. Camazotz can easily handle the Bylillys, but once the Fear Doirich has possession of my body, he'll chew through the bat god like a goat in a field of clover. Then, he'll give Ernesto possession of your gateway to the underworld, and set him up to terrorize this entire region. You want that on your conscience?"

She frowned and shrugged. "I'll be dead and gone if that happens, so what does it matter?"

"I think you care a lot more for the fate of the people you protect than you let on. And I think you know there are things worse than death—things the Dark Druid would do to you simply for opposing him."

La Onza stood statue-still as she glowered at me for several uncomfortable seconds. Finally, she spoke. "If I help you, you must promise to leave Camazotz locked in his cage to protect my cave."

"I promise that old *Camazotzes* will remain to protect your cave after we're done dealing with the Dark Druid," I replied, stone-faced.

La Onza's brow furrowed, then she turned and walked off into her lair. "Larry will be at your camp when you return, and he will help you find the place where the Dark One resides. I will join you at the battle. Now, go—I must prepare."

17

"You guys ever been to the Mariscal Mine?" Larry asked as we snuck up the backside of a ridge that overlooked the mine from the south.

It was late in the afternoon, and the sun would be setting soon. The sky was overcast, so we'd have darkness on our side at least. Or course, it wasn't the ideal time to take on a necromancer, a specter, and a couple of skinwalkers, but I had my reasons for hitting them at night.

"No, Larry," I groused, signaling everyone to stop. "It's not like we've been doing a lot of sight-seeing since we got here."

Undaunted, the chupacabra continued to run his mouth. "Oh man, you guys have really missed out. It's one of the most popular tourist attractions in the park. They used to mine cinnabar here, and turn it into mercury. You can still see the smelting pits, some of the buildings, the whole bit. Lots of miners died here—I guess mercury poisoning is a sorry way to go."

"Meaning, there'll be tons of unmarked graves and a lot of angry ghosts nearby," Fallyn remarked.

"Plus, the cinnabar acts as a sort of magical heat sink," I said. "That's likely why the Dark Druid chose this as a hide-out, because no one would ever notice him here."

"That's true," Larry said as he licked his anus. "La Onza woulda never guessed he was here, unless I'd overhead Stanley mention it."

"Oi, do that somewhere else, wouldja?" Hemi protested, hiding his line of sight with one hand.

Larry stopped and looked around at everyone, hunched over with one leg splayed in the air. "Oh, like you guys wouldn't do this if you could."

"Sshh! Enough," I said. "We're damned close, and I'd like to scope the place out without being discovered. Fallyn, let's go take a peek. Larry, you stay here with Hemi."

"Why do I have to babysit the cur?" he asked.

"Cur? I'm not even a dog, you poor man's excuse for Dwayne Johnson," Larry replied between licks. "You're like a reject from a Disney movie, a walking cliché if I ever saw one. Can't even tell if you're Hawaiian, Maori, or 'other' the way you talk and dress. I—"

Hemi had the chupacabra by the throat, squeezing just hard enough to cut off his air. "One more word, and we're gonna see if cursed mutts can die," he growled.

"Hemi, please put him down. Larry, shut up or I'll be the one cursing you." I turned to Fallyn, who, despite the general mood, was trying hard not to laugh. "Let's go do some recon before we get caught."

Fallyn pinched my cheek, giving it a little shake as if I were a child. "Oh, you're so cute when you get all bossy and stuff."

"No respect," I mumbled as we crawled the rest of the way to the peak of the ridge. Right before we reached the top, I cast a "look away" cantrip on us, then we popped our heads over to see what we were up against.

"That's not good," Fallyn said, so softly that only I could hear her.

"Nope, it's not," I whispered back.

Below, the ruins of the mine swarmed with animated skeletons and undead tourists. Some were obviously the shambling kind, while others moved with a bit more pep in their step. I counted at least three-dozen zombies and skeletons, that many more ghouls, and a few dozen revenants.

"There has to be at least a hundred of them," Fallyn whispered.

"They aren't the only things we have to worry about. Look," I said, pointing at the mine entrances. There, dark ethereal shapes flitted about in the shadows. "What do you want to bet La Llorona is hiding down there, too?"

We slowly crawled backward until we were well hidden on our side of the ridge.

Fallyn pointed with her thumb behind us. "Tactically, we have the high ground, but numbers are on their side. Even if we place snipers on all the high points and overlooks, we could still be overrun as soon as the fighting starts. So, what's our play?"

"Is the Pack ready to go?"

She nodded. "Waiting about a half-mile from here with Samson, and itching for a fight. I guess you're not as much of an outcast as you think," she said with a wink. "You want me to call them in?"

"Uh-uh, not yet. I prefer to have the Pack acting as rear guard when we go in the mine to take out the skinwalkers and La Llorona. Plus, I don't want to risk a lot of losses. I have a better plan for dealing with the Fear Doirich's little army."

I reached into my Craneskin Bag, pulling out the flechette I'd recovered from Jesse's shoulder. It was still encased inside my stasis spell, and thus it hadn't been broadcasting its position. With a few arcane gestures, I removed the stasis spell, then examined it in the magical spectrum to ensure the damned thing was still sending out a strong signal.

Loud and clear.

I grabbed a baseball-sized rock, and with a little druidic coaxing, the flechette was soon encased inside it.

"How good's your arm?" I asked Fallyn, knowing that her strength far exceeded mine at the moment.

"I spent three years pitching on a select team when I was in high school. Our high school coach kept me benched all the time, so Dad enrolled me in a private league." She shrugged. "Where do you want it?"

I pointed to the northeast, toward the main road leading to the mine. "About a half-mile that way."

Fallyn stood, still hidden on our side of the ridge, bouncing the rock in her hand to gauge the weight and balance. Then, she wound up and delivered a pitch that any major league scout would have drooled over. The rock and its payload went soaring off into the distance, well past the undead sentries and hopefully right where I wanted it.

The she-wolf cocked a hand to her ear, and stood absolutely still for the span of several seconds before giving a short nod. "I might have been off by a hundred yards or so."

"Meh, horseshoes and hand grenades. As long as nothing and no one at the mine notices, we'll be fine."

"So, what do we do now?"

I smiled. "Now, we wait."

About three hours later, we heard the faint "whoomp-whoomp-whoomp" of helicopters approaching from the northeast. We were sitting close to the top of the ridge, so we had a good view of the skies toward Austin.

Time to gear up.

I pulled a short-barreled pump shotgun from my Bag along with a bandolier of ammo—some of my leftovers from the Hellpocalypse that I'd been loath to part with. Next, I strapped my tactical belt and pistols around my waist, then checked to make sure I had several mags loaded with ammo in my mag pouches. Finally, I slung Dyrnwyn over my shoulder, and finished by checking my pockets to make sure I had various other surprises handy. Then, I searched the skies to the east for Mendoza's black helicopters.

No lights. Fuckers are flying dark. I guess Cerberus doesn't answer to the FAA, either.

"They got here fast," Fallyn remarked.

I squinted as I did some calculations in my head. "Figure we're about four hundred-some miles from Austin as the crow flies, and a military bird cruises at a hundred-eighty mph—yeah, Mendoza must still be super-pissed to have scrambled his troops like that." I inclined my head at the top of the ridge. "Let's go see how this all plays out, shall we?"

Although they were flying on blackout—no running lights whatsoever—the noise of the engines and rotors echoed off the canyon walls like thunder. Soon, four UH-60 Black Hawks landed just east of the mine area, and roughly forty agents in tactical gear carrying black rifles and other more exotic weapons poured out of them. The noise and movement was more or less a dinner call for the undead below, who went absolutely apeshit crawling all over each other as they ran, trudged, shuffled, stumbled, and crawled toward the noise.

A hundred undead against forty heavily-armed agents. This ought to be good.

Hemi grunted. "We, uh, gonna help 'em?"

"Nope. Serves those fuckers right for busting into my junkyard like they owned the place." I looked at Larry. "Any sign of La Onza yet?"

His tongue lolled out of his mouth at an odd angle, hanging like a pinkish-grey tapeworm between two of his messed-up teeth. "Oh, she's around, believe me. Once the fighting starts, she'll do her part."

Fallyn started to strip, immediately garnering all Larry's attention. This earned him an ear thump from Hemi. "Manners, mutt!"

Larry growled before looking the other way. I noted that one of his bug-eyes looked downhill in the direction he was facing, while the other somehow turned of its own volition to watch the werewolf. I grabbed a rock and beaned him in the snout.

"Ow!" he exclaimed. "Alright, I know when I'm not wanted. Don't die before you kill Ernesto, druid." Then, he faded out of sight.

"Good riddance," Hemi said under his breath.

"I heard that!" Larry said from somewhere down the hill.

By the time I turned my attention back to my companions, Fallyn had already shifted into her half-human form. She glanced over her shoulder and caught me looking. The she-wolf's hips swayed seductively as she swished her tail side to side with a wink. I didn't know whether to be aroused or repulsed, but I was leaning toward arousal. And honestly, I didn't know how I felt about that either.

"Is the Pack in position?" I asked, shifting the attention to me in hopes of avoiding any questions from Hemi later on werewolf mating habits.

Fallyn answered in a slightly deeper, rougher version of her normal voice. "They are."

"And they know that when we go in, their job is just to watch our backs, right?"

"I'm the Pack Alpha's daughter, Colin," she growled. "I know how to convey orders."

"Right—sorry, I'm just a little nervous." I looked at them both each in turn. "Remember, your job is to take care of Ernesto and Stanley so I can go after the Dark Druid. What-ever happens, do not follow me, do not try to intervene, and get the hell out of there once our battle starts."

"Still can't see why we can't jump in and help," Hemi pouted.

"Because, it's going to be a big, messy clusterfuck," I answered. "Once we engage each other, spells are going to be flying everywhere, and the Fear Doirich doesn't deal in kiddie magic. He's going to be out for blood, and if he can use one of you as leverage, he will. It'll make things a lot easier on me if I know you two are out of the way when I face him."

Both my heart and mind were racing in anticipation of the coming battle, so with nothing better to do, I began to stealth-shift, wanting to conserve my full Fomorian form for the Dark Druid. The noise from the helicopter rotors died down while I was in mid-shift, only to be replaced by small arms fire. First it was just a few scattered shots, then we heard sustained automatic weapons fire, along with a lot of shout-ing, growls, and the moans of the undead. As I finished my transformation, I couldn't help but laugh at what happening to Mendoza and his goons.

"I do believe that's our cue," I said.

"You're enjoying this way too much," Fallyn remarked.

"Let a bloke have his fun," the Maori protested. "It's not every day you get to face your archenemy." He patted me on the shoulder with one of his huge, meaty hands. "Kick his arse, Colin."

"Oh, I fully intend to," I replied.

And if that fails, I plan to take the fucker out with me.

"Fallyn, you're our link to the Pack. Once we enter the mine, call them in and have them guard our rear flank. Also let them know that they are not to engage Mendoza's people. If the feds make it through the undead and start to advance on the mine, the Pack should retreat to a safe distance and conceal their presence."

"Samson's not going to like leaving us in a pincer between the Dark Druid and the feds," Fallyn said. "Dad might not show it, but he is *very* interested in keeping you alive."

"Tell him I plan to give him a big hug next time I see him, just for showing up. That'll make him abandon my sorry ass in a hurry." I gave them both a grim smile. "Alright, let's go storm the motherfucking castle."

With the undead out of the way, we leapt off the ridge to the plateau below. Fallyn and I landed lightly behind a crumbling limestone building, the only sound being the *caliche* crunching under our feet. As for Hemi, he made a bit more noise than I would have liked as his three-hundred-fifty-pound frame landed in the gravel. A couple of the ghosts flitting back and forth around the main entrance of the mine to the south must have heard, because a couple started floating our way.

I frowned at Hemi and mouthed, *Dude, really?*

He yawned and cracked his neck in response. "Don't worry, mate. I got this."

Before Fallyn or I could react, Hemi strolled out from behind the ruins, calmly walking toward the tunnel entrance —and at least a dozen angry spirits.

"Well, shit. I hope he knows what he's doing," I whispered to Fallyn. She grinned wolfishly—the only way possible in her half-human form—and settled in to watch the show.

The ghosts shrieked in an awful chorus of rage and delight upon seeing the big Maori walking their way, and the lot of them made a beeline straight at him. Undeterred, Hemi began his haka. His tattoos began glowing with pale blue magic as he started chanting, stomping, slapping, waving, and making the scariest damned faces at the oncoming ghosts.

One would think that an angry spirit who only existed to seek revenge on the living would be unimpressed by such a display, no matter how large or intimidating the person performing it. And, if you thought that, you'd be wrong. Instead of increasing their pace, the ghosts began to slow, gradually coming to a full and complete stop in midair. Within seconds, their contorted, tortured faces were frozen in mid-scream, their ghastly voices trailing away to silence. This happened to each ghost in turn, until every last one of them was under Hemi's spell.

Then, Hemi began to pick up the pace. He chanted louder, leapt higher, stomped deeper, and made scarier faces —if that was possible. And while the tattoos on his body continued to glow that same sky blue, the black ink in his *moko* began to writhe and twist into entirely new shapes. Simultaneously, his unmarked skin in the spaces between the ink began to glow with a white, eerie luminescence, the light ebbing and flowing in time with his voice.

And just like that, the spirits started to shrivel up and fade away, one by one, each releasing one last haunting cry that trailed off into nothingness as they were banished. As the last ghost disappeared from sight, Hemi stood up and gave one final stomp and victorious battle cry. I was just about to congratulate him when a lithe, translucent female figure in a lacy black dress rose up from the ground behind him.

I knew what would come next—La Llorona would scream, using her magic to freeze him in place, and then she'd go for the kill. I opened my mouth to shout a warning, just as that deadly keening wail began to emanate from the specter's featureless face. Knowing Hemi wouldn't hear the warning in time, I covered my ears and attempted to make a run for it, even though my legs were already turning to jelly.

Just then, Hemi spun on a dime and grabbed La Llorona by the neck in one of those huge hands of his, cutting her voice off with a single, powerful squeeze. My jaw hit my chest and Fallyn released a short, quizzical whine beside me. I had no idea how my friend was hanging onto a ghost, but he was, and obviously it was as much a surprise to the specter as it was to everyone else.

Behind Hemi, the ghosts of children began appearing, one by one—La Llorona's victims, I was certain of it. There were hundreds of them, sad little forms that filled the valley with their numbers. Once all had arrived, they slowly advanced on the murderous ghost. In response, La Llorona began kicking and scratching, fighting and clawing for all she was worth to get loose, but the Maori warrior held her fast.

"Now, *kurī uwha*, you'll know the terror these children felt," Hemi said with an almost casual conviction. Then, he turned his head and spoke to no one in particular. "Mum, I'm ready."

A magic portal opened beside my friend, shrouded in dark mists but translucent enough for me to spot a familiar face on the other side. Between the strong, slender build, high cheekbones, full lips, nearly ashen skin, deep brown eyes set in a permanent glare, and that full mane of hair, well —there was no mistaking her. After my adventure in Hemi's homeland, I'd have recognized his mother anywhere.

But this time she wasn't "Henny," the stern, no-nonsense mother I'd met on Stewart Island. Now she was Hine-nui-te-pō, the Maori goddess of night and death, shrouded in shadow and darkness and beauty. The weight and force of her power and station was evident in her very stance and bearing. Unfortunately for La Llorona, she'd answered her son's call across space and time all the way from *Te Reinga*, the underworld where she reigned supreme. And by the look on Hine-nui-te-pō's face, it was clear she'd come to mete out justice on the wicked specter as few other gods or goddesses were able.

A long, graceful hand reached out of the portal, grasping La Llorona by her straight black hair with a vise-like grip. On cue, Hemi released the specter, eager as he was to hand his quarry over to his mother's unforgiving supervision. Without a word, Hemi's mom yanked that evil bitch back through the portal, in a manner that was by no means gentle or kind.

That moment would be etched in my memory for all eternity. As La Llorona was pulled into the portal, her freaky blank face faded away, revealing the features of a twenty-something Spanish girl underneath. This young woman was exotically beautiful, with light brown eyes, dusky skin, a slightly hawkish nose, and full lips that betrayed her Moorish heritage. She was absolutely stunning, but what I found most striking of all was her expression.

Never had I seen anyone look more terrified than La Llorona in that moment. For an instant, we locked eyes. I saw not defiance there, or rage, or the pain of grief and loss. Instead, what I witnessed was the knowing certainty that she was about to pay for the centuries of grief and sorrow she'd caused, and the hundreds of lives she'd snuffed out, far, far too soon.

I felt a small twinge of sympathy for her, then remembered what she'd done to her own children. Once I'd reminded myself of that initial, unforgivable act—the reason why she'd been cursed in the first place—any compassion I might have felt for her vanished.

Have fun in hell, bitch.

As soon as La Llorona had been sucked into *Te Reinga*, the ghosts of her victims began to leave. One by one, they walked toward a pinpoint of bright light in the distance before fading out of sight.

Realizing the portal was still open, my eyes snapped back to the goddess. Hine-nui-te-pō winked at me, an incongruous act that shocked me back to my senses. Then, the portal snapped shut. Hemi stood there, shoulders back and head held high, looking every bit the Maori warrior he was.

And that's why you don't fuck with the son of the goddess of death and night.

18

"Um, Hemi—think you could get your mom to help us with the Dark Druid?" Fallyn asked with a gleam in her eye.

Hemi shook his head. "Naw, sorry. Mum tends to avoid getting mixed in the other pantheons' biz. Professional courtesy. This one was a personal favor, and a one-off at that."

"Too bad," Fallyn said. "I like her style."

With the ghosts and the issue of further divine intervention settled, we checked each of the mineshaft entrances for signs of foot traffic, inspecting them closely to see if the iron grates covering them had been disturbed. All were intact except for the main shaft, the only place where Fallyn detected the recent passage of skinwalkers. It would have been an easy guess which way to go regardless, as the heavy iron grate had been ripped off and carelessly tossed to the side, leaving the shaft exposed and uncovered.

Apparently, the Dark Druid wants me to find him. Peachy.

According to an old survey map I'd found online, this entrance was a vertical shaft some three hundred feet deep with horizontal tunnels branching off it at intervals. In the distant past when the mine was active, a lift had taken miners down and brought ore back up. But now, no such equipment existed on site, which meant we'd be descending the hard way. It also meant it would be that much more difficult to retreat, should it come to that.

I uncoiled a length of climbing rope that I brought from the campsite, tying it off on some old discarded heavy equipment nearby. Hemi pulled the grate away from the mine shaft, and I tossed the rope down the hole. It was darker than pitch twenty feet down the shaft, so I cast a cantrip to enhance my vision, sharpening my senses even more than they already were in my stealth-shifted state.

"I go in first, then Fallyn, and finally Hemi," I said. "We'll take the first side shaft we come across. Most of the tunnels are above one-hundred-fifty feet, so that's where we'll likely find them. Remember, once we deal with Ernesto and Stanley, I want you two to beat feet back to the surface. Leave the Fear Doirich to me."

"Naw, mate, no can do," Hemi protested.

"Same," Fallyn growled.

"We've been over this before," I sighed. "Neither of you are equipped to handle the Dark Druid. And, it's going to be much easier for me to fight him if you two aren't in the way."

"Hey, that stings," Hemi replied.

"He's right. You would just be in the way," a female voice said from nearby.

The others spun to face the new arrival, ready for action, but I already knew who it was. "Hemi, Fallyn—meet La Onza."

The diminutive witch inclined her head in greeting. "Leave the Dark One to the druid, and help me take care of the skinwalkers. Once that task is complete, I'll lend the young druid whatever assistance I am able. I swear to it."

"Yeah, but—" Fallyn began.

"But nothing," I said, cutting her off in the kindest tone possible. "Look, you two—this guy's been practicing magic for two thousand years, almost as long as Finnegas, and he's simply out of your league. No offense, but it only makes sense to leave the magic battles to the people who actually know magic."

Hemi crossed his arms over his chest. "And just how good is your magic? I remember you being soundly trounced by this fella back at the graveyard."

Everyone looked at me, including La Onza.

"I'm a different druid now, Hemi. My connection to the Druid Oak gives me magic that I didn't possess before. It's a power the likes of which I've never known, and it gives me an edge I lacked the first few times I faced him. Heck, you remember how scary dryad-Jesse was when she was connected to the Druid Oak, and she didn't even have full control of its powers. I do."

"Still sounds risky," Fallyn said. "I'd feel better knowing we were there to back you up. Or, if we sent Dad down there with you instead."

La Onza snorted. "For all your skills and talents, the Dark One would snuff you out like a candle, *Loba*. Your father as well—oh yes, I sensed his presence the moment he set foot on these lands. He's a wily and powerful werewolf, but even he lacks the necessary skills to deal with an ancient magic-wielder such as the Dark Druid."

"And Hemi?" Fallyn asked.

La Onza's voice was taut—it was clear she wasn't accustomed to being questioned. "The demigod might last longer, and surely his death would be avenged. Yet his presence would make little difference in the outcome of this encounter."

Fallyn looked at me, her yellow wolf eyes flashing in the dark. "Can you do it, Colin? Can you beat him?"

I honestly wasn't sure, and I didn't want to lie to Fallyn and Hemi. But I also needed them well out of the way if I was going to face the Dark Druid.

"I can stop him," I said with certainty, knowing that much at least was true.

"Colin is very powerful," La Onza said, coming to my rescue. "But, I also sense that his power is raw and his control is—unrefined. The Dark One is a highly skilled magician and a dangerous necromancer, but he does not have access to the same reserves of magical energy as the young druid. It will be a battle of brute force versus finesse, but your friend does have a strong chance of winning the encounter."

So, I get a vote of confidence from the centuries-old witch. Good to know.

I waved my hands back and forth. "Enough debate. We stick to the plan, and that's the end of it. You guys help La Onza take out the skinwalkers, then you retreat, and La Onza sticks around as my back-up. Deal?"

I got grudging nods from my friends in reply, but it'd have to do.

"Well, then, let's go kill some skinwalkers," I said.

———

We descended the mineshaft one at a time, except for La Onza, who said she'd find her own way in. It was quite a ways down before we came to the first side tunnel. I pushed off the side of the shaft and swung over, landing inside the pitch-dark tunnel in a crouch as I let go of the rope. The air inside the tunnel smelled stale, with undertones of minerals and bat guano—and also death magic. Fallyn and Hemi were still making their way down, so I reached out with my druid senses to scan the mine ahead.

It always amazed me how much life was present in the world all around us, a bustling ecosystem hidden from human eyes in the walls of our homes, the trees above, and the earth beneath our feet. Mammals, birds, and insects had their own thing going on, blissfully ignoring the lives of humans for the most part while they went about their own. For us druids, such creatures were our eyes and ears, a communication network that kept us informed no matter where we went in nature or civilization.

And this mine complex was no exception. Cave spiders and other small insects were everywhere, dotting the three-hundred-sixty-degree picture in my mind like tiny points of light. Along with those creatures were those that preyed on them—Mexican long-nosed bats who lived in these mines during the day, only to exit them at night to feed. Still, a few of them remained, and those were the animals in which I was most interested.

Some of those left behind were sickly and old, but I found one that was healthy but simply lagging behind the rest. I reached out to the little flying mammal, teasing her to drop from her hiding place and spread her wings. From there, it was merely a matter of encouraging her to flit here and there, all the while tapping into her sonar to get a complete three-dimensional image of the upper mine tunnels.

While she flew around, a couple of times I sensed a presence that she couldn't detect with her acute and finely-tuned senses. I had no idea what that meant, as it could have been anything from more ghosts to inter-dimensional beings left to guard the various tunnel junctions. I made note of it and steered my little helper around the mines, taking every turn and exploring every side shaft I came across.

Finally, we came to a large stope, a man-made cavern some sixty feet long and perhaps twenty-five feet wide. I noticed a side tunnel leading off the far end of the chamber, and encouraged my little tour guide to head that direction. She started flying that way, but upon approaching the tunnel, she panicked. Despite the great deal of mental suggestion I exerted on her, the creature refused to explore those tunnels.

However, she did get close enough to give me a sonar image of what lay just past the tunnel entrance. There was another long, straight tunnel that branched off at ninety degrees about twenty feet past the stope exit, and a vertical shaft further on that likely dropped down to the next level below us.

The Dark Druid is down one of those corridors—I'm sure of it.

I made note of the location, then released the now frightened bat to head topside for her nightly hunt.

Thank you, little friend, I said, sending her reassurance that all was well. Soothing her frazzled nerves was the least I could do for the help she'd just provided.

"Taking a nap?" a gruff voice asked from nearby.

Chuckling softly, I opened my eyes. Fallyn stood a few feet away, still in her half-human form and scanning the dark for threats. In spite of her casual banter, it was clear she was on edge. I'd sensed her presence, of course, connected as I was to the wildlife around us. Hemi swung into the tunnel behind her, tattoos already glowing and lighting up the space around him.

I stood and brushed my knees off. "Just getting the lay of the land. C'mon, I think I know where the Bylillys might be hiding."

We crept down the tunnel for about fifty feet until it opened into the first stope the bat and I had discovered. There, we headed left down a slight decline, descending deeper into the tunnels toward the area where I'd first felt that hidden presence.

"Be ready," I whispered. "We're not alone."

Hemi began mumbling, and soon his tats cast a soft pool of blue light around us, signaling our presence to anything that might be lying in wait ahead. I honestly didn't expect to get the jump on Ernesto or even Stanley, so from a tactical perspective it didn't matter that Hemi had lit up like a night-light. It wasn't long before the skinwalkers proved me right.

Ernesto's voice echoed off the walls of the stope. "Come to get a taste of my magic, druid? The Dark One said he'd let us toy with you, before he robs your body and imprisons your soul.

"How generous of him," I said, sweeping the cavern with the barrel of my shotgun, "to set up a play date for us like that."

"You'll not be laughing when we're done with you, McCool. Especially after I send your large friend back to the underworld."

"And I have my way with the female wolf," Stanley said from somewhere nearby.

Fallyn answered with a snarl. Hemi merely chuckled.

"Don't reckon she agrees, ya doongi," Hemi remarked. "And I welcome the chance to give you both a hiding. Why not show yourselves, aye?"

"Oh, but that would ruin all our fun," Ernesto said.

Without warning, a hairy gray-black hand shot out of the darkness, raking Hemi across the face with a wicked set of claws before any of us could react.

And like that, we were assaulted from every side by the two *brujos*. The skinwalkers popped in and out of sight at will, slinking past with a swipe of their claws or a slash of their teeth, only to fade like black mists before we could respond in kind. We'd turn to face them in one direction, only to be attacked from our flanks. Soon, we started fighting back to back, but then they simply came at us from odd angles above and below.

The bizarre thing was, Fallyn and I could see every corner of the cavern clear as day. Yet I couldn't get a handle on their location, because it seemed like Ernesto and Stanley were everywhere and nowhere at once. They slipped in and out of the shadows like smoke, almost as though they were traveling from one location to the next via the darkness itself. It made me think of the "shadow dimension" where Camazotz was imprisoned, and the possibility that Ernesto and Stanley were ducking in and out of it at will.

My body had been supernaturally toughened when I'd shifted under my skin. Yet the skinwalkers' claws and teeth seemed to be quite capable of tearing through even my tough skin and flesh. I was bleeding in a dozen places, and it was starting to piss me off. A glance at my companions told me they fared no better, although Hemi's wounds were less severe since his wards provided better protection, and Fallyn's injuries healed soon after they were made.

Still, I can't help but think they're simply softening us up for the kill. And where the hell is La Onza?

"You guys doing okay?" I asked.

"Fine, just pissed," Hemi replied.

"Same. You need to do something about these pricks pronto, Golden Boy," Fallyn snarled in frustration.

"Alright. When I give the signal, close your eyes," I replied, firing the last of my rock salt, iron, and silver shotgun rounds at a shadow that flitted away from me. Dropping the shotgun, I reached into my Bag for one of the surprises I'd brought along: a common thirty-minute road flare.

As a druid, I could do a lot with ambient energy and the forces of nature. Unfortunately, there wasn't much to work with down here, but I'd expected as much so I'd brought some kit. What I wanted right now was light—a lot of it—and my usual flashbang cantrip wasn't going to cut it. I needed a stronger light source to borrow from so I could disrupt the skinwalkers' gameplan.

Only need a second to expose these fuckers, then Fallyn and Hemi will do the rest.

A shadow flashed past, swiping me across the face. I roared in frustration, ignoring the pain as I ignited the flare. Holding it high overhead like Lady Liberty carrying her torch, I reached out with my magic and *pulled* on the flame.

Whoosh!

Instantly, the entire flare consumed itself under the influence of my magic, and all that light and heat was drawn into the stub that I still held in my closed fist. Still focused on holding all that energy, I shut my eyes and reached out to the dark spaces around me with my senses. This time, I wasn't looking for an animal to mind-link with—I was dialing into the air molecules in the room, attuning my senses with every little eddy and air current in our immediate vicinity.

Soon, I felt the Bylillys moving around as they slid in and out of the shadow plane that was just beneath our own. It was a neat trick—not true teleportation, mind you, but almost as effective. They'd duck into the shadows, sprint to another spot in the room while still in the shadow dimension, and then they'd attack, only to fade away before we could respond.

But there was a pattern to their movements. Obviously, they'd trained this tactic together a lot, and in order to coordinate their attacks they followed a template. I took a few moments to figure it out, then waited for my opening.

"Now, guys!" I shouted.

I lashed out, opening my hand to release the flare's pent-up energy. I'd thrust my hand out in a palm strike, fully meaning to hit one of the skinwalkers in the face as I released my spell. The flash of light and heat caught Stanley Bylilly square in the eyes, blinding him. I knew this because I recognized the sound of his voice as he screamed, and I felt his eyeballs boil and pop open in my hand like two eggs in a microwave.

"Damn it, Colin—you blinded us too!" Fallyn cried, blinking furiously in an attempt to regain her vision.

"I warned you, didn't I?" I asked.

"You said 'close your eyes,'" Fallyn complained. "Not 'blindfold yourself because I'm about to release the sun inside a pitch-dark cavern!'"

Hemi stood beside her, also batting his eyes at the fading light and evidently not much better off than Fallyn. As the spellcaster I wasn't nearly as affected, and still retained my ability to see. But that also meant I was the only one of us currently capable of defending the group.

Aw, hell.

"Um, I meant to say 'cover your eyes'—sorry!" I said. "You guys just sit tight while I deal with Ernesto."

I held my arm extended as the spell ran its course, ensuring that the entire chamber remained lit with searing bright light until the spell was fully spent. Stanley lay writhing in agony on the floor, out of the fight for the moment. I quickly scanned the room in an effort to find the other skinwalker.

There.

Ernesto stood no more than fifteen feet away, scraps of shadow falling off him like paper ash floating away on the wind. The elder Bylilly spared his son a momentary look of scorn, then bared his claws and leapt at me.

The timing couldn't have been worse, as I was out of shotgun shells and without another weapon in hand. Additionally, I was still in my enhanced human form—the one that lacked natural weapons like claws and long, sharp teeth. Sure, I'd survived fighting baby vamps and feral 'thropes like this back in the Hellpocalypse, but never something like Ernesto.

This should be interesting. Here goes nothing.

19

E rnesto came at me like a honey badger on meth, a hundred miles an hour and all teeth and claws. His first attack was sheer rage and aggression, pretty much a spazzed-out, head-on charge, so I simply pimp-slapped him as hard as I could across the head and face. People always underestimate the power of a good slap, but one delivered with timing, back-up mass, and bad intent could do a hell of a lot of damage.

Not only that, but I was juiced up in my stealth-shifted Fomorian form. When I hit him, it wasn't with my normal peak-human strength, but with the enhanced physical power and speed of a young higher vamp or 'thrope. My hand connected with skull-crushing force, enough to send him straight to the cavern floor at my feet.

And the fucker looked up at me and *smiled*.

Should've packed a lunch—looks like it's going to be a long day.

Ernesto pushed himself off the ground like a character from the Matrix, with a one-handed push-up that sent him spinning in a flat trajectory that defied gravity and physics. As he spun, he raked me across the legs, stomach, chest, and face with his razor-sharp claws, in one rapid succession of rotational movement. Honestly, if I didn't hate the fucker so much, I'd have been impressed as hell—but after having our asses handed to us by Ernesto and his son for the last few minutes, all it did was piss me off.

The skinwalker kicked off me with a flip and landed just out of reach, but I'd already decided I wasn't going to let him get his footing. I stepped in with a solid combination of kicks and strikes, a mixture of French *savate*, Muay Thai, Krav Maga, and this crazy style of Celtic boxing that Finnegas had taught me. Side stomp low to the knee, flip that into a roundhouse to the nuts, hammerfist to the arms, body, and head as I stepped in, then headbutts, elbows, and knees in close.

I connected with just about everything I threw at Ernesto. I felt bones snap, cartilage crunch, and internal organs tear. Still, the crazy evil bastard fought right back, blow for blow, giving as good as he got. And the messed up thing was that he had better weapons than I did—claws hand and foot, and a mouthful of fucked up teeth—so he actually gave *better* than he got.

This is going sideways fast. Time to regroup—but where the hell is everyone?

I threw a hard front-thrust kick right in the skinwalker's midsection, tossing him across the chamber and into the limestone wall ten feet away. That gave me time to sneak a glance over my shoulder. Stanley was out of the fight for good now—Fallyn had located him by sound and smell and ripped his throat out. Looked like it hurt. Despite that, she and Hemi were still blinking and feeling their way around like a couple of drunks.

Damn it. I gotta keep Ernesto away from them.

I wanted to beat the snot out of the guy with my bare hands, really I did. But I still had the Fear Doirich to contend with, La Onza was nowhere in sight, and my friends were compromised due to my somewhat poor choice of tactics. So, I did what any reasonable druid-trained hunter would do in that situation.

I blasted the fucker with a lightning bolt that would've done Thor proud.

Lightning is a funny thing. For one, it moves faster than even a very powerful vamp can react, about one-third the speed of light. So, there's no damned way anyone is going to avoid it once it's cast. Second, it hits like a freight train. A hundred thousand volts was nothing to sneeze at, that was for sure. And third, it's fucking hot, like five times hotter than the surface of the sun.

Fireballs are fun, but lightning is the real killer.

So, when my lightning bolt struck Ernesto in the chest, I figured I was going to flash-fry his ass right back to the Middle Ages. And oh, I hit him alright, smack in the center of his gross, malformed, hairy ribcage. No holding back, either —he got both barrels in one pull of the trigger.

And here's the kicker—that lightning bolt left a charred, smoking hole in Ernesto's chest that I could stick my fist inside. His fucking lungs were visible, behind the ends of ash-white ribs that had once been attached to his now vaporized sternum. I could see his heart pumping in there as well, and let me tell you, it was freaky as hell.

But you know what that hairy shit-stained sphincter of a skinwalker did in response?

He laughed.

"Oh, druid," he chuckled, looking down at his chest. "I

will admit, that tickled a bit. Now, it's time for you and your friends to die."

He spread his arms wide, and out of that hole in his chest spilled a flood of evil spirits that looked like they were made of black silk and smoke. And how did I know they were evil? Because their eyes glowed red, and they were screaming that they were hungry for souls. Not that I understood their language, but their message came across loud and clear inside my head.

As those demonic freaks flew across the cavern at me, I figured I was done. I'd never been very good at dealing with restless spirits, and these looked like the very worst kind. They weren't your garden variety haunts, but the kind of spirits left behind by truly evil people, shades that should've gone to some hell or another when they died. Instead, they stuck around out of sheer spite and hate, just so they could pull more souls down with them.

Angry as they were, they'd rip me apart body and soul. And without blessed salt, a good protective ward circle, or a handy exorcism spell, I had no way to prevent it. As for my back up, Hemi still couldn't see what was going on, otherwise he'd be doing his *Ghostbusters* bit on them. Fallyn was good with flesh and blood, not so much with incorporeal beings. And La Onza, well—she looked to be a no-show.

That double-crossing bitch, I thought as the first spirits neared me. *I'll come back from the afterlife to haunt that dwarf of a witch—I swear it.*

Crunch!

The sound of bone and flesh being crushed was unmistakable, as I'd heard it too many times over the course of my young life. And it was loud—I even heard it over the dead people's screeching. In an instant, those same spirits vanished, leaving Ernesto standing there with a seriously surprised expression on his messed-up skinwalker mug.

I heard another loud *crunch*, just before Ernesto's head sort of flopped forward onto his chest, where it hung momentarily by nothing more than a flap of skin and gristle. Like a puppet with its strings cut his body followed, and the evil bastard tumbled to the ground in an awkward, deanimated heap. Behind that lifeless jumble of limbs, fur, and blood sat the biggest freaking mountain lion I'd ever seen, licking her paws and wiping the skinwalker's blood off her face and whiskers.

When she was done cleaning herself, the *bruja* transformed back into her human form. Unlike the way 'thropes shifted, her change was instantaneous and obviously the work of magic instead of any inherited skill or ability. La Onza looked around, taking in our condition as well as Ernesto and Stanley's corpses. She frowned at me and shook her head.

"Don't you know anything, *gringo*? You can't kill skinwalkers that way, not after they've slipped their skin. Have to shoot them in the neck with ash-blessed bullets, or cut their heads off. They'll laugh off anything else you do to them."

"I, uh, noticed that," I said with a sarcastic smile. "And as for your timing—fuck that! You could've jumped Ernesto at any time. Why'd you wait until I was about to get butt-fucked by an army of angry spirits before you stepped in?"

"I had to wait until he was distracted to strike, *mago*. Although if you'd hit him in the neck with your lightning, you could have ended it like that," she said, snapping her fingers. "Now, are you ready to face the Dark One?"

I suppose it makes sense, and I can't blame her for fighting smart. Still pisses me off, though—and it makes what I might have to do a hell of a lot easier.

I wiped blood off my forehead with the back of my hand. "Geez—give me a sec, will you?" I turned to check on Fallyn and Hemi. "You guys alright?"

Hemi leaned on a rough-cut stone support column that had been left behind when the mine had been excavated centuries prior. He was covered in scratches and cuts, but the bleeding had stopped so it looked like his healing wards were kicking in already.

"Yeah, bro, vision's starting to clear. Warn a bloke properly next time, aye?" he said as he rubbed his eyes.

"I second that shit," Fallyn grumbled as she snapped Stanley's neck. Hemi and I looked at her, mouths agape. "What? You heard the witch—if you don't do it right, they shake it off. 'Thropes know the score—we learn it from the time we're kids. Go for the kill or go home, right?"

"I don't think that's how the saying goes," I said.

"Whatever." She looked around the chamber, curling her lip in a silent snarl. "Guess it's time for us to bail on you, huh?"

"La Onza has my back. Besides, I need you to see what happened with Mendoza and his thugs. If they're waiting for us, sneak out another tunnel and meet up with the Pack at the rendezvous point."

Fallyn eyed the stone faced bruja, who stood off to the side with her arms crossed. "Double-cross him, and I'll strangle you with your entrails," she said. "Let's go, Hemi."

The big guy gave me a reassuring smile and a bro hug. "This is your moment, cuz. Go finish it."

"See you topside, buddy," I said, patting him on the back.

La Onza waited until they were both long gone before she spoke. "If you are killed, I will do my best to make sure your body is unfit for the Dark One's purposes."

"Wow, you're good at these pep talks, aren't you?" I quipped, scratching my head. "Look, I'm fine with you doing the same number on the Dark Druid that you did on Ernesto. Stay hidden until you know you can tip the scales. No sense in both of us going down today."

The dwarfish little witch gave me an inscrutable look, then she transformed into a mountain lion. La Onza headed into the dark, her voice fading as she stalked away from me.

"I will give you what assistance I can, druid. Just be sure to keep your word as well."

With that, she blended into the shadows and was gone.

I checked my gear and took one last look around the chamber, just to make sure I wasn't forgetting anything. For the hell of it, I torched the skinwalkers' corpses, making sure they were burning bright before I turned my attention to other matters.

You're stalling, Colin, a familiar female voice inside my head said. It wasn't really Jesse, but just my conscience speaking to me in her voice. Or maybe my subconscious wishing she were here. This was about the time she'd normally show up, when the shit hit the fan or thereabouts.

Even though I knew it wasn't her, I answered that voice just the same.

Yes—I am stalling.

You can't delay the inevitable, so you may as well get it over with, Jesse's voice replied.

I never wanted this, you know. I wish we could just go back to the way things were, before the Avartagh showed up.

You can't go back, slugger. There's no rewind button in this life. I died, and you're stuck with it.

Ah, but I'm learning time magic, I answered back.

Don't get any bright ideas, please.

I chuckled, because my conscience was a real smart-ass. Jess would've approved.

"Fine. Time to send this fucker to hell."

The Dark Druid was right where I thought he'd be. The moment I exited the last stope the bat had shown me, the signs of his passage were everywhere, in the most literal sense. Senses on high alert, I stopped to examine his work.

Well, this is a new level of fucked up.

Fresh human corpses—sacrifices, obviously—lay in twisted, desecrated heaps at intervals up and down the tunnels. As he'd done at the graveyard chapel, the Fear Doirich had used his victims' life energy to power necromantic spells that he'd painted in blood on the walls, floors, and ceiling of the tunnels. Some spells I recognized, since I'd been studying up on death magic and necromancy since our first encounter—those spells had been used to raise and control the dead. Others were unfamiliar to me, but I could take a guess as to their purpose.

When the time came, he'd trigger them and use them to force my spirit out of my body so he could take it over. And, if my hunch was correct, he'd trap me inside another phylactery, then torture my soul over the course of many, many centuries. I'd heard of necromancers forcing captive spirits to inhabit human corpses, animal carcasses, dead fish, you name it—sometimes for the sake of experimentation, and at other times, for the sheer pleasure of torturing their souls.

Could he do it to me, now that he had possession of Jesse's weird life and death magic? I had no idea, but I was betting that I'd still have some residual resistance to necromancy left over from the time I possessed Balor's Eye. I also theorized that being in my full Fomorian form would provide me with additional resistance, but it was a theory I'd never tested.

Maybe the combination would be enough to combat the Dark Druid's necromancy and Jesse's powers, maybe not. One way or the other, I'd know for sure soon.

As I followed the Fear Doirich's handiwork further down the tunnel, I checked the corridor for wards and traps along the way, but there were none. Now that he'd gotten what he wanted, the Dark Druid had no need for subterfuge, nor for concealment. To quote a certain famous sorcerer, we were in the end game now, and at this point the prick *wanted* me to come and find him.

Oh, and I'm coming with bells on, I thought as I called my Hyde-side forth.

After shifting into my full Fomorian form, I took a deep breath and drew Dyrnwyn. It was more like a short sword in my hand now than a full-sized blade, but I figured it might give me a slim advantage. For my final preparations, I readied a few spells and sent some instructions to the Druid Oak, then marched down the corridor toward my destiny... or doom.

Sixty feet in or so, the tunnel opened into another long, narrow stope chamber. This room was roughly thirty feet across and eighty feet long, with a few smaller side chambers where miners had chased veins of cinnabar until they'd petered out. As in the other stopes, the miners had used room and pillar mining techniques, leaving a ceiling high enough for me to stand with a bit of head room, although I had to duck my head when I came near the hourglass-shaped pillars.

Save for the graffiti, the entire room glowed with a sickly green light—not the bright neon used to portray radioactivity in the movies, but the diseased viridian hues of algae-covered swamp water, of pond scum on an alligator's back, or maybe green mold on old plaster. It pulsed softly, coming from everywhere and nowhere, illuminating the chamber in pestilent light that, to my magical senses, stank of piss and shit and decay and death. That magical "scent" was layered on top of the odors my physical senses took in, which were just as horrifying and overwhelming.

Just like the corridors leading in, the walls of this room had been painted with necromantic symbols and runes. More bodies were scattered across the floor at random intervals, slain and discarded with no concern for decorum or solemnity. Some appeared to be from across the border, others looked like vacationers and hikers who had been in the wrong place at the wrong time, and still others wore park ranger uniforms. I lost count at fifty, and soon simply diverted my eyes because I was starting to lose my shit—not due to fear, but anger. I needed to be clearheaded to win this fight.

The Dark Druid stood at the other end of the chamber, hood pulled back to expose the putrefied flesh of his face. Maggots squirmed beneath his skin, and pus ran in rivulets from wounds and sores. Dark, gangrenous veins stood out under what intact skin remained, and all that remained of his hair were a few stray wisps of gray.

He might not be locked in that body, but he damned sure looks to be suffering in it. If I can keep him from jumping ship, then I just might have a chance.

The old necromancer observed me with keen interest as I entered the room.

"I knew you'd come," he rasped.

I glanced around the chamber and tsked.

"You might know necromancy, but you're a shitty interior designer," I said. "Two thousand years of extended life, and yet here you are rocking the Dark Ages necromancer from hell look. Although the green lighting is a welcome break from your past work, you really should consider expanding your color palette. The 'Christmas in Hell' thing is so passé."

This sort of banter annoyed the Dark Druid, although I'd never throw him off his game with it. He was too old, clever, and controlled to let a little shit-talking trip him up. So, the only reason I did it was because I was petty like that.

"Are you done?" he asked.

"Well, now that we're on the subject, we really need to talk about your wardrobe as well. I—"

A loud rumble cut me off as the tunnel entrance crumbled behind me.

Gulp.

"Jest all you want, McCool—you won't delay the inevitable."

Now, where have I heard that before?

"The inevitable? The colonization of Mars? The end of the two-party system? The nationwide decriminalization of marijuana?"

The Fear Doirich licked the corner of his mouth with a sickly gray tongue that reminded me of a hagfish's tail. "I grow weary of your games, apprentice, and I'm impatient to inhabit that wonderful Fomorian body of yours."

I grimaced and held my hand up, palm out. "Whoa, whoa, whoa! Hate to tell you, buddy, but this thing called the hashtag-metoo movement happened, and that kind of talk is just *not* socially acceptable anymore."

"Enough!" he rasped, slamming his hand on a rune painted in blood on the wall behind him. All those runes that I didn't recognize lit up at once with the same sickly green glow that was coming from the walls, floor, and ceiling above. Yet the runes flared brightly with luminescence, and within that light were flecks and streaks of black.

Life and death magic together, just like La Onza said.

I had little time to reflect on the Dark Druid's methods, because as soon as he triggered the spell, I immediately felt as though I was being pulled apart at the molecular level. It was like each cell in my body was being forced to split in two all at once, and every neuron lit up with excruciating, burning pain. The only way I might describe it was that half of me was being ripped out of my skin, cell by cell, by a million tiny invisible hands.

"Oh, I don't feel so good," I said as I stumbled to my knees, vomiting bile and blood all over the place.

20

The Dark Druid calmly walked toward me, rubbing his decaying hands together slowly as he explained what I was experiencing.

"Ah, yes—that's the wonderful effects of the former dryad's magic at work," he said in a casual tone. "Normally, life and nature magic cannot co-exist together in a single magic-user or spell casting. However, your young lady friend was a very unique creature. After living in the realm of the dead, and then being raised again as a kind of nature goddess, then becoming human—well, death and life found a way to co-exist within her, it seems."

"And then you killed her again, you fuck—gah!"

I vomited again, and was starting to see double. Or, at least, that's what I thought I was seeing. Then, I realized what I was really seeing were two versions of me being ripped apart, one human and one Fomorian.

"What are you doing to me?" I demanded in two voices at once.

"You must be referring to the fact that there will soon be

two of you. That's the brilliant thing about the way your former paramour's magic works—or rather, worked, until I killed her and stole it. As you'll recall, formerly I couldn't use necromancy against you because of the immunity granted to you by Balor's Eye. But recently I realized that immunity had to be hidden within your Fomorian DNA, because no human could wield—much less retain—even a smattering of the Eye's magic."

With a monumental effort, I lifted my heads to look up at him—now I was really seeing double as my body and soul split into two separate entities. In that instant, I could feel my spirit being ripped apart, with my human spirit energy going with my mortal body and the beast going with my Hyde-side. Neither one of us liked it, but there wasn't a lot we could do about it at the moment except groan in agony and vomit more bile and blood.

"But..." I struggled to get the words out, because I was controlling two mouths, two voices. Or maybe two people were trying to say the same thing in unison—it was hard to keep it all clear. "There'll be two of us to fight now, instead of just one."

The Fear Doirich stood close now, and he knelt down to look me in my eyes—or rather, he looked back and forth between both sets. "Ah, but that's the delicious thing, you see. Once you're split, it'll only take me a moment to imprison your spirit so I can inhabit your human body. Then, before this"—he gestured at my Fomorian half—"beautiful, powerful beast can respond, I'll rejoin your two halves and have the benefit of your full powers, all in one glorious, immortal body."

"I'll kill you for what you d-did to Jesse, a-and everyone e-else. I swear i-it."

He smiled and licked his pale, decaying lips with that disgusting gray-green tongue. "She felt every bit of it, you know. The agony you're experiencing now? That's nothing compared to the feeling of having your magic, your life essence, and your soul sucked out of your body all at once. Connected as I was to her at the time, I heard her in my mind, screaming for mercy and to make it stop. My only regret was that I couldn't capture her soul—a pity, really. I could've tortured you both together, for eons. Now, wouldn't that be romantic, hmm?"

"A-all this because a young girl wouldn't love y-you. Y-you're pathetic."

"Ah yes, Sadhbh," he croaked. "But as you'll recall, I had my revenge. I always have my revenge."

At this point I saw two of his dead, decaying, sneering face, and seeing one of that fucker was enough. It occurred to me that I was about to lose this fight before it had even begun, and that pissed me off almost as much as what he'd done to Jesse. I struggled to move, to attack him, to do something—but when I tried to get my bodies to respond, both refused. I was completely locked within the grips of the Dark Druid's spell and Jesse's magic.

So weak. Have to fight this—but how?

A voice echoed in my mind.

-You have the means, although you are unaware of it.-

La Onza?

-I told you I would lend what assistance I could. Since I'm no match for the Dark One, I'm lending you my hundreds of years of knowledge and insight—wisdom that you, in your youth, lack.-

I'd rather you bite the Dark Druid's head off.

-If I show myself, he'll kill me. There isn't much time, so listen

closely. This magic he uses, he stole from that young girl who was your companion, yes?-

Yes, but—

-¡Escúchame, pollino! Where did that magic come from?-

From the Druid Oak, but—

-Are you so foolish that you can't understand what I'm saying? Who is the master of that magic now?-

The truth of what she was hinting at *hit me like a ton of bricks.*

I am.

-Then, what are you waiting for? Reclaim what is yours, and end this.-

La Onza's voice faded away inside my head. The split was almost complete now. I could tell because the double-vision effect was fading away, and my connection to the beast was becoming weak and tenuous.

Okay, let's see if she's right.

With a thought I reached out and called Jesse's magic to me, and to my surprise it obeyed me instantly. My body soaked it in like a sponge soaking up water. Sapped of all the energy behind the Dark Druid's spell, the effects dissipated. Once the spell failed, the two sides of me snapped back together, like a rubber band that had been pulled taut and released. This resulted in a tremendous backlash of magical energy that sent the Dark Druid tumbling across the chamber.

I looked down at my hands and arms, and thankfully saw only one set. Yet the form I'd taken when my two sides rejoined was somewhere between my full-on Hyde-side and my human body. My skin was thicker and hairier, my joints were knobbier, my teeth and nails had grown longer, and my muscles were larger, yet I was only slightly taller than normal. If I had to describe it, it felt like I'd fully shifted, just without the bulk of my full Fomorian form.

Weird. Hope I'm not stuck like this.

Across the chamber, the Dark Druid pushed himself to his knees. His eyes met mine, first wide with shock, then they narrowed as his face contorted into a rictus of pure, impassioned hate.

"Impossible!" he howled as his hands began to glow with silver light. "There's no way you could have broken free from that spell!"

"That magic was borrowed from the very beginning, asshole. It didn't belong to you, any more than it belonged to Jesse." I raised my hand in front of my face, closing it into a fist as thick bands of warm, green, translucent magic appeared around it. "I'm its master now—and I do believe that makes you my bitch."

"You think too much of yourself, apprentice," the Fear Doirich rasped as a silver ward circle appeared on the cavern floor around him. "You might possess power, but what you lack is the knowledge and experience to use it. Allow me to show you what a master druid can do, since your mentor never saw fit to teach you himself."

The sickly green light was gone from the chamber, replaced by a healthier green glow that emanated from me, juxtaposed against the silver light that shone from the Dark Druid's hands and the runes on the floor around him. That silvery glow meant he was using druidic battle magic, and to be honest that had me worried. Before he'd become a necromancer, the Fear Doirich had been only second in druidic skill to Finnegas, and he'd mastered the entirety of the craft —including druidic battle magic—nineteen hundred years before I was born.

Me? I'd barely scratched the surface of that branch of druidry in my studies with Finnegas. Not to mention the asshole had kicked my tail with battle magic before. I certainly didn't want a repeat of *that* performance.

Think, Colin! What's your advantage here?

I snatched Drynwyn off the floor as I ducked behind a support column, chewing my thumbnail as I thought the situation through.

For one, he's made himself immobile. That ward circle will protect him, but only so long as he stays inside it.

Second, we're surrounded by rock and stone. I could use that against him.

And third, he's afraid of me—else he wouldn't have spent precious moments casting those wards.

"Duck!" Larry's voice yelled from somewhere to my left. I complied, just as a molecule-thick sheet of compressed air sliced the column in two where my neck had been a moment before.

Guillotine spell—lost an arm to that one last time, as I recall.

"Larry!" I yelled as I dove and rolled to another column. "What the hell are you doing here?"

"I felt the skinwalker's curse lift," the chupacabra's disembodied voice answered, now from my right. "So, I thought I'd come say thanks. Good thing I did—looks like you could use an extra set of eyes about now."

"Never thought I'd say this, but I'm pretty fucking tickled to hear your voice. Just don't let the Dark Druid see you!" I yelled as I crouched and ran from my hiding spot.

A second later, that column disintegrated in a cloud of

acrid smoke, the result of a nasty cone of acid spell that my enemy had cast at me.

Well, that's a new one. Gonna have to get Finnegas to teach me some of this stuff—that is, if I make it out of here. Speaking of which, it's time I went on the offensive. But with what?

The problem with being so far below ground was that hardly anything grew down here. Sure, I had the full force of the Grove's magic at my fingertips, but I needed stuff to work with. Grass, vines, trees, and so on—and there was none of that in the mines.

But what I did have was rock, and plenty of it. So, I called on the Grove's magic, connecting it with the stony walls and floor around me. Just as I had back in the Void, I grew missiles to throw at the Dark Druid—long, slender blades of hardened stone that sprang up from the ground beside me. I sent one whistling at him, but it shattered against his protective wards.

"Master of a Druid Grove, and you have no idea what to do with all that power," he taunted, flicking his hands at me.

Sheets of silvery power like flat panes of glass shot toward me, one after the other. I leapt and spun, contorting my body in impossible ways to squeeze between those deadly guillotine spells. But not quite—one of them caught me, slicing an inch-thick section of skin and muscle the size of a small saucer off the front of my thigh.

I landed awkwardly behind a column, bleeding profusely and with limited ability to support myself on the affected leg. Now that I was also more or less immobile, it would only be a matter of time before another guillotine of compressed air and magic did me in.

First, the Dark Druid hit the column with a cold spell, presumably to freeze the stone and make it easier to destroy.

Then, as expected, he threw more of those deadly guillotine spells at me, one after another, slicing and chipping away at the stone support above me. Sheets of frozen rock began to fall and shatter all around me, and with each successive spell he sent my way, the column shrank in height.

"Druid, you gotta move!" Larry yelled at me.

"You think?" I yelled back, looking around the chamber for another hiding place, and finding none near enough to reach with a bum leg. Another guillotine spell sliced the column neatly about six inches above my head, shaving off another thin layer of stone that broke like tempered glass as it fell on top of me.

For some odd reason, I noticed that this last piece of column was different. Rather than the yellow-white of lime-stone, it was a rust-red color.

That's it!

"Larry, what was it you said they mined here again?"

The chupacabra responded immediately in his thick Brooklyn accent. "Cinnabar—you know, mercury ore."

Mercury absorbs and conducts magical energy, which is why it's sometimes used in magic amulets. And like any good conductor, it can also disrupt the flow of the energy it conducts when it's used as a ground.

I dropped flat to the floor and closed my eyes as I extended my magic and druid senses out to the rock around us. At first, it was difficult to tell the difference between the porous sedimentary rock and the cinnabar deposits. Yet with only a little searching, I was able to spot the mercury-containing rock veins in the cave walls around us.

Now, to get what I need to do this asshole in.

Using the magic of the Druid Oak and the control I'd learned while repairing the Grove in the Void, I pulled every single bit of mercury out of the walls, floors, and ceiling around us by heating the rock up and boiling the metal out of it. But instead of drawing it into a single huge ball of quick-silver, I sent it crawling along the floor toward the Dark Druid.

While I worked, another guillotine spell whooshed past, just above my face. I needed more time.

"Wait, don't kill me!" I shouted. "Maybe we can work something out."

"There was a time when I might have considered it, McCool," The Dark Druid replied. "But you've been a thorn in my side for far too long. First you imprisoned my son again, after I'd spent centuries breaking Finnegas' first imprisonment spell. Then, you foiled my initial attempts to get Balor's Eye. And locking me in this body, not to mention the loss of my hand and the Eye in our last meeting—do you know how hard it was to find a mummified Fomorian's hand? No, I've reached the end of my patience with you. If I can't inhabit that body, then I'll see you dead."

Thank God this freak likes to monologue, I thought as I sensed the small streams of mercury I'd collected working their way underground toward the Dark Druid. *Almost there—now!*

I directed the mercury to work its way up to the surface around his ward circle, and then to flow across the circle, lines, and runes in little rivulets from a dozen different directions. At first, my efforts met with resistance. I mean, if it was that easy, wizards and witches would just toss globs of mercury at each other when they wanted to break another magic-user's wards.

I needed some serious juice to make this work, so I connected the mercury with the power of the Druid Oak and pushed in on the Dark Druid's wards with every bit of will I possessed. This effectively turned the mercury into a sort of magical grounding circuit that shorted out the Dark Druid's wards while siphoning energy off. Instantly, his protections fell away and the shimmering wall of translucent silver magic was gone. Temporarily weakened, the necromancer stumbled to his knees, the result of a great deal of magical energy draining from him all at once.

Now, to use his tactics against him.

I rolled out from behind the column and threw Dyrnwyn in a flat trajectory. As it left my hand, the blade lit up like a blow torch from hilt to tip. Everything I had went into that throw, and the blade sailed like a missile, spinning through the air and crossing the distance between us in the blink of an eye. Dyrnwyn's white-hot blade sliced through the Fear Doirich's neck, severing his head from his shoulders and cauterizing the wound as it did so.

The blade finished its trajectory by burying itself tip-first in the wall of the cavern beyond. The Dark Druid stood there for a moment with a surprised look on his gray, black-veined, decaying face. He opened his mouth to speak, then his head tumbled off his shoulders, bouncing to the floor and rolling to a stop on its side several feet from me. As for the rest of him, the lot of it collapsed in a heap of dust, bones, and parchment-dry skin behind him.

My leg was still bleeding, but it was beginning to heal, so I pushed myself off the ground and limped over to where the Dark Druid's still very animated head sat. He glared at me as I approached, his jaw working as he spat silent curses or spells at me—I couldn't tell which. With no voice to speak nor hands to gesture, the Fear Doirich was now as powerless as a newborn.

"Damn, that's messed up," Larry said as he coalesced into view on my right. "You'd think getting your head cut off would do a guy in, ya know?"

I stared down at the Dark Druid's severed head. It was shooting daggers at me with its eyes and silently cursing me to seven different hells all at once. Although he was harmless in his current state, it occurred to me that so long as the thing was alive, I'd never truly be rid of him.

My mind quickly ran through the many ways I might do him in, just as quickly discarding each. In every scenario, the possibility remained that someone or something would locate whatever was left of the Dark Druid's remains and resurrect him. That was not a risk I was willing to take.

Boy, would he be pissed if he came back after I killed him. Naw, I need to make sure he doesn't return to haunt me, ever. Time to follow through on that deal I made.

I closed my eyes and located a thin, shadowy thread of magic that had connected me with Camazotz' prison since he'd allowed me to leave with my life. A small tug on that thread was enough to trigger the minor alterations I'd made in La Onza's containment spells, changes that were small enough to escape her notice. And once my spell had been initiated, the wards that kept Camazotz trapped in the shadow world inside La Onza's cave disappeared.

Immediately, the bat god stepped through a magic portal before me.

"You kept your bargain, *Mago*. What is your price?"

I pointed at the severed head at my feet. "I need to make sure this one dies, for good."

The bat god crossed his arms, cradling his chin in his

hand as he considered what remained of the Dark Druid. "Hmm... powerful magic preserves him, even now that he has lost his body." Camazotz turned to look at me. "Did you consider burying it?"

"I did, but I was concerned his friends would come along with another body. He's kind of connected in the world of the Celtic gods."

Camazotz rubbed his chin. "Yes, that's a possibility. You could burn it, until nothing remained."

"I thought of that too, but I have the same concerns. His spirit would be tied to this place then, and if someone came along and gathered his ashes, well—"

"The Void, then. You have access to it. Toss his head in." Camazotz brushed his palms off. "Done."

I shook my head. "Too risky. The things that roam out there—all it'd take is for some eldritch symbiote to find him, and I'd have a far more dangerous enemy than he was before I cut his head off."

The bat god raised a hand. "I see your point. I am a god of death, after all, so I could break the spells that preserve him. But, if he's as connected as you say—"

"You don't want to take the blame for killing the Tuath Dé's pet druid," I finished for him.

"It could cause complications I do not need, so soon after being freed from my prison. In my current weakened state, I would not care to risk it."

"I understand," I said.

Camazotz whispered to me behind his hand. "By the way, is the bald coyote with mange a friend of yours? I could use a quick snack."

"That's it, I'm out of here!" Larry exclaimed, disappearing.

I chuckled. "Sorry. I owe him a debt, so if you could avoid eating him I'd appreciate it."

"As I owe you," the bat god stated with a nod. "And Camazotz pays his debts. So, I will take the head of the necromancer with me, and keep it safe and hidden until you have the means to dispose of it yourself. Does this even the scales between us to your satisfaction?"

"It does, mighty Camazotz, bat god who is the night."

"Indeed," the giant bat-guy said, scooping up the Fear Doirich in one huge hand. He inclined his head in my direction. "Farewell, Mago. Until we meet again."

"Goodbye, Camazotz."

With a wave of his hand, another portal appeared. The bat god stepped through it carrying the Fear Doirich's head tucked under one of his ginormous arms. Even as they departed, the damned thing was still glaring and cursing at me. I flipped him off, purely for shits and giggles.

Petty, I know—but it felt good just the same.

"Beware, Bob Kane," I heard Camazotz mutter in a dangerous voice as the two of them winked out of sight. "The night comes for you."

After the portal closed, Larry whispered from the darkness.

"Is the scary roided-up bat freak gone?"

"He's gone, Larry."

"Thank goodness," he said with relief. "Got any Funyuns?"

21

"You did *what*?" Upon hearing that I'd freed Camazotz, La Onza was livid, as I'd expected. "You broke your word, even after I helped you defeat the Dark One!"

"Now, hang on a minute—I kept my word," I said. "To the letter, actually."

The small-statured witch fumed as she paced back and forth across the tunnel. After the fight, we'd found her waiting for us near the main shaft where we'd entered the mines. Larry sat nearby, ignoring us as we argued. La Onza stopped pacing and got in my face, pointing her index finger at me as she read me the riot act.

"You told me Camazotz would remain to guard my cave and the portal to the underworld, did you not? Yet now, he is free from his prison—and free to hunt me, and the people I protect." Her eyes flashed gold as she glared at me. "What do you have to say for yourself, druid?"

"I told you *camazotzes* would guard your lair—and indeed, they will. A few of Camazotz's offspring are still around, also known as camazotzes, plural. And he promised to send them in his stead to guard your place. Problem solved."

Her eyes narrowed, and her irises took on a deeper shade of gold. "And the bat god, when he decides to seek revenge? What should I do then?"

It took an effort to keep myself from sighing with impatience.

Probably not a good idea—she might try to turn me into a frog. Or Larry.

"I spent a good deal of time negotiating the deal I made with Camazotz. Among the terms of that agreement were stipulations that he was not to seek revenge on you, nor was he to prey on the inhabitants of the areas you protect."

She threw her hands up in the air. "Great! Now he's simply going to hunt elsewhere. Your deal solved nothing, druid—nothing!"

"You're right, actually. He will hunt elsewhere—but with conditions. For one, because of something I may have mentioned in passing, Camazotz is now obsessed with becoming a sort of hero to humans. I, er, might have encouraged that obsession by telling him that today's humans worship in a different manner than they once did, through social media instead of human sacrifice."

Suddenly, I had La Onza's attention. "Go on."

"And in the spirit of becoming a hero instead of a villain, I explained the concept of vigilantism to Camazotz. Thus, another condition of his release was an agreement that he will prey only on those who harm other humans—murderers, rapists, pedophiles, and the like. I assured him he would not go hungry."

La Onza squinted at me, her fists balled up on her hips.

"You are lucky, druid. If you had not made such a clever deal with Camazotz, I would have turned you into a rabid bat."

Bullet, dodged.

Larry's ears perked up. "Trouble coming," he said before disappearing.

I began to reach out with my druid senses, but La Onza's voice stopped me.

"Don't bother, I already know who comes. It is *Los Federales*, coming to investigate the mines in their search for you and the girl." She closed her eyes and nodded. "They had many casualties, and the battle was a near thing. When you defeated the Dark One, you saved dozens of agents."

I twirled a finger in the air. "Yay, me," I said in a flat voice. "Have they found the mine shaft yet?"

"They're climbing down the rope you left," La Onza said with a nod. "Come, I will lead you to an exit they will not find."

She took off at a jog, not bothering to see if I'd follow or not. Since indefinite incarceration was low on my bucket list, and because I really didn't want the deaths of a couple dozen agents on my hands, I made the very wise decision to tag along.

After leading me down several side tunnels, we came to a vertical shaft that was hidden behind a pile of rubble in a caved in section of the mines. She jumped in, dropping twenty feet to land lightly in a section of tunnels that weren't on the maps. After making numerous twists and turns, we came to a dead end. La Onza waved her hand, and a section of the wall swung away, revealing another tunnel behind it that led upward at a forty-five-degree angle.

After we entered, the wall swung shut behind us. From there, it was a straight shot to a hidden entrance on the other side of the mountain ridge. It was bright outside, and the sun was coming up in the east as we exited the mines.

Looks like it's going to be a beautiful day.

A nearly invisible trail led down the slope, which we followed until we reached a fork in the path. La Onza stopped to face me with a hard look in her eyes.

"This is where we part ways, druid. *Por favor*, the next time you decide to hide from *Los Federales*, do so anywhere but here."

I chuckled in spite of myself. "Next time I'll probably just leave the country."

Her expression softened as she looked at the chupacabra sitting in the dirt near my feet. "Larry, be good."

"Not on your life," he said. "Take care, *doña*."

La Onza's form shimmered. One moment she was human, and the next she was a pony-sized mountain lion. She bounded away, her outline blending into the vegetation and terrain until she effectively disappeared from sight.

"Magical camouflage. Not as good as being invisible, but decent," Larry remarked. "By the way, your girlfriend said to tell you she'll see you soon."

"You mean Fallyn? She's not my girlfriend, Larry."

"Uh-uh, not her—the other one."

I rubbed my face, because I needed sleep. "The Spanish girl? We broke up."

"Wrong again. I mentioned that I see dead people, right?"

I knelt down in front of him. "Jesse? You saw Jesse?"

"I did. She watched your fight, which was about all she could do. Her spirit's still weak since she just died, and that makes it hard to manifest. Anyway, she told me to tell you that while you were busy talking to that creepy bat-dude. Then, she split."

Aw, Jess.

"Thanks for letting me know."

"Don't mention it—least I could do." He stood up and wagged his mangy, rat-like tail. "You ready to blow this joint?"

"I am. You coming with?"

"I got nowhere else to go. You mind?"

I thought about it for two heartbeats. The chupacabra was weird and annoying, but he'd also proven himself to be loyal and goodhearted.

"Not at all, Larry." I reached out in my mind and called for the Druid Oak, which zapped into existence right before our eyes. "And what do you know—here's our ride."

When we arrived at our rendezvous point on the mesa, the Pack had already split up. The plan was for them to melt into the park posing as tourists and campers, and then head back to Austin separately in small groups so as not to attract attention from Cerberus. But that ended up being an unnecessary measure.

After their disastrous run-in with the Dark Druid's undead army, and finding zero trace of us in the aftermath, Mendoza and Cerberus left the park. Samson's government law enforcement connections informed him that Cerberus had gathered their dead and wounded and headed back to their secret hideout to lick their wounds. Word was, the entire operation had been categorized as a complete and utter disaster, leaving Mendoza in hot water with his superiors.

Once Samson told us it was safe, I called Maureen to see how she and Finnegas were doing. Kenzie Kupert of Borovitz and Feldstein, Attorneys at Law, had called earlier to inform us that the Department of Homeland Security had called off their investigation. Even so, I doubted we'd seen the last of Agent Mendoza.

Although the feds had backed off, Maureen seemed to think it best that I steer clear of the junkyard for a while. Finnegas agreed, saying a little time away wouldn't hurt anything, as we all needed breathing room to process what had happened. Just in case Cerberus came sniffing around again, we had Borovitz and Feldstein do some asset protection trickery on the property, transferring ownership into a trust that had so many layers of ownership that no one could possibly trace the title back to me. Then, Maureen gave everyone notice that I was taking a break from my job as Druid Justiciar.

Once all that had been taken care of, I took Fallyn and Hemi back to Austin. Hemi was eager to get back to his apartment and domestic life with Maki, but Fallyn, not so much. Since time moved much more slowly in the Grove, the werewolf stuck around for a few days to help me get situated. I won't say the company wasn't welcome.

It's kind of weird, living inside a sentient pocket dimension that anticipates your every need. If we were hungry, fruits and nuts would fall from the trees, perfectly ripe and ready for harvest. Or, the Grove would portal us somewhere that Fallyn could hunt for game. And while we didn't need shelter there since the weather was always perfect, I still spent time crafting a cottage from the inside of a massive redwood tree trunk the Grove had provided for the purpose.

Once I was done, Fallyn and I stood back to admire my work.

"Looks like some elves should be baking cookies in there," she remarked drily.

"Hmm—I guess it does have a sort of Keebler vibe to it," I said as I looked it over. "But to be honest, I was kind of going for the whole 'hobbit-hole' look."

"Then why didn't you build it in the ground, doofus?" she asked.

"Doofus? Now you're just being mean. Anyway, it'd take way too long to create all the interior woodwork, plaster, and lathing needed to make an earth home cozy."

"Duh! After all that time we spent in caves recently, and you didn't think to use stone?"

I rubbed a hand along the bark next to the door, which I'd fashioned using my druidic control of the Grove. Here, I could pretty much make anything with enough time and imagination—that is, within the limits of the raw materials available, and so long as it didn't offend the Grove or Oak.

I shook my head. "Staying away from caves and stone was kind of the point. I'm not too fond of being underground, you know." I took her by the hand and led her to a nearby bench that I'd formed from the tree's roots. "Come, have a seat. We need to talk."

She frowned slightly and her eyes narrowed. "You'd better not be dumping me before we've even gone on a date."

"What? No, it's not that. Just—sit down. Please." I patted the bench beside me.

She hesitated a moment longer then did as I asked, pulling her hand away so she could cross her arms.

"Alright, speak," she said, her voice devoid of emotion.

"Guarded much?" I asked. "Sheesh. All I was going to say was that I want to keep spending time with you. But in light of recent events, I thought it would be wise to keep things, you know, platonic."

The tight set of her lips relaxed as her eyes lit up with amusement. "Holy shit, Colin, is that all? And what made you think you were going to get into my pants in the first place?"

"Wait—what? I never said..." She laughed and slugged me on the shoulder, hard enough to leave a mark. "Ow!"

"Oh suck it up, you big baby." Fallyn crossed her legs, resting her forearms on them as she leaned in to look me in the eye. The look she gave me was warm, friendly, and altogether unsettling. "Colin, I appreciate where you're coming from. And honestly, I still feel guilty about maneuvering for you the way I did back at the park, right before Jesse died. So sure, take your time. I'm not going anywhere."

I cleared my throat. "That's just the thing, see? I'm going to be in here, training with Finnegas, Hideie, and—er, others, while you're in the real world. You've seen how time passes here, right? It might seem like weeks have passed here for me, while for you it'll only be hours, if that."

Her almost-yellow hazel eyes bored into mine. "So what you're saying is, you might want to take the next step sooner than later?"

"From your perspective, yes. Although I might spend months or years in here before that happens."

She smiled and reached out to cradle my cheek in her hand. At first it was a gentle gesture, then she patted my face in a playfully rough manner. "Sounds like a pretty damned convenient arrangement to me. You take your time—in here —but don't you dare forget about me while you're learning how to be a jedi or whatever."

I chuckled and rubbed my cheek. "Wouldn't dream of it."

The next night, I dreamed of Jesse.

We were outside the Dagda's cottage in Underhill, walking through fields of wheat that were ripe and ready for harvest. Birds, bees, and dragonflies flitted and flew lazily overhead and amidst the rolling acres of grain. The sun was shining, a soft breeze blew, and the air smelled like honeysuckle and rich, moist dirt.

I glanced around, taking in our surroundings. The entire place had a dreamlike, fairytale quality to it, like that scene in *Gladiator* when Maximus finally reaches the Elysian fields and is reunited with his family. It was like looking at a photo-processed Thomas Cole painting, awash with a permanent golden light and soft-muted so only beauty showed through, sans the harsh details of reality.

I looked over at Jesse, who had the same ethereal quality about her, from the flowers in her neatly braided hair to the long, gauzy, flowing dress she wore, to her perfectly clean bare feet. She looked exactly like she had the day before her first death, in the full bloom and beauty of her youth and health. More than anything, that's what tipped me off with regards to our location.

"This isn't Underhill," I said.

"No, it isn't. Part of my deal with The Dagda was that he'd take me to Tír na nÓg once my task was complete."

"And what exactly was that task?" I asked.

"Haven't you figured it out? He needed you to bond with the Oak and Grove, to become its master. Druidry was dying out, Colin. I'd died, you were reluctant to continue your studies, and Finnegas doesn't have much time left. If Finn had passed on without completing your training, there'd be no one left to keep druidry alive."

"Except the Fear Doirich," I remarked.

"And what a horrible legacy for The Dagda to leave," she replied. "Do you think he wanted that, for all that knowledge to be left in the hands of a madman?"

"It's hard to say what the Tuatha want, Jesse. Their motives are as twisted and warped as those of the fae. Even the ones history and legend call 'good' can't be trusted."

"But sometimes, they tell the truth. Like when the Dagda told me I wouldn't last long after you bonded with the Grove."

"That's why you were so sullen after you became human again," I said.

"I couldn't tell you," she replied. "Because I knew you'd try to stop it. And you needed the Grove's magic—all of it—to help you survive facing the Fear Doirich."

"Yeah, Jess, but if I'd known, I would've kept you away from him and protected you instead of leaving you alone."

"I'd have died regardless, and you would've blamed yourself. It was better that I die at his hands."

"You let yourself be taken."

She smiled, but her eyes were wet with tears. "Once you claimed the Oak and bonded with the Grove, the magic that sustained me was supposed to pass back to you, fully. I wasn't even supposed to come back again—my spirit was meant to move on to Tír na nÓg. The only reason why I came back was because you wouldn't let me die. The Grove sensed your desires, so it left some of its magic behind with my mortal remains."

I nodded—now it all made sense. "And that left you somewhere in between life and death."

"It wasn't supposed to happen that way, but yes."

"Why'd you do it, Jess? Not being taken, I mean, but the whole thing?"

She looked away in an attempt to hide whatever emotions were written on her face. Sadness, mostly, with traces of regret. "The Dagda showed me a thousand futures where you faced the Dark Druid without having claimed the Druid Oak or bonded with the Grove, and you died every single time. As I said, the only chance you had of surviving that confrontation was with the Grove's magic. There was no other way."

I laughed, mirthlessly. "And typical of the gods, he failed to understand human emotion and motives. He figured the spirit of the Grove would be irresistible to me cloaked in your form."

"And with my spirit cohabiting the body of the dryad, he thought it'd be a done deal from the start."

I exhaled heavily. "You knew better, Jesse. Again, why'd you do it?"

She took my hands in hers. "Because it was a chance to be with you, one last time. I've never stopped loving you, Colin, and my love has never changed. It broke my heart to watch you move on and become involved with Belladonna. But I also knew it was the best thing for you at the time."

I snorted. "Yeah, that worked out well."

"She was your rebound girl, slugger. Did you really think it'd last?"

"Belladonna is a good person, Jesse. She didn't deserve what happened to her—to us."

Jesse gave me a sad smile. "Life's not fair, Colin. And you can't go back—you can never go back. If this whole experience should have taught you anything, it's that."

My cheeks were wet with tears. "I still wish I'd never have

asked you to come with me that day at the baseball fields. I should've just left you to get ice cream with your family, instead of dragging you into this life with me."

"I don't really think that was your call," she said as she brushed a tear from my cheek.

I looked around at Tír na nÓg, at the fairytale perfection of the place. "You don't belong here, Jesse. You should be somewhere else, where you can be reunited with your family and loved ones when they pass."

"This is just a rest stop, Colin." She smiled at me with bittersweet warmth. "I was with you from the start, and my heart is with you to the end. Until you need me again, I'll be here, waiting."

"Will you be okay?"

Jesse nodded. "I will, don't you worry." She stood on her tiptoes, leaning in close as if to give me a kiss. Instead, her lips caressed my ear as she whispered, nearly inaudibly. "The gods have their eyes on you, McCool. Whatever you do, don't let anyone know about your relationship with the Welshman. Your life depends on it!"

She pulled away quickly, looking over her shoulder with worry in her eyes. "Colin, I—"

The next moment, I was awake in my bed in the Grove. Only Roscoe and Rufus were there—I'd refused to leave them at the junkyard, and they'd seemed happy to chase the Grove's rabbits and lounge all day in the sun. As I swung my legs off the side of the bed, Roscoe walked over and nudged my hand.

I wiped a few tears away as I absently rubbed his neck with my other hand.

"It's alright, boy. I'll be fine. It's just going to take some time."

EPILOGUE

A ustin, Texas, 3:17 am.
(A large oak tree suddenly appears in the Barton Creek greenbelt near Zilker Park, close enough to local retail stores to get a decent Wi-Fi signal. A young man steps out from behind the tree with two pitbull mixes in tow. He sits down with his back against the trunk, pulls out a smart phone, and brings up a live feed of the local news. The dogs sniff around the tree and start doing dog stuff.)

Male News Anchor: *"...and now we go to the latest weird news story from Mexico City. Susan, what can you tell us about this bizarre situation?"*

Female Reporter: *"Well, Bob, reports have been pouring in from Mexico's capital city, where eyewitnesses claim they've seen a—well, a giant bat committing acts of heroism. One woman says the bat pulled her baby from a burning building, a skydiver says the giant creature saved him after his chute failed to open, and yet another eyewitness saw what he described as a 'bat-like man' swoop in to catch a suicide jumper before he fell to his death. And footage has even been floating around the internet of an* attempted robbery that was supposedly foiled by this bat creature."

(The news cuts to grainy footage of an apparent convenience store robbery. A man in a mask pulls a gun, then a dark blur swoops in and the gunman is suddenly gone...)

Female News Anchor: *"Wow, Susan, that certainly is some amazing footage. But honestly, does anyone really believe that giant bats are fighting crime in Mexico City? What's next, chupacabras sniffing for drugs at the border?"*

(The news anchors and reporter all share a good chuckle, then the studio cameras cut back to the news anchors.)

Female News Anchor: *"And in other news, law enforcement officials south of the border are seeing a massive uptick in drug-related killings as the war between the drug cartels heats up. The latest victim was the leader of the notorious Garcia cartel, Rodolfo Garcia himself. Mexican police report his body was found in his bed, completely exsanguinated, with no signs of gunfire or struggle."*

Male News Anchor: *"Now, for the local weather..."*

(The young man releases a sigh as he shuts off the phone screen, just as one of the dogs returns to lay its head in his lap.)

"Well, Rufus, I guess we'd better brush up on our Spanish..."

This concludes Book 8 and the second tetralogy in the Colin McCool urban fantasy series. Be sure to subscribe to my newsletter at https://MDMassey.com to get a free book, and to be among the first to know when I release my next Junkyard Druid novel!